D0504140

Andrew Greig is the author of six acclaimed books of poetry and two books chronicling his Himalayan expeditions of the Eighties. His first novel was shortlisted for the McVities Prize and the Boardman-Tasker Award. His second was shortlisted for the Romantic Novelist's Award.

THAT SUMMER

It is late June 1940, and Len Westbourne, a young and inexperienced fighter pilot, and Stella Gardam, a radar operator, meet at a dance and fall in love, knowing their time may be short as the War becomes an epic struggle between the Luftwaffe and the RAF: The Battle of Britain. She is his eyes on the ground, he is her protector in the air, and as the battle intensifies so their affair gathers pace. Class and national barriers begin to break down amid a heady whirl of parties that distract from the more serious business at hand.

ANDREW GREIG

◆

THAT SUMMER

Complete and Unabridged

ULVERSCROFT
Leicester

First published in Great Britain in 2000 by
Faber and Faber Limited
London

First Large Print Edition
published 2001
by arrangement with
Faber and Faber Limited
London

British Library CIP Data

Greig, Andrew, *1951* –
   That summer.—Large print ed.—
   Ulverscroft large print series: romance
   1. Britain, Battle of, *1940*
   2. Fighter pilots—Great Britain
   3. Radar operators—Great Britain
   4. Love stories
   5. Large type books
   I. Title
   823.9′14 [F]

   ISBN 0–7089–4445–0

Published by
F. A. Thorpe (Publishing)
Anstey, Leicestershire

Set by Words & Graphics Ltd.
Anstey, Leicestershire
Printed and bound in Great Britain by
T. J. International Ltd., Padstow, Cornwall

This book is printed on acid-free paper

To the vanishing generation

Firstword

Above my bed, when I was young, the Airfix kits, the Hurricane, Spitfire, Messerschmitt, spun on their threads in the draught.

One by one they will return, throttling down over perimeter wires of forgotten airfields, then taxi up to abandoned huts. Down the bramble-choked lane come the women and men on bicycles, others on foot, the sound of their voices light and drifting as a summer swarm as they pass through the rusting gates, waving to the CO gliding by in his Lagonda.

The pilots jump down from their planes, knees bending as they hit the ground. A few stumble, awkward with their parachutes bumping at the back of their things. Some wave, some call, but their voices are so light they are borne away on the summer breeze. A faint rain is starting to fall and clings, shimmering, to their grey-blue uniforms.

The two groups meet and mingle. Handshakes and pats on the back. A hug and a light kiss on a cheek, postponed for sixty years. A black Labrador runs through legs and is greeted by a bulky man who kneels to embrace him. As they tussle, some drift over to the aircraft whose manifolds steam in the drizzle. These are mostly men, the fitters, riggers and armourers. They stroke the wings, run fingers over the blown-away fragments of cloth that once covered the gun ports, curse quietly.

Others look around in the rain at the rutted grass, the cracked concrete where the youth of the town race motorbikes and go-karts at weekends, the husks of Nissen huts. The control tower still stands though its windows are blank, the aerials bent and rusting. Some of the WAAFs move towards the concrete filter room, passing over the foundations of the communications hut. In the mud on the floor of the Anderson shelter one crouches and digs up the remains of an old *Picture Post*. She peels the pages apart and out falls a wizened French letter. She shrugs, others laugh. The youngest bites her lip.

Nearly all smoke. They pass cigarettes between them like benedictions, like tokens of belonging. After all, they need take no heed of health warnings, even if there were any on the packets they slip from breast pockets, flip open, light up, then breathe into the warm, damp air.

They talk in small groups. The pilots

gesture with their hands, showing how it happened. They argue still over numbers and formations. One shows with the side of his hand dropping earthwards how he had peeled away, then steadied and came up behind his other hand, flying level. Then both start to shake. The others nod and laugh, quiet but persistent as memory.

So they talk and drift till the drizzle slows then stops. Cigarettes are squashed under shoes and flying boots, ties are pushed up under collars, caps are straightened or set at precise, jaunty angles that pass just inside regulations. The couple who have been entwined since the beginning come back from the woods by the perimeter fence. The bells of the bicycles ring faintly as they fade up the lane. The propellers blur as the engines rev in whispers. Then one by one they take off and climb above the clouds where it is always blue, burning and burning at that summer's end.

There are some radio telephone signals from that summer — pilots taking directions from the women who controlled them from the ground, or screaming at each other to get in formation — that have become trapped between the ground and the Heaviside layer. They bounce back and forward like tennis balls in some endless rally, for they don't decay. Once in a while a radio ham, idly skimming the airwaves late at night, will suddenly be listening to men and women controlling, flying, singing, cursing, dying. All present in the headphones though they are long gone.

And among the few trees that are left beyond the rusting perimeter fence, there is a trunk with large distorted letters bearing a name and a date. It was carved by the other one, the lanky tired one who stands half in, half out the bedroom window of a house in the post-war estate, his tan boots sunk a foot below the floor. The one with his long back turned, whose right arm hangs slightly crooked, who is always starting to turn round, who never fully turns round, whose face would be so familiar. Who speaks in the dark:

1

Late June 1940

First time I saw Tad he was standing in the Botanical Gardens near the station with a brown trilby shading his eyes and his foot on the stump of a 300-million-year-old fossilized tree. He was staring at it like a hunter gazing down at the lion he'd shot. The same look of awe and regret and . . . something.

I lowered my heavy kitbag and stood near him, reading the plaque. Tried to imagine this part of England near the equator and covered in steamy swamps, the huge primitive trees towering over our heads. Thought of the great changes that had taken place, and of the one that was happening right now, and then it didn't seem quite so important and that was a relief.

The figure beside me stirred then straightened up. I felt his eyes flick over me, my uniform still blue and stiff, my kitbag.

'Yes, my friend,' he said, as though continuing a conversation. His voice was throaty and quite strongly accented. 'This is very old, you see.' He tapped the stone tree with a spotless brogue shoe. 'But we are alive and it is not. So we are one up.'

I nodded. So that had been the other part in his expression: quiet triumph. I nodded as though addressing strangers was normal, put it down to his foreignness. And the War.

'Yes,' I said. 'But what will be left of us?'

He laughed then. An easy laugh that I hadn't expected from his heavy, serious face.

'Nothing, my friend!' He held out his hand, it was surprisingly small. I automatically took it, as though this was quite normal. But then, very little was normal recently.

'So you are the gloomy type,' he said. 'I am Tadeusz. I am from Poland but not gloomy, you know.'

I didn't know if Tadeusz was his first or second name. He said it as though it was a title.

'Leonard Westbourne,' I said, 'though people call me Len.'

'Ah yes, the English nickname of intimacy! In that case, you may call me Tad, I think it simpler for you.'

His face suddenly lit up in a smile that brightened the grey day around us. But it wasn't directed at me. With a gesture at once formal and natural he removed his hat and inclined his head as he clicked his heels together. I looked round. A tall and strikingly pretty woman was approaching us.

'Good day, madam!' he said, 'I trust you are well?'

She hesitated. I watched several impulses chase across her face. *Who is this lunatic? Have we met before?* Then something in the warmth of his smile, the deference of his gesture must have reassured her.

'Very well, thank you,' she said. Then she walked on and past us but something about the set of her head suggested she was smiling.

Tad looked after her as if it pleased him to see something so fine. Then he clapped me on the shoulder.

'You see, Len,' he said, 'life is short but there are many possibilities. Was she not beautiful?'

'Maybe,' I said. I hefted my kitbag onto my shoulder. 'But I've a train to catch.'

Then without the trilby shading them, I saw his eyes. They were near-black, hot and restless and suddenly serious.

'Yes,' he said. 'We do not forget the War. Never!'

He said it with such conviction as if it were a curse, such passion that could never be English. Then he put his hand on my arm.

'Come, my friend, let us go to the station and join our squadron and fight this war.'

I stared at him, at his expensive suit. He was quite short and wide, big-boned. With his hunched shoulders and large mobile head and hot dark eyes he suddenly reminded me of a hawk. That same concentrated force. He looked back at me and chuckled at my astonishment.

'You are Sergeant Westbourne, are you not? I am told you are joining with me and you will be catching this afternoon train. Why do you think I introduce myself? My luggage awaits at the station, you know.'

He put his trilby on and adjusted the brim down over his eyes.

'If we hurry, there may be time for a drink of your warm beer at the station bar. There were two women there, very pretty . . . '

★ ★ ★

I hesitated outside the pub. In front of me was the public bar, which looked seedy, especially for someone as immaculately overdressed as my new companion. I suggested we went in the lounge. More comfortable.

He shook his head, sorrowfully it seemed.

'Leonard, I am not bourgeois!' he announced grandly. 'Lounge bar is for the stuffy and the bourgeois. But Tadeusz

Polarczyk is intelligentsia and you are a peasant, yes?'

He pronounced my peasant status in such a matter-of-fact way it was impossible to be offended.

'Yes,' I said. 'I suppose I am a peasant.'

'So we drink in the public bar among the people!'

'Fine,' I said. 'You're buying and please don't call anyone else in there a peasant. They mightn't like it.'

Inside we quickly drank to our good health, then caught the train at a run. So many possibilities, he'd said, and I felt them all around me that evening as the train ground south towards the coast, as solid yet ghostly as that once-living tree turned to stone.

So I just caught the bus at a run as it left the end of Green Road. The conductress stood watching inside and she wasn't smiling.

'It's forbidden to join a moving bus, Miss,' she announced.

I paused halfway up the stair to get my breath back.

'You might have waited for me,' I said.

This time she positively scowled. She wore brown heavy-rimmed glasses and they were just made for scowling.

'If we waited for everyone who's late, we'd never leave the station. Then where would we be?'

'In the station, stupid,' I muttered as I turned and went on up the stair. I half expected her to add *There's a war on, you know*, which seemed to have already become a catch phrase justifying any shortage or stupidity. People had said it as a joke during the phoney war, but now with the fall of France it wasn't so funny.

Upstairs was packed and smoky. There was one place left next to a woman with a pile of yellow hair.

'Excuse me, please,' I said.

She picked her bag off the seat, put it on her knee then glanced at me. She was younger than I'd thought, my age. I felt her take in my uniform, the new duffel bag containing my papers from the training school.

'Thank you,' I said, and sat down.

She took the cigarette from her full mouth, tapped the ash on the floor.

'You're welcome, love.'

Then she buried her head in the magazine she was reading. One of the cheaper, gossipy sort. The conductress came up and I paid my fare. She didn't go away but stared at the magazine my companion was half hidden behind.

'Fare, please,' she snapped. 'I'm talking to you, Missie.'

There was a long pause then the magazine came down. Big blue eyes set around with make-up.

'I've forgotten my purse,' she said. 'Sorry. I'll get off at the next stop.'

'Sorry! There's honest people on this bus pay their fare, but not you. Don't you know there's — ?'

'It's all right,' I said. 'She's with me. I'm paying.'

'Thanks,' she said. 'Thanks so much. Did you see that old bat's face?'

'Yes,' I said. 'That was well worth a few pennies.'

'Like a smoke?'

She held out the packet. Du Maurier. I'd tried as a child, then again at university, but never really got into the habit.

'Thanks,' I said.

We lit up together and I tried not to cough. I blew smoke out into the thick blue-grey fug. Hard to remember what it was like, upstairs in buses in those days.

'I'll pay you back,' she said. 'You're on this bus regular. I seen you before.'

'No need,' I said. 'Really.'

'Thanks. I thought you were toffee-nosed but you're a good sort. Still, doing the bus company is one thing, doing a pal is another.'

I sat with the warm glow of that 'pal'. Truth is, I was lonely in my billet in the town, getting my training through the week, going home at weekends. My university friends had gone their ways, and as for boyfriends, well, I didn't want to think about that.

I finished the cigarette and got up.

'My stop,' I said.

'Tell you what,' she said. 'Let's go to that

Lyons across the street and I'll get you coffee and a cake.'

'But I thought — '

She smiled then, big and wide. Lots of white teeth. I'd see that smile, hear that laugh many times before we were through with that summer.

'I was at school with a waitress there,' she said. 'We used to skip off lots together. If I ask, she might just lose our bill. So?'

I contemplated this world in which people tried to avoid paying on buses, lost bills and didn't go to school, and didn't even feel guilty about it. My mother would be shocked. Alarmed that I would even associate with such a person, as though such a condition might be contagious. As though I might sink back into the class she'd striven to climb out of, the steamy swamp of the Unrespectable.

'Thanks,' I said. 'That sounds great.'

And as we stepped down from the bus, she said, 'I'm Maddy, by the way.'

'Stella,' I said. 'Stella Gardam.'

Then we went for coffee and cake in Lyons and the bill never appeared. I have to say the cake tasted all the sweeter for it, and the coffee had an edge I rather liked. And she told me she was a Naval VAD and how she had her hands full with an outbreak of mumps but the sailors were a load of laughs.

I told her I was training in signals but it was hush-hush and I mustn't say more about it. Work with Radio Direction Finding — what would become Radar — was still a big secret. We'd yet to find just how important it was, back at the end of June that summer, before the battle had really started.

We stood outside on the pavement. I was about to say goodbye and walk back to my digs.

'Here,' she said. 'Fancy going to a RAF dance on Friday? I know the drummer in the band, we can get in free.'

I thought about it. A weekend at home with my mother and respectability. Dad out with the ARP. And I had revision to do.

'That sounds fun,' I said. 'I'd love to.'

And so Maddy Phillips and I met, and so we went to the dance, and so . . . everything.

2

Early July

Yet how light a girl is when you dance, how far removed from a machine! She was pushed my way at the dance once Tad had bowed, clicked heels, seized her friend and whisked her off onto the dance floor. This one looked startled, then amused as we introduced ourselves. I missed the moment to shake hands and just nodded and grinned at her like an idiot, though an enthusiastic one.

'I expect you want to dance,' she said neutrally. Beyond her name, her first words to me.

'Well, yes,' I said. 'Do you?'

She glanced across the dance floor where Tad and her pal were spinning through the crowd. Then she looked me carefully down and up. When she smiled, two faint vertical lines appeared between her eyebrows.

'Yes,' she said.

We looked at each other a moment. I was sweating but wasn't going to let her have it all her own way.

'So,' she said at last, 'are you asking me?'

'I expect so,' I said, then she laughed and I took her right hand and for the first time placed my hand on her firm waist as we caught the beat and swung into a quickstep.

Stella Gardam looked good to me — glowing, chin up, pretty and funny and clever, you could tell. And probably way out of my class. Finished university, no less, now training at something she couldn't tell me about.

'Hush-hush,' she'd whispered in my ear as we turned a foxtrot at the corner of the crowded hall, Tad and her friend having disappeared.

'Oh, go on,' I said. 'Do I look like a spy?'

She leaned back in my arms and looked up at me.

'You look like an honest man,' she said eventually. 'But it's hard to tell these days.'

'Go on,' I said. 'Please.'

The clarinet squawked, the violin went *Aaw* and made it sound almost like harmony.

'All right,' she said, then stretched up to my ear.

'Radio Direction Finding,' she whispered. 'I'm learning to see what's coming our way.'

For a moment I looked into her eyes — wide-set, grey, looking straight back at me, calm and measuring.

'I don't know if that's such a good idea,' I said, and it came out more serious than I'd meant, and made her look away for a moment.

★   ★   ★

Tad and Stella's friend, a cheery bouncing blonde called Maddy, reappeared as the band was packing up. They seemed wrapped in some secret glow or joke. Tad proposed we all met up again soon as possible. I made with the eager nods while he kissed hands and bowed all over the shop and generally cut a dash. To my amazement the women were persuaded, we found a date we could all make, and a place — they were billeted just a couple of miles away. So: the Darnley Arms, twenty hundred hours, God and Goering willing.

Outside in the warm dark, she kissed me on the cheek. Then, as I hesitated, kissed me again, however briefly, on the mouth. Her lips were warm, dry, light. She went back down onto her heels and looked at me.

'Sometimes forewarned is forearmed,' she said. 'I didn't know I was going to do that. Did you?'

A sparky girl. Something in her look is a challenge I would rise to.

'It was a dead cert,' I said. 'Didn't need no RDF to tell me.'

13

I got a quick grin, then she squeezed my arm and walked away. Two shadows detached themselves from behind the hall and Maddy came into the light again and caught up with Stella, straightening her dress. Well, Tad had made his intentions clear enough (*I want rolling that Maddy from here to Cracow*) and she seemed to have no objections at all.

We walked home through the warm darkness, humming 'Red Sails in the Sunset'.

'Did you and Maddy — ?' I asked. No answer but his laugh.

He's not what I'd pictured. Not even an officer, for a start. No moustache (not many of them do, that's for the older ones, the desk men left from the last war). And he's not posh — quite a marked West Country accent, his father works a lathe in some factory, and while my mother would doubtless describe his background as 'salt of the earth', I doubt if she'd want it sprinkled on her back garden, or on her daughter. (Not that it will come to that.)

He's a bit gangly and gauche is Mr Len Westbourne. Maybe this is what I liked about him, that he was embarrassed and stood there like he didn't know what to do when Maddy pushed me towards him at the dance. Because I didn't know what to do either — I mean, I'd only gone to keep Maddy company, not looking for a man.

So I teased him to relieve my own embarrassment. As I waited for a response I wondered if he was slow, and I can't stand slow. But he stood up for himself and forced me to ask if he was asking, because I suddenly did want to dance. No harm in having some fun, just because there's a war on.

To my surprise he danced not badly and was good in the turns. He led well, not bossy, just letting the rhythm push us both around. He knows it's *funny*, dancing, and for that I liked him. I hadn't had a man hold me like that since Evelyn, and before that, of course, Roger of cursed memory.

Anyway, though we'd accepted the date, we'd no real intention of going to meet them at the Darnley. At least, I hadn't. Far as I was concerned, if Maddy wanted a roll under the hedge with our admittedly well-groomed Polish friend, there was no need to drag me along. But though I'd only nodded, I felt somehow implicated, and his face had lit up so . . .

No, I had other things to concentrate on. I'd keep my head well below the parapet on the romantic front for a while yet.

Then we heard the guns around Gravesend as they hit the docks again, broke off the darts match to step outside and watch the show. It wasn't much at that distance, looked more like a nuisance raid than anything big. Since the fall of France we were still waiting for the real thing; it had to come sooner or later. In the meantime, we were free to fanny about.

'So why ain't you lads up there, knockin' 'em down?' one of the locals asked.

I said nothing, just watched our search-lights drain to nothing in the dark. It was rumoured the ack-ack was a waste of time, couldn't shoot high enough. But the gunners had to keep their spirits up, and reassure the public something was being done. I felt for those blokes, running around with their helmets slipping over their eyes, banging off rounds at invisible aircraft while knowing their shells fell short. So pointless, so human.

'His momma is not letting Lennie fly at night,' Tad growled. 'It stunts his growing, you know. And me, I have never liked the overtime.'

In the dark street I smiled to myself,

though our return fire was just a gesture. I'd noticed Tad's English was good except when it suited him, like when dealing with an irate CO or teasing the natives.

'Let's hope you shoot better than you speak English, mate,' one of them said.

These lads were set on beating us, and with their home crowd looking on it was friendly, but a bit of needle too, no doubt. We shrugged, turned away and went back into the pub, nothing we could do. Tad was right, we were no night-fighters.

And I'm no darts player, never have been. Too much time to get tense, to start to doubt myself. As a lad with my dad's old .22, I was always better at a moving target. So exciting to have that power at a distance, hear the crack, feel the recoil and see the rabbit fall over just like that. And I loved rabbit stew. It was the bit in the middle I didn't like, the glazed eye, the blood.

In any case, draughtsmanship has always been my thing, not chatting up women. Though I'd thought this time I'd got lucky. But there was still no sign of Stella and Maddy (a wild one, suitable mate for Tad, I reckoned). I glanced at my watch as Tad picked up the darts. An hour late. Not much chance they'd be coming now. I thought again of those ack-ack gunners, shooting off shells knowing it was useless.

Our opposition, Dave and Tom, two local lads we'd met that evening while jostling for bar space in the Darnley, were frankly in a different class. But we'd had a couple while waiting for the women, and we'd hit one of those hot streaks that comes once in a while, and we were holding them. With their mates watching and making with the wisecracks, it had turned into a bit of a do. Not what I had in mind for the evening, but it was all that was on offer.

So I took a quick drag and went up to the mark to throw. Went for 19, hit treble 17, pinged one off the wire then on impulse switched to 20 and picked up a double. It had been like that all evening. Lucky in darts if not in love.

We won that game. Three-all. A last decider. I got another round in first. No hurry, after all we had nothing better to do.

Shame, really. For a moment I'd thought it might happen.

But our date had always been a speculative shot. We weren't officers, I'm no Clark Gable, and Tad's just too different for most. I checked my watch again. Nearly an hour and a half late. Finish the game, one more drink then leave.

They got away first throw but so did we,

and chased each other down great style from 501. Suddenly I was standing with 50 to shoot, three arrows in my hand, the local aces needing only double tops to wrap it up.

'When the going gets tough . . . ' Tad whispered. 'You can do it, Lenny.'

I put down my cigarette, casual like, and toed the line. With the room silent and all eyes on me, I hit the 10. Then went for tops. Tensed on it, hit the ruddy wall. Someone laughed, I hesitated, and in that bright room felt alone, not tough at all. Certain of defeat, I drew my arm back anyway.

The street door opened. I saw Stella's eyes on me, wide forehead beneath that permed-up sweep of auburn hair, and Maddy right behind her. I glanced, turned back to the board, threw.

The moment it left my hand I was sure. Nothing, no bombs, no ruddy war could change it now. My dart slid through the smoky air and thudded into double 20.

Hubbub, laughter, Tad's whoop. Mine host set us up a pint apiece while we shook hands with Dave and Tom.

'Won't be so lucky next time,' Dave muttered, and I rather agreed as we pushed over to our girls. She smiled, I smiled. For that moment there seemed no flap, no worry. Though she had class, I had my moments and that might do. Would blooming have to!

'What was all the fuss about?' she asked.

'We got lucky and won against the run of play,' I replied.

'I see,' she said. 'Maybe it's as well we were late. Missed the boring bit.'

But she took my arm, just like that, as we went through to the Snug. And when we were seated with the beers and gins and she turned to me again, I seemed to see what she'd say next, what I'd say, how it would all turn out, as though a searchlight had just leapt forward in the dark and we had always been its mark.

When I got back to my billet that evening — the dour bulk of Mrs Mackenzie standing guard as usual just inside the door — I wasn't about to go anywhere, particularly not a smoke-filled noisy pub. I was tired and headachy from a day in front of the screen, trying to learn to read those cursed blips and dips, and there were pages of Operational Notes to study. I phoned Maddy and told her. We had a brief falling out then made up again.

Then after the evening meal — eaten in near-silence as always, to the rhythm of Mr Mackenzie's chomping and her complaints as though the War had been started to inconvenience her personally — I studied awhile then lay down, looking at the ceiling and thinking about my past love life. For a while I felt sorry for us all, then I sat up in bed and threw the Signals textbook into the corner. Damned if I'd let those sad affairs spoil my life. Anyway, it was only a night's fun and chat. And that poor pilot would be so sorry if I didn't show up.

So I went downstairs and phoned Maddy,

then got dressed up — not so much, just enough to look good without being desperate. By the time she got round and we cycled through the blackout, feeling our way between dark roadway and deeper darkness of the verge, hearing the not-so-distant drone of bombers, and finally got to the village, we were badly late. So late we even discussed whether we dared show our faces and if they'd still be there, and we stood outside in the dark, suddenly unsure of ourselves. There was a burst of laughter inside and I felt excluded, wanted to leave yet longed to join in.

'This is ridiculous,' I said. 'There's nothing to stop us having a drink before we bike back.'

And I pushed the door open into the brightness and saw him and he saw me then he threw a dart and there was a lot of noise and cheering and I was glad we'd come. So pleased I forgot all caution and took his arm as we went through to the Snug.

I looked round at us and raised my glass.

'Happy outcomes,' I said.

Don't think I didn't catch you looking at me, young Len, as Maddy and that eccentric friend of his — apparently I must learn to call him Tad — ran through their routines. I felt your eyes brush over me like very light hands, but they were at least respectful, amused, wondering, and you kept them (in so far as a man can) above rather than below my neck. But look you did, till I had to laugh my way back into conversation.

We talked of nothing important and with a couple of gins inside it was fun. They tried to explain about darts, we swapped histories in brief. He's Volunteer Reserve, the non-officer lot, transferred only recently to the RAF with no combat experience as yet.

'Takes all my time just to fly the thing,' he said. 'And stay in formation. The sky's so huge and bright, you've no idea.'

As we talked there were soft thuds from the direction of the docks like someone clearing their throat or coughing and I noticed how he cocked his head a moment, paused, then came back into our conversation as though it was nothing. At least nothing that need concern us, and that I both appreciated and resented.

'Stella tells the future,' he said to Tad, and I realized he was a little drunk. 'She sees what's coming. Like how many and at what height.'

I shrugged modestly.

'That would be anything to do with the tall masts?' Tad said. 'Or are you just psychic, you know?'

'Of course she is,' Maddy said. 'And so am I.'

'Prove it to me,' Tad said.

'Well, I'll tell you what you're thinking about.'

She bent forward and whispered in his ear while Len and I didn't look at each other.

'You *are* psychic,' Tad whooped. 'So correct! Or maybe you are just hearing your own thoughts?'

I had to smile then, thinking of the blips I'd been spending the last weeks with, those shifting echoes. The trick is learning to read them, I thought vaguely through my third gin.

*　*　*

We had no need for them to walk us home. I pushed my bike, which came usefully between us. Tad and Maddy drifted further behind and disappeared somewhere in the darkness.

It was a mild night, not long past midsummer and not entirely black though the moon was down. The stars were faint through the sky, the searchlights had gone to bed. He crossed in front of the bike, came round to my side and put his arm round my waist. We walked on a while in silence, both suddenly incapable of speech. The air was soft and moist. I smelled nettles in the ditch then something sour-sweet that may have been hawthorn. Blackout sharpens the sense of smell, I thought, then realized I'd said it out loud.

'You lose one thing and gain another,' he replied. 'That's how it goes.'

We walked on, his hand now firm on my waist, gripping and not slipping down. And for some reason I was annoyed at his saying so, or doing so. I was supposed to be in charge here.

'So what have you lost recently?' I said.

'Certainty,' he replied straight away. 'Like everyone else. I don't know what happens tomorrow, next week or next year. We could have an invasion. In a month there could be paratroopers coming down this lane.'

I shivered. It seemed wildly unlikely, yet it was true ever since the fall of France, everyone knew it. And, I confess, part of that shiver was excitement.

'And gained?' I asked.

A long pause, so long I'd started to look at the sky again, thinking I'd been too personal. And I hadn't been fishing, honest.

'A life,' he said quietly, and his long-fingered hand gripped my waist tighter for a moment.

We stood at the crossroads, waiting for the lovebirds if that's what they were. Honestly, I think it's happening under every hedgerow in England. Which is no reason why I should add to the numbers. Eventually they appeared out of the darkness. He was pushing her bike, which squeaked; she was hanging on to his free arm like a willing satellite. The four of us stood there a moment, Maddy still straightening her hair. The conversation lit up, fizzled, went out. I was very tired now and ready to get home, look at the ceiling and let sleep come quickly.

My young man — how I love to patronize him, it saves being alarmed by him — had put his hands in his pockets and run out of words. Was swivelling on his heels, looking down then over my shoulder. I took pity on him, took him aside and on impulse kissed him firmly on the lips though we kept our mouths closed. And again. This time he got the idea, though he seemed a little out of practice. Then we said good night and went our ways, Maddy already debriefing me, incredulous I hadn't dragged him into a ditch and had my way with him.

I said nothing, but laughed along with her. It had been a good, merry, insignificant night, a fine way to relax after a hard day with the blips.

Admit it: said Yes to a date next week, just the two of us, my beanpole pilot and me. Wasn't apologizing to Evelyn. Wasn't mourning Roger as I fell asleep.

3

Early July

Woke around five, my head still thick from booze and cigarettes. Bit of a carry-on last night! Thought of her face at the pub doorway, my throw, that moment when everything fits. I wondered if it would be like that for my first kill, or if I'd get it first, cannon shells crashing into my tiny cockpit, the plane catching fire and going down with me screaming and trying to get the hood back before —

Some carry-on. At least two drinks too many. Did we really make complete asses of ourselves? How far did Tad get with Maddy? Should I have pushed things further with Stella so she'd remember me? Even if she wanted to. Her kiss had caught me off-balance and my response had been clumsy.

I blushed in the dimness of my billet. If I had another opportunity, the suave or witty things I'd say, the certainty with which I'd kiss her . . .

Her lips had been warm. Not unwilling, I

29

thought. How does one know the meaning of these things, or if it means anything more than an evening's pleasure snatched during a war? The spark of a cigarette in the blackout . . .

Seeing her next week. The game's not over yet, this war has hardly started.

Then I was on my feet on the cold linoleum floor, drinking a glass of water held to the dawn light. Then another. I changed into running gear, tied my gym shoes then went out the door, glancing at Johnny Staples on his back, arm across his face as though to protect himself. He'd downed two and a probable in France and though only a sergeant like myself, had been promoted to the Hon. Harry St John's wingman. One of the insiders, while I was still the new boy, getting the jokes too late and struggling to stay in position.

I stood outside the door, feeling cold water sloosh round my muddy guts. There were low bands of mist wrapping the poplars that lined the flinty road, just their tips showing, still and unmoving. In the farm across the way, a Land Girl was leading horses into the yard. As I tried not to stare at her trousers, thinking what my mum would have said, she saw me and waved silently.

I waved back, did a few stretching

exercises, then set off on my sobering-up run. Loped across the common, feet already damp with dew, then through a stile and down the hawthorn lane. Then ran past the lightning-blasted big tree, turned onto the ridgeway and up across the fields. There was me leaping and dodging nettles and cowpats like squashed hats, scattering rabbits and pheasants, whooping after them. My arms and legs were going like bilge-pumps, emptying my carcass of last night's slop.

Into the trees, the big oaks and beeches. Cool in there, soft forest floor under my feet, spotted fox holes but no fox. I came to forks in the path and for once chose on impulse, without hesitation, in love with summer and my youth and the onrush of it all.

Came back down the hill, sun up and already steaming off the dew, through the village, past the row of sleeping houses up Saracen Lane. Grabbed a cold shower, kitted up, picked up the roll-neck sweater because it would be cold at 20,000 feet. Bolted down some breakfast, signed the chit then jumped into the truck — old Goosey driving, 'Been out wenching, son?' — as we rattled down the lane and took the short cut through the orchard where the apples and pears were starting to plump.

Blokes were talking and laughing but I

wasn't listening. Thinking of how I'd be seeing her next Thursday, God willing. For once there were no worries, no fear. We're alive till we die, that much is certain. And it's going to be a scorcher, you can tell.

The green blips sank and squiggled. My head ached and my eyes wouldn't focus. My uniform was itchy, the blouse clung to my skin, and I could already smell the warm reek off my armpit.

Sergeant Farringdon leant closer and insisted. We were informal on good days but this wasn't one of them.

'Reading, Corporal,' she repeated in her posh drawl. I knew she'd been at some smart boarding school because she was always saying how the Forces were just the same but softer. 'Distance, bearing, height,' she demanded. 'Estimated number.'

I leaned closer to the screen and tried to make sense of a bunch of squiggles. I repented of that last gin the night before. I repented too of that kiss and that date. Right now I wanted to be left alone for a long time. Maybe I should have done nursing like Maddy, something simple. Trouble is, often I don't like people much and I can't stand complaining. In fact, I'm not really a very nice person. Which Maddy, for all her sexual carry-ons, is.

'Fifty miles,' I said. 'Bearing — '

'*Hostiles, fifty miles*,' Farringdon said too loud and close. 'You've got to identify them as hostiles.'

'But they're not,' I said.

'For the purposes of this exercise, they are, Corporal Gardam. Don't pretend you hadn't forgotten. Believe me,' she added as I grappled with the dial, 'they'll be hostiles soon enough. We're on our own now and Mr Churchill isn't asking for peace, as far as I recall.'

'Wouldn't mind some peace,' I muttered, hating her and all her class, then read off the bearing. She nodded, corrected a little on the calibrated dial.

'Now height,' she said.

I fed in the range and bearing and waited till height came up on the calculator.

'Twenty-three thousand,' I said. 'Angels twenty-three.'

'Estimated number,' she demanded.

I squinted at the tiny screen, the falling and rising blips. Only experience could help me here, and like my pilot I didn't have enough.

'Sixty?' I ventured. 'Maybe more.'

Farringdon shook her head. 'No. See the way it falls?' She pointed with her pencil. 'The width and rate? More like thirty, unless they're stacked, in which case the line is

34

thicker. Say thirty-five.'

'Sorry, Sergeant,' I said. 'I'm not at my best today.'

She glanced at me then. A quick, hard, undeceived glance.

'Try getting to bed earlier,' she said briskly. 'I'd suggest you restrict your contact with pilots to R/T rather than the pub.'

I glanced at Jean Finlay and Mo sitting along from me, but they were suddenly very busy looking at their screens.

'An alternative suggestion, Corporal,' Farringdon said more gently. She put her hand on my shoulder a moment. Her nails were long and perfect, like her teeth. 'If you're going out on the bash, drink plenty of water before going to bed, and try to make sure you've a morning off next day. When we do this for real you'll need to be at your best. It'll come soon enough.'

Then she smiled and passed on to Jean, leaving me to go through another couple of exercises, and for the next hour I was much too busy to think of pilots and dates and sweet clumsy kissing.

The Battle of Britain, it was decided later, began on 10 July, a Wednesday. It dawned with cloud and rain, which cleared to brilliant heat. Had Stella Gardam been entrusted with a live screen on the Chain High radar network, she'd have seen enough activity to bring on another headache.

The first major attack was on a Channel convoy. Len Westbourne's squadron was not one of those sent to intercept the attack. Instead they waited in their huts as it rained, then put out the deck chairs when the sun came through. They read the papers, flicked through the *Picture Post* and *Lilliput*, played cards and argued about tactics and pubs and what had gone wrong in France.

Some wore shirt and tie and polished shoes, as if respectability was needed to kill or be killed. Others wore roll-neck sweaters under their Mae West flotation jackets, and sheepskin flying boots — they were mostly veterans of France, entitled to this casual dress, like senior pupils in a school. Entitled to sit and sweat and feel the tickle under their arms as the sun grew higher.

France, it was agreed, had been a shambles. They'd been shot up on the ground, messed around, retreating from aerodrome to flying school field to finally sleeping in tents. Orders were conflicting, sometimes impossible. Without a warning system, they had to fly wasteful standing patrols, which amounted to — as St John put it — *flying all over the shop while the buggers blow up the airfield behind your back*. It was agreed they were much better off like this, fighting in their own back yard.

But the tight formations they'd worked so hard at were proving a liability. Some grew heated on this point, especially those like Billy (Shortarse) Madden, who'd been *blown out of the sky, so busy keeping an eye on my No. 1 I never saw the bastard*. The looser German *Rotte* grouping, worked out in Spain then honed through Poland then Belgium, Holland and France, was much better for fighters.

Then the CO strolled by and reminded them that tight formation was still official policy and would be adhered to as long as he was in command, though he might condone the use of a tail-end Charlie, weaving at the back to protect the rear.

Len sat and listened, knowing he would, as the least experienced pilot, be that tail-end

Charlie, and wondered who was going to protect him.

'This is very silly,' Tad muttered. 'What need of formations? We fly, we get close, we kill them. That is all, you know.'

The pilots in earshot stirred uneasily. Better to complain or make a joke of it. Not talk of killing and being killed. Better to say *We down a few kites, and the odd chap will buy it. Drink to him and carry on, that's the form*.

They were stood down, and went to get some lunch, though it didn't sit well on some jumpy stomachs. Rumours came in from the Channel that there'd been a do involving Hurricanes and Me109s stacked above Me110s and Dornier bombers. Most of the convoy had got through, the losses were said to be ten to four, and two of those had bailed out. Billy Higson was said to have gone down in flames.

A moment's silence, a blip in the gossip and speculation. Len exchanged glances with Tad, who nodded like he'd expected that then went back to dealing his patience hand. Neither of them had ever really known Billy, but he had just become one of those whose name would only be mentioned in a certain sort of way, with a short pause before and, like as not, a joke after. *Good old Billy!*

Remember that time in Deauville when he flagged down that taxi and told it to drive to Paris — and it did!

Good old Billy, Len thought, dead somewhere in the Channel. Had he had a hot date too, before the machine-gun bullets smashed into his cockpit and then the flames? Tad just seems to accept that, but I can't.

He blinked, shook his head to flick away the thought. Then he turned another page of *Mr Standfast*, the glare bouncing off the paper making it hard to focus or pay attention for long.

★ ★ ★

They don't know what has just begun. They don't know about the Battle of Britain; it's not called that yet. On the other side this phase would be known as the *Kanalkampf* or Struggle for the Channel. While the RAF pilots have the tension of uncertainty and waiting, the *Luftwaffe* pilots know from their orders of the evening before exactly when they'll be flying and where — which generates its own sort of tension, sitting for hours watching the clock inch on. Unlike the RAF fliers, they can play chess or tennis or read a book, knowing the length of time that has to be filled.

39

None of these people know the outcome of anything — the War, the next week, who will survive and who won't, if the troopship barges amassing across the Channel will shortly be launched. They are the most up-to-date people on the planet and still they don't know.

That's what keeps them on their toes. It makes breathing shallow and stomachs jumpy. It makes Len long for Thursday, to see Stella again. Only then will he know where his life might go.

Remember: far as they're concerned they are as up to date as anyone alive, the last word in modern, with all the outcomes still unknown.

4

Mid-July

There's a scratchy pause between the Tannoy switching on and the announcement that follows, and it jerks in the gut like someone has pulled a string. What comes next could be music, or one of the CO's jokes, or it could be time to get off our behinds and do what we're paid for. *Scramble!*

Even as we run for our kites with Tad on my right stuffing cards into his battledress pocket, I notice the relief of an end to waiting, like a child finally going into the dentist's room. I smell the heat coming off the turf, feel my parachute bumping awkwardly off my legs, hear the shouting and behind it somewhere a wood pigeon cooing in the woods and for a moment wish myself among the cool trees, reliving my boyhood.

But I'm running, in my prime, keyed-up and trigger-happy, eyes sharp and reactions spot on. As I jump onto the wing and clamber in and Fred Tate the engine mechanic starts up and the whole airframe begins to roar and shake, I feel myself come fully alive. He helps

41

me strap in. I sign Form 700 whereby I accept this perfect machine in full flying order. The airframe mechanic Evans, a tall, silent, grim man with a stubby moustache, pulls away the trolley accumulator. Fred gives me the thumb then jumps down. I glance over at my section leader; he's starting to roll already. They pull the chocks away and I begin to go.

Tail up. Roar, rumble, thump as I go over a bump. *Come on, come on!* over the R/T. Controls starting to respond. Bump, thump, feel sick, which could be nerves or uneven ground, check airspeed then ease the stick back and we're off. That's better. Wheels up, whine, clunk. OK, look to my No. 1. Can't see him. *You've overshot me Leonard. Get in tight.*

I do. Bo Bateson — a hearty type, too many backslaps and bad jokes for my liking but then I'm an awkward so-and-so and he is a good pilot and of course he's been to France, shot down three and a half — is already in tight on the other side. I look in my mirror, see Red section is right behind us, Tad out on the right. Mirror's shaking, hard to see well, got to learn to cope with that.

We've rehearsed this often enough, I've even been allowed two sessions of gunnery practice, but this is not a rehearsal.

42

Controller's voice spattering in headphones. *Climb to 20,000 feet. Expect bandits. Repeat, bandits coming your way.*

I'm looking and looking, swivelling between watching Geoff Prior's wing tip and looking up ahead and above. It's so bloody bright, and the cockpit frame shakes. And so much sky, planes just disappear in it. Then in seconds they're on you. The first times are when you're most likely to get killed, everyone agrees on that. Fifteen thousand. Seventeen. I wonder if Stella's following us on her screen. Can't even picture what she looks like. Just those grey-hazel eyes, looking straight back at me for a moment.

Shake head, keep looking. The air's thin up here, the plane's just sliding about in the sky. *Bandits! Two-o'clock. Line astern — here we go!* Can't see anything. Shake my head, blink my eyes and look again and there they are. Not that many, a dozen maybe. Bombing Channel ports, most like. Soon put a stop to that.

Red section has peeled off behind me. Slip in line astern, push throttle through the gate, feel the big surge. Remember to set gun sights for Heinkel wingspan, feel pleased about that then look above for fighters coming down.

Suddenly, so suddenly I'm in among the

43

bombers. Fire off at a Heinkel, swerve to miss the next one, fire at a third and see the formation break up. A Hurri, maybe Tad, right up the arse of a bomber. Bits flying off in all directions. Then a bright flash and it's gone. Tad roaring triumph in my earphones.

Rattle across my wings like someone running a rod along railings. The plane shakes, staggers. Damn! Stopped looking! Throw the stick to right corner, everything goes grey, just see a Me109 flash past me. Try to turn, get a wild shot in but he just dives and is gone. Don't feel sharp enough to turn on my back and go down after him. Turn after the bombers. They've split, one is going down in flames. God, this happens so quick. Which one to follow? Look behind!

Here's one, below me, a fighter. I dive on it, press the red button and even as I feel my kite slow with the recoil I see the wing shape of my target and know it's a Spitfire. Hell! But I miss him and he's gone. I look around. Nothing anywhere. Check behind. Nothing. Where have they gone? Where is everyone?

Empty sky. Right wing looks ripped a bit, controls sluggish. Lucky man. Get out while the going's good. Last look around and head for home. Somehow I've fired all my ammo, all fifteen seconds' worth. Must get closer next time but it's so quick, so damn quick . . .

Feel tired going home. Then glad, throttling down over perimeter wire, the trees, those deep green trees. Thinking of tea, some grub, a cigarette. All those appetites returning. Thump, rumble, feel sick again. Taxi up, cut engine. Sit a moment and listen to the silence. My first contact.

★   ★   ★

'Do some shooting, then?'

Evans the airframe mechanic strokes the wing, the blownaway patches over the guns. I climb out awkwardly.

'Yes,' I say. 'Didn't hit anything.'

He looks disappointed, almost disgusted. His little moustache twitches.

'Think two bombers went down,' I say. 'All our chaps OK?'

He points across the field. 'That's the last of them back now,' he says.

I walk over the grass, exhausted yet fizzing inside, needing to talk about it. Prior waves and waits for me. I feel good, walking over the fresh-cut grass towards him, joining the club.

Strange idea of a date. He was standing outside the Darnley Arms and instead of going in he asked if I minded going for a walk. I smiled to myself, imagining full well what this might entail, but said yes just the same.

We took a path into the woods when the sun was low, and followed it towards the next village. He didn't say much. Not, I think, because he had nothing to say but because he was too wrapped up in what he needed to say.

As we walked, hands hanging loose but not touching each other, he asked how my training was going. I told him as he struggled to listen. He sharpened up when I told him I'd be on the receiver for real in another week.

'Congratulations,' he said. 'That's wonderful.'

I nodded modestly. 'It's a big responsibility,' I said. 'You feel it. My heart beats faster just thinking of it. Those blips are real. Real planes, real bombs.'

He nodded, listening hard, I felt, to something inside himself.

'Yes,' he said at last. 'I have to admit we rely on you to point us in the right direction. In fact we're blind without you. We'd have to be up on standing patrol all the time, and we haven't got the resources.'

We walked on through the heavy leaves. He kicked them over, frowning. He told me he was a country boy, a peasant, as his friend Tad called it. He waited to see if I'd laugh, but I just nodded and he went on. His father had been a gamekeeper till the estate let him go, then a joiner, then worked a lathe. Now working in one of the new aircraft construction factories in the town, but still living in the country and going in on his motorbike every day.

One sister, he didn't say much about her. She wasn't living at home any more. His father was away working all hours. They were all scattered by the War. Everything had changed.

'But this,' he said, and wrapped his big hand round a head-high branch, 'this doesn't change. It's still summer, then it will be autumn, then leaves will fall and it'll be winter. In fact,' he said and laughed apologetically, 'I often think I prefer trees to people. They've got more dignity and they don't suddenly up sticks and move.'

He looked at me anxiously, but because he

was showing me a bit of himself, I didn't laugh.

'Still, their conversation must be limited,' I said. 'The trees, I mean. Though their leaves do turn gorgeously.'

He looked to see if I was taking a rise, and I was but just a little bit. I told him I was born in a new street right on the edge of town so I knew what he was talking about and how he felt. As a child I'd spent a lot of time by myself in the fields. But since the War had started I was trying to be closer to people. In fact, I found the part of town I'd been billeted in rather too quiet. I wanted to go to London with my friend Maddy. I felt protected in a crowd.

He sat down abruptly, leaning against a big oak at the top of the rise. The sun was just going down, splintering through the leaves, and cattle bugled hoarsely to each other from the next field. There was no one in sight as he patted the ground beside him.

Here we go, I thought, but sat down anyway. He began by picking up a big wizened chestnut leaf and began to shred it, very delicately, with his nails. He picked at it, frowning to himself, till it was a skeleton. Held it up to the last of the sun then threw it away and raked for another. He certainly knew how to keep a girl waiting. I edged closer then, seeing he was fully occupied, began on a leaf myself.

He began to talk. Quietly, as the dew came down. Talked about his first attack earlier in the week. About how big and empty the sky was before and after, and what a shambles it was in between. How everything happened too fast, how he wasted ammunition, how he'd nearly shot down a Spitfire with a reflex shot. ('Luckily I missed,' he said. 'As usual.') How he'd had his best chance with a dive bomber but overshot.

'Maybe I'm just useless at it,' he said and laughed. 'Still, at least they're giving us practice. They haven't come in strength yet, mostly just attacking shipping. I guess the Navy wouldn't agree!'

They'd shot down seven in the week, plus two probables. A man called Bentley in the next flight had been killed. Prior had been shot down but baled out, was slightly concussed but would be back soon. Tad had got another probable Junkers 87, which translated as a Stuka. Tad hated them above all aircraft, called them *the bully boys*. Apparently he had memories of them from Poland, screaming down on the infantry and just a few old biplanes to defend with. Tad had this theory that getting close was the key, but you had to be a great pilot or lucky to do that, and in any case the guns weren't synchronized for close, and it was dangerous . . .

I let him talk because he needed to. And, yes, because I was interested. Those blips were real. Those squiggles translated to tons of flying metal, to fighters and bombers and, above all, men sitting sweating inside them, soft flesh and blood inside their uniforms as they fired at each other.

It horrified and fascinated me because this man talking quietly beside me, shredding leaves and talking as though he was groping towards some destination, had made it real for the first time. Real and frightening, as I could hear in his voice he'd been frightened. Real and frightening because as I sat beside him while the light faded, I began to care about that particular flesh and blood, those hands, that catch in the voice, that apologetic laugh, and I began to tell myself this was a bad idea. A very bad idea, quite different to but on a par with Roger.

He stopped talking, and looked through the wood and over the field. Then he turned his head and looked at me and it seemed he was really seeing me, not just a woman but *me*. He took my hand and laughed.

'Waste of good drinking time,' he said. 'Quite unacceptable.' He got up and pulled

50

me to my feet. 'Sorry to be a bore,' he added.

When he laughed he seemed quite different, suddenly lighthearted and young, as he should be.

'That's all right,' I said. 'I'm interested, though I am quite thirsty.'

He laughed again as if I'd said something delightful. Then as I smiled uncertainly, he leaned closer and kissed me, just like that, and it was very acceptable.

★ ★ ★

It is really not a good idea to get interested in this man. I have eyes, I have ears. I read the papers. Even if the scores are true, his survival is not, I think, very likely.

In the Darnley Arms I drank gin too fast and laughed too much and kissed him too long as we said good night. What else can we do? In bed my thoughts drifted sleepily towards prayer. Let him at least live first, I thought. Let us live.

5

Mid-July

'*There is reason*,' Tad said.

'A reason,' I corrected him automatically.

'Yes,' he said. 'There's a reason why we doing this.'

He was sprawled next to me on the grass in the shade at the far side of the dispersal hut. We were on stand-by after flying twice already that day, no contact made. Every so often one of us would get up and hurry to the toilet block. It was a strain on the guts and bowels, climbing to near 20,000 feet in an unpressurized cabin, then coming straight back down again. The biggest strain was expecting to be shot at any moment, bullets clattering in out of a clear sky, the whole body tense as you wait to kill or be killed. And then — nothing. No contact. Fly home and wait to do it all over again. Exhausting. It's as well we were young and immortal, of course we were.

'Remind me,' I said. 'Is it for the money?'

Tad glanced up at me sharply as though checking something. His eyes were hot and black, a shock, as if as a child I'd just touched the surface of my mum's stove. He always seemed relaxed and leisurely, but I'd begun to notice how his knee jumped continuously when he was sitting. Even when he was lying like this he was never quite still.

'You English,' he said. 'Always kidding.'

He nodded and finished laying out his patience deck. Then as his hands moved steadily among the cards, he told me his story.

He was born in Cracow. The most beautiful city in the saddest country. On a childhood visit to his uncle's estate — he loved his uncle but was bored by adult talking and endless fields — he heard a buzzing-saw sound. Like ripping in the sky. It got louder then came roaring over the house. The wings — it was a biplane, you know — rocked from side to side then it flew on away. Low and level. He stood transfixed, all boredom and impatience shaken away.

A brown haze came from under the plane. Spraying of crops, his Uncle Stefan explained. The family headed back into the house, only Tad stood on the porch, watching the plane turn, come back again, thunder low over the house then rise up and away, all thoughts of knights and heroes driven out of his mind.

'I could not believe this,' he said as he

moved a stack of cards, 'that our neighbour owned one of these, bought in France. That he, a man I knew, flew it. I knew we must go to visit him. I do not rest until we do.'

Small boy reaching up to touch the wires. Runs his hands over the strange covering material. Lifted up into the cockpit, feels the stick in his two hands, looks back and sees the rudder turn. Half stands up to see forward, leans into the breeze coming over the fields, feels the possibility of flight. Yes, I could see him all right. It hadn't been so different with me.

Tad straightened the cards carefully. 'So I learned to fly when I leave school,' he said. 'Happy as Larry boy. My father, he is a professor, you know. He teaches history and he's not so happy with me. Get a real job, he says. Get education. But I insist. I pass my licence. Started off with commercial work, freight, you know. Then at an air show I meet this American guy, Tommy. He does acrobatics like I have never seen. We talk, we like each other. He shows me tricks. I learn quickly, a pilot falls ill, I join his barnstorming show and we went all over, making folks gasp. This was when I learned better English too. Also I speak German, French, some Russian.'

Right enough, Len thought, I'm a peasant

and Tad's probably the best acrobatic pilot in the squadron. Only he doesn't do it often in case people think he's shooting a line.

'Yes, we went all over,' Tad continued. 'First the States and Canada, then Europe. England of course, then France . . . then Germany.' He paused, turned over another card, pulled a face and turned over the one beneath. Either this was a new form of patience or he was definitely cheating.

'That was 1937,' he continued. 'Not a nice time. We saw the new Messerschmitt, I flew it once. It was some machine, much ahead of anything we'd seen. Fast, turns quick, lots of gunpower — it's a bitch to land, though.'

He pulled down a line of cards, laid them as an extra column then turned over the one he'd exposed and played on.

'We had days off in Hamburg and Vienna and Berlin. Things we saw in the streets . . . '

He paused, came to a standstill on his patience and cheated again, flipping over another card and carried on.

'Where I grew up in Cracow then Lvov,' he said, 'we had plenty Jewish neighbours. There was an old man I used to visit, you see, a special friend to me when young. A girl I used to play with — I suppose you say I fancied her. Other children in my class at school . . . They were just people, you know? Lots of

Poles talk bad of Jews and gypsies, but my father is Liberal and he doesn't agree. And I honoured my father, in this I agree. But in Germany all kinds of people are not people any more. My father . . . '

His hands stopped moving. He leaned forward toward me, bending into his shadow.

'What we saw there was bad stuff,' he said. 'Beatings, breaking windows, making them register and wear . . . I knew then there would be trouble, trouble for us all. You can't imagine, Len, not in this falling-asleep country. Nothing ever happens here, till now.

'Their pilots were OK. You know flyers. Some had been in Spain and learned much. They were open to us about this. What I notice is that for them bombers are the hot number — dive bomber to support ground troops, the twin engine bomber to destroy cities and factories and kill morale stonedead. The bomber always gets through, that's what they say.'

'Not if we can help it,' I said. 'Seems to me you can break up a sky full of bombers with half a dozen fighters.'

Tad flipped another card over, shifted it to another column.

'We'll find out soon,' he said. 'But these German pilots, they are keen. They are hot to trot, you know? And I think: trouble. They say they have best planes, best pilots, best tactics, and I think they are right. They are the best, it is a fact. Look at what they do in my country. Then in France. They destroy our little air force, mostly on the ground. Bombs and bullets and cannon — no defence. We fight in our silly planes but it is hopeless. Many brave friends die. Stukas bomb crap out of Army. We fight hard but every day going back, back. Then we plan a counterattack. Next day, the damn Russians invade. My country is finished.'

'How did you get out?' I asked.

'I flew to Bucharest,' he said. 'Last day, I see my father and family. I want to stay but my father say No. I must leave and fight. That is hard, you see? He is Liberal and I fear for him. I fear for my brothers and my sister. My mother is long dead, you know. We all say goodbye outside house in Lvov. It is a fine autumn day, flowers in gardens, and tanks they are coming. We embrace. Many tears. I say I will stay, but my father drags me to the car. I look back and see them for the last time. Later I hear he is . . . '

A long pause. His big head went down over the cards and the day seemed to get darker. When he continued his voice was quiet but thick in his throat. How much older he felt than the rest of us.

'The Germans come, round up all Liberals. My father, he is dragged from our house. They tie his hands. They say he is a traitor. He says nothing, just looks at them. All Liberals they take to square. A major makes a speech. Then they are hanged. Takes long time to die, you know, hanged. He tries to speak, but no one can hear what he says. Then he is dead. Each man gets one bullet in head to be sure. End of my father.'

He moved two columns, piled up cards on his aces, working fast now.

'One brother escape. In hills, I think. The other taken by Russians because intelligentsia, I am told he is sent to Siberia for labour. No news. My poor sister . . . '

He tailed off but his hands kept moving, sorting, stacking, forcing the game to work out.

'Think I give a damn about British Empire, Lennie? That's not why I leave good night life in Bucharest, get to France and steal a plane — a Morane, it's a heap — talked myself into goddamn Limey air force. I am here for my father and family, my destroyed country. My sister. I don't want to tell you the terrible thing that happens to her. But all this I will revenge.'

He gave a grunt of satisfaction as he piled on the last jack, queen, king. Then he looked up and somehow smiled.

'And the chance to kiss some pretty girls! So I say, there is a reason. There's a reason why we're shooting at those maybe decent guys who are shooting back at us. Why we must kill them. End of my long lecture. Sorry, my friend.'

There was a long pause between us. Part of me wished he hadn't spoken. But he had and I could feel it hanging like a sack of dirty water in my gut.

'You cheated,' I said at last.

'Of course,' Tad replied. 'What else do we do when we attack out of the sun? Everybody cheats. This is serious, no game. You think I am reckless, but it is not so. You guys are brave enough, but you love the amateur too much. Now let's play poker, penny a point.'

'I can't play poker.'

'Much the better.' Tad grinned. 'I learn from American Tom. Lemme show you.'

I'd never heard him talk about his family before. It made me uneasy, not just because he spoke with such feeling but because it sounded like some kind of last statement he wanted to make. So that someone in this foreign land would know him before he died. It gave me a queasy feeling in my stomach, the way Stella did sometimes.

'Fine,' I said. 'Always happy to fleece the intelligentsia.'

* * *

A bunch of us lay on the grass, learning how to bluff in Tad's poker school. Has to be said some of the blokes were naturals at it, like all good pilots bluff. I'd gone inside the dispersal hut for a brew when the Tannoy clicked. Then the announcement. *Scramble!*

Running across the grass, into the plane. Strap in, check parachute, the prop catches, revs, becomes invisible. And this has become invisible, has become routine. It tugs us forward like the airscrew, bouncing over the grass, pulls us into the air and tucks us neatly in formation.

This time we actually pick up the enemy around 17,000 feet with height on our side. Their bombers with a fighter escort circling above. We have our instructions: go for the bombers. Let the faster Spits take on the Me109s. No heroics.

For the first time it doesn't happen so fast. For the first time the shaking of mirrors and cockpit and the aircraft bouncing in the air isn't so distracting. For once it's not like trying to thread a needle on a bobbing cork. We dive down past the fighters straight into bombers, taking them head-on. Perfect.

This time my prey is lined up, a juicy thin-tailed Dornier come to bomb hell out of the convoy below, and I'm cool and angry. Think of Tad, his family, father choking at the end of a rope. Check my tail, swerve and come closer till he fills my gun sight.

He sees me, starts to turn. Get in a burst as he comes across, then I turn and follow. Swing to avoid the sparkling burst of tracer from the rear-gunner, then come in from below, give him another. Nothing happens at first. Then a few bits start to fall off, the plane slumps sideways and down. I fly into smoke. Cut away, pull up to avoid the Me109 streaking by, let him go. Lost my Dornier, into light cloud then lost everyone. Empty sky at other end of cloud. Check compass and head for home, thinking of what I've done.

A probable? Definitely a possible. Bo Bateson backs me up at the debriefing, thumps me on the back.

'Good one, my son,' he says.

'Wizard,' St John says as he lights up. 'They call it a possible, but far as I'm concerned you downed him.'

★ ★ ★

I talked to Tad on the way to the pub that evening, a bunch of us cutting down through the orchards in a light mist. Complained about our lightweight armoury, eight machine guns but no cannons. I'd given that Dornier ten seconds worth for very little effect.

He nodded, reached up and plucked an apple and crunched into it with a big grin.

'Must get closer, Lennie. Only way, I'm always saying. Two fifty yards maximum. That's why when I hit a plane, he blows up.'

'Two fifty!' I protested. 'The guns are synchronized at six fifty.'

'This I know,' he said. 'But Mr Tate has reset mine.'

'Blimey!' I said. 'That's against some rule or other. How did you persuade him to do that?'

'Bottle Polish vodka,' he said. 'That is persuading! I advise you do the same.'

I thought about it. True enough, at 650 yards an enemy plane was a small bouncing toy it took a fluke to hit. But 250! If it was possible to get that close and the plane blew up, it would be very dangerous. Then again, what we were doing anyway wasn't exactly safe.

'Three hundred,' I said. 'I'll do it. Got another bottle you can lend me?'

Drinks all round that night in the Leather Bottle. Slightest pause as we raised our mugs to the absence of Junior Johnstone who the others had known from France. He'd been blown apart when his plane exploded. Then someone told a joke and from then on the only serious thing we got down to was drinking.

Me, I drank deep as anyone, still flushed and jittering from the day's events. Longed to phone Stella and tell her, but thought that might be shooting a line and anyway I might have killed someone, which suddenly didn't seem something to be excited about. Rather think I did, actually. I don't see that Dornier getting back across the Channel. Found myself wondering what its crew was — three? four? — and how likely they were to be picked up.

Then it was time for another round. I put my hand in my pocket and called it.

6

Mid-July

I lay across the bed in my room, writing up notes for my signals test while trying not to listen to the complaints of Mrs Mackenzie floating up from below. The blackout, rationing, an insolent air-raid warden, the things the young get up to when they're away from home. If only she knew.

I rolled onto my front, listening to the Scottish accent cut into the quiet morning. I'd once talked like that, protective colouring, automatically taken on during that couple of years in St Ninians. The move had been one of Dad's bright ideas.

I wondered where they were now, all those people I'd known in my primary class. Shonagh and Betty Inglis — were they in uniform or nursing or in one of the factories? And then, for the first time in a long time, I let myself remember *them*. Porky Pig and . . . Fando Fillamon.

It was hot behind glass in the afternoon sun, and I sweated as I gripped my notebook and saw it all again.

Fando Fillamon tripped Porky Pig neat as anything when they came into the class just ahead of me.

I was right behind Fando, watching him, and I saw how neatly it was done. I saw his tanned leg twitch sideways, his tackety boot clip Porky's ankle, saw the fat white legs tangle then blur and thump and Porky went falling into Dewar's desk. The tall pile of blue jotters began to topple, then Porky was on his knees in tears with books still slithering onto the floor. I reached out and caught the last one in mid-air. Patrick Geddes, English, Primary 7.

'Paterson! Are you in the furniture moving business, man? Get up!'

Fando winked at me.

'Nice catch,' he said.

I went red and put the jotter on the desk.

(I still feel the soft roughness of that blue card cover. Patrick Geddes's jotter, a classroom in July years back, with the smell of sweat and chalk. And cut grass and hawthorn wafting in the open windows and the faint clatter of the mower out on the football field. I see Shonagh among the girls looking worried and excited, and Fando. Of course I see Fando now as his blue-green eyes approve my catch, I feel my pleasure and anger at him and the tickle of sweat under my eleven-year-old armpits — but I can't see Patrick Geddes. Not a trace. Fallen through a crack in my memory, as I probably have in his. Gone for ever.)

'Get up, Paterson!'

Porky pushed up off his fat white knees and his head crunched into the corner of the desk. Fando had his hands in the pockets of his dark green shorts as he waited as the class waited.

'He tripped me, sir!' Porky wailed.

Dewar shook his head and blew softly and his breath quivered his dark moustache.

'Did you trip Paterson, Mr Fillamon?'

Fando looked straight back at him.

'No.'

'No, sir,' Mr Dewar corrected him..

'No, sorr,' Fando said, broadening the Irish. 'Our feet got tangled as we came in the dorr. Sorr.'

He had a way about him, the exotic bird of passage, blown into the school for that summer when the gypsies camped by the river. Part-Irish, part-Tinker — a double outsider, doubly strange. I was just a single outsider, just English, though that was bad enough.

Dewar's moustache quivered. He looked

66

down but I noticed the side of his mouth tug, knew what that meant. As an incomer I'd learned to watch the signs. Porky sniffed, Fando stood still and relaxed but I saw his right knee turn out and knew he was ready to run.

'So what's your version, Miss Gardam?'

The class, those hyenas, shifted. Porky looked at me with watery blue eyes. Fando's eyes were green today, he was the tallest boy in the class, exactly my height.

'Well? A tangle or a trip, Miss Gardam?'

I was sweating in my clumpy shoes and mum's cut-down print dress. With all the eyes on me, I heard my mother telling me one thing and my dad the opposite. Honest Injun versus Cheerful Charlie.

I chose neither.

'It looked like a . . . tango, sir.'

'A tango?'

'Yes sir, like they were trying to dance but Peter fell. Sir.'

Spluttering from the girls in the front row, laughter from the thickies at the back. Dewar's hand brushed over his mouth then thumped onto the desk.

'I'll tango you. Ach, away and sit down all of you.'

I went and sat down beside Shonagh. Fando winked as he went past. Shonagh

67

passed me a sweetie under the desk, the first I'd been offered since I'd arrived at the school. Porky sniffed in the corner.

They got out their books and I sat for a while feeling confused. You could tell the truth or you could tell a lie but there was a third way. You could make them laugh. A joke was neither truth nor lie.

I stared at my writing and sucked the sweetie quietly. Make them laugh sometimes. Be anybody. It was like finding a new way home.

★ ★ ★

He was sitting cross-legged in the shadow under the big hawthorn at the end of High Field, fiddling with something in his lap.

'Nicely done, colleen,' he said without looking up.

I hesitated. I stopped and looked down at him, fingers looped round the cord of my duffel bag.

'My name's Stella,' I said. 'And it was mean to pick on Porky when everyone does.'

He looked up.

'We call all pretty girls colleen.'

Nobody spoke to me like that. Well, except for my family and now Shonagh, almost no one spoke to me at all. And I knew I wasn't pretty. I was skinny and scraggy and had reddish frizzy hair.

He uncrossed his legs and leaned back against the trunk and stared at me.

'I know why you didn't tell,' he said.

Maybe he did. He seemed so sure he knew something about me I didn't. I reached up and held a branch and swung slowly from side to side and stared back.

'I still think it was mean,' I said.

He opened his hands. He had a knife, an odd white knife with a long thin blade. I stared back at him, still swaying slightly from the branch. Under the tree things smelled at once strong and sweet and sick.

'Imagine being fat and slow and everyone getting on at you all the time,' I insisted.

He held the knife between his finger and thumb by the tip of the blade. He held his arm up and squinted like he was going to draw me.

'Sure it was a devilment, colleen,' he said.

That wasn't his real speaking. I wasn't stupid. Fando grinned very white teeth and drew his arm back. I stopped swaying and stood dead still with my arms clasping the branch above my head.

'My name's still Stella,' I said. His arm brushed quickly across his face then a flash and a thunk and the knife was quivering in

69

the trunk. I blinked but didn't move. Even in dreams I'd never been afraid of Fando Fillamon, not that at all.

'But if they weren't picking on him, it would be on you or me, wouldn't it now?'

He rolled over and plucked out the knife and rolled back quick as a wolf, neat as me catching the falling jotter.

'And you know that's true, colleen.'

'They wouldn't dare pick on you,' I said.

'Paddy? Pape? Tinkybum?' He spat. 'If there was enough of them they would.'

'I haven't seen a knife like that,' I said. 'Is it a gypsy one?'

He grinned, flexed his hand and the thin blade disappeared.

'Na. You'd best be looking, then.'

I dropped the duffel bag and sat down beside him. He shifted away, just a little, and then I felt dizzy and full of myself. I lifted the white shaft from his brown palm and examined it. The handle was long, white and cool, with two silver hoops and a black button at one end.

'It's a flick-knife. Himself got it in Paris from a gangster.'

I turned it over. Paris. Gangsters. Flick-knife.

'The handle's ivory,' he said.

'From elephants' tusks? Real ivory?'

I saw his eyes glitter as he nodded and I knew we were kin.

'How do you use it?'

His fingers brushed my palm. He wrapped the handle in his long fingers then bent his wrist away from me, pressed and whipped his wrist and then the blade was pointing at my heart.

'That's great!' I said. 'Let me try.'

He shifted away, rolled on his back and looked up at the sky through the leaves, still clutching the knife pointing up.

'Ah well,' he said.

I leaned over him. He kept looking at the sky. It was hot in the hollow under the tree and inside my dress I felt myself full and buzzing and looking for a new home like a summer swarm. I took the tip of the blade by my thumb and finger and drew it gently from his hand and rolled away with my prize.

I soon got the hang of it. Press the button, fold the blade. Bend the wrist, pause, press, turn and — click! Every time I did it I felt stranger and more confident and swarming inside. It was like stroking yourself over and over till that part of you felt different, not even part of you.

'Strike upward if you really want to hurt,' he told me. 'Aim for the heart. If you want to cut, strike down. I've sharpened both sides.'

I pictured Porky falling, crying, his head hitting the desk.

'I don't want to hurt anybody,' I said.

'And why would you indeed?'

That wolfish grin and brown hair flopped over his eyes. He reached out one hand towards me and I knew what would happen and there would be kissing and rolling round and for the first time I could almost see why people did that. But he took the knife back gently, slipped it in his pocket and stood up. He held out my duffel bag, I tugged down my dress.

'Can I come with you to the camp?' I blurted.

'Na. Himself will be there.'

'My dad drinks with your dad,' I said.

'He's the only one here who does,' he replied.

'My dad drinks with anyone who'll listen to him.'

He glanced at me, then giggled.

'Mine too. But he wouldna stand for it. We don't mix.' He looked down and shrugged. 'Sorry, colleen.'

Then he ran down the path towards the river where the caravans were and I took the short cut home through the cornfield, which grew much higher then. On the way I tried different ways of walking in my mum's dress then forgot about it and broke off a stalk and ran home with it in my right hand, striking upwards at the heart with every second stride.

⋆　⋆　⋆

I got up and went through to the little alcove curtained off from my bedroom, feeling the tingling in the back of my knees as I lit the single ring and put the kettle on. Hard to connect that free, solitary girl with myself now. A different person, almost a stranger, but one I shared my life with. Now I was meant to be ladylike, now I was more . . . restrained. It seemed there were fewer options when you grew up, not more. I'd never expected that.

I poured boiling water into the pot then put it by the bed. I sat and clasped my feet in my hands, the way I'd done as a child. What had happened to that physical freedom, that boldness? Perhaps it was still there, to be poured over some lucky man in a way I'd never quite done.

I thought of Len's long hand firm on my waist, and wondered if it would be him. I stared into the steam rising from the spout, remembering how it felt then.

* ★ * ★ *

I slipped the window up and went out headfirst. The moon was a pale round disk like one of my mum's ornamental seed pods, the drainpipe was already dew-damp on my hands.

I got my knees onto the ledge, glanced down at the flowerbed where the square of light from the kitchen window below fell on the groundsel and stock. I tightened the cord of my dressing-gown round my old pink pyjamas, then without pausing to think about it — that was the trick like with catching a jotter in mid-air — I stood up on the ledge, facing in. One hand squeezed between the pipe and the wall and the other gripped into the ivy and I stepped out and down onto the little sloping ledge that ran right round the house one floor up.

The ledge was rough on my bare soles. Three steps sideways clinging to the ivy, then my foot was on the lead skews. I groped for the roof-ridge then pulled myself onto it, turned round and sat astride and looked out.

I could hear the murmur of my parents' voices below and a jazz record playing. I looked along the street to the left, the neat new gardens. Then off to my right over the wall and down the dip where the trees and

74

river and gypsies were. The voices rose. '*You just please yourself!*' I heard, then Dad's giggling laughter that sometimes worked and sometimes didn't. My mother said something else I didn't quite catch, then the clink of a glass and another giggle. Then the window was pulled down and the voices were cut off.

I pulled a cigarette, pinched earlier from my dad, from the top pocket of my dressing-gown. I ran it under my nose, all smooth and cool and white like the ivory knife, and smelled the smoky gypsy smell. It was quite true: I didn't want to hurt anybody. I just didn't want much to do with them. In my daydreams, the struggles, the chases, the plots and secret understandings were all about escape. That was the excitement, getting away. Of course Dad pleased himself and was totally unreliable and people thought he was a great laugh. Of course he wanted to help me and show me things, but what he taught was only what pleased himself, not me.

I jabbed and parried at the moon with my cigarette, then stuck it in my mouth. I thought about Porky, the white of him falling.

I leaned down and cautiously struck a match on the slates. The moon made a haze in the damp air, like a pale waterfall pouring silently past. I sucked in and blew out. I would live in a cave behind a waterfall, sitting on a rock and watching the screen pour past, and be wild and free and please myself.

I smoked quietly, trying not to cough, thinking how I'd be leaving the little school tomorrow. And how I'd heard the gypsies were leaving for Blairgowrie and the raspberry picking, and I'd never see Fando again. I kept getting bigger and learning things, and there was nothing I could do about it. At best I could only stay alert, and catch the jotter as it fell.

★   ★   ★

I stirred on the bed, wanting a cigarette though it was bad on my breath. Anyway Mrs Mackenzie's house rules included no smoking in bedrooms. I'd have one on the way to training school.

I drank my tea then glanced at my watch. Forty minutes. Sometimes life seemed one long sequence of schools. You think you're done with it, then university. Leave that and suddenly you're studying and being examined all over again. There was something to be said for life behind the waterfall.

I twitched, embarrassed at that childhood fantasy. It had been so real, so important at the time. Perhaps it lingered yet, in little traces and blips. I'd thought I'd been in love since, with Roger at least, but perhaps no one had ever found me. Perhaps I'd never let them.

I gathered up my notepads and jotter, put on my cap and straightened it in front of the mirror, then went down the stairs and out of the door.

'Lovely morning, Mrs Mackenzie!'

Today was the final test on the console. As I walked to the bus stop I thought of Fando. I'd read something of what had happened to gypsies in Germany and the countries it controlled. I hoped he wasn't there, that his family had gone back to Ireland. Maybe it was just propaganda.

The girl I'd been still whispered in my ear once in a while. Like when after Czechoslovakia was invaded and I saw a notice in the newspaper saying trainees were wanted in Signals. A little inner voice, a hatred of bullying perhaps, or the memory of Fando, made me write down the number and join the WAAF instead of continuing with teacher training.

Maybe I had lost something when I grew up, some kind of freedom and boldness. Yet when the bus came along, I seized the rail and jumped on, pleased to feel it pull away and take me towards the future and all that waited there.

* * *

Sunlight splitting white beams through trees like at the pictures, angled down from projector to forest-floor screen. Late afternoon, stood down, I walk right into it. A clatter, flash and I flinch. Black and white crosses, sun in my eyes: two magpies.

In the fringe of the wood among hawthorn, hogweed and nettles. A sharp reek in sunlight. Each leaf outline traced sharp and clear. My youthful twenty-twenty vision.

That's what it is: like I'm finally on-screen, not onlooking. I'm in it, alive like never before, moving among heroes and pals, not to mention lovely gals and bang bangs. Loads of action. Everything sharp to the last leaf, the last chewed fingernail. Living in focus for the first time since childhood. Some feeling.

I look up where the birds had gone, feeling the fizz rising though me. It comes clear: you stop acting, and act. Be regardless, as they say, the true fighter pilot. Be light. Everything else is bollocks.

Much simpler this way. If I could but follow it.

7

Late July

Jean Finlay took off her headset and slid out of her seat, rubbing her eyes.

'All yours,' she said. 'Good luck.'

I took her swivel seat, felt the warmth she'd left behind, the slick of sweat on the calibration dial. A deep breath, on with the headset. Sergeant Farringdon pulled up a seat next to me and sat with her hands crossed in her lap. Her back was perfectly straight and her head was high. I pictured hours of deportment lessons.

'The morning wave's gone through,' she said. 'You can expect a bit of a lull.'

It was quiet and dim in the receiver hut, which doubled as an operations room. There was a steady flow of chat and phone calls and chain-smoking on the other side of the hut. On mine there was only the towering bulk of the receiver with all the switches, fuses, buttons and dials that had become familiar to me. But this time it was different. This time I was in charge. My first big day.

For a long time we sat together and

watched the green line. Some excitement when blips started and I was about to post it up when I recognized that the signals came from IFF transmitters our planes carried, so they were friendlies. I dropped my hand from the calibration dial, rubbed it on my skirt, waited. And waited.

I rubbed my eyes and saw the green line blip and bounce. I put down my fist and it was still bouncing. I could feel the pulse in my throat as I turned the dial for the bearing. I screwed up my eyes to read the range and prepared to enter it into the calculator. We were away.

I gabbled the figures. Hostiles' code number, range, bearing, height, number. Farringdon steepled her fingers.

'I think you've overestimated again,' she said quietly. 'But not by much. Very good. Just keep doing that and don't get in a flap and you'll be all right, Corporal.'

She patted my shoulder and got up to go. Even as she did so, another blip started and I went into action, sure the approaching aircraft could tell I was a fraud. My back was beginning to hurt. To my right, a WAAF I didn't know calmly pulled up a seat and began to record my hostiles. She worked out the Tizzy angle and passed on the likely point of interception for the squadrons on their way. Her voice was calm and easy, almost bored, as she spoke into the mouthpiece hung by her lips.

She caught my eye and grinned. She was middle-aged, reminded me of my mother only more relaxed.

'Jessie Walker,' she said. 'It's a piece of cake, dear.'

Reading is a queer affair. I'll be sitting in the deck chair sweating in my Mae West looking at a page of *The Three Hostages* but really the letters might as well be sundial spikes.

Because all that's happening is I'm watching the sun move across the page, while trying to follow the languid slang passing between Bunny and Coco, Dusty, Boy and Bo — the university types all having such nicknames. (Sergeants don't have nicknames.) Then I'm thinking about Stella last time I saw her, and how I wasted so much kissing time just walking and talking under the trees.

Right now I'm sulking and nervous because for the rest of today I'm to act tail-end Charlie while we're flying a wing of four. Me, Prior, St John, Bo Bateson. And everyone knows that position is for new boys and those about to die soon. The only way out of it is to be promoted through other people being knocked out, or by shooting down a few yourself.

The next thing I'm *inside* the book, like I've gone through a door in the page. I'm in there with Hannay and Dominic Medina, and the airfield has gone faint and the voices are whispers off-stage. Even the sunlight isn't the light of this world but of that. And when the Tannoy goes and my heart leaps, it's like a mighty rope has tugged me from one world into another and I'm still sprawled on the back of my mind as I take in that it's only one of the COs' blasted morale-boosting announcements. It's his birthday so there'll be a bit of a do in The Cock tonight. The famous Spitfire squadron down the road might join us. Oh, jolly, jolly good. Bunch of publicity-grabbing line-shooting pretty boys.

I'm worried, too, because during the night the underside of my Hurri has been painted pale sky-blue. This isn't a joke but a good idea we've finally taken from the opposition — that much harder to spot from below. But I don't like it because I feel superstitious about my plane. It seems bad luck to change it.

My feet are cramped and moist inside these shoes. Would it be good or bad luck to start wearing the leather gloves my mum sent? Just get through another three days and I'll be seeing Stella. What do I want of her? What does she expect of me?

The Tannoy clicks, pauses, then blares. It's us up, along with Blue section. I mark my page with a leaf of grass, grab my parachute and start running.

★ ★ ★

In the last sector of our climb, Prior orders us to fly away from the hostiles and gain more height before turning back into them. We're fed up with always meeting the enemy higher than us, so we're going to add a couple of thousand whenever there's time. The controllers on the ground can like it or lump it.

I'm weaving at the rear like a drunk going home. Head turning and turning, checking the mirror, staring into that blue acreage of sky. Above all checking my tail so I won't get knocked off. There's a lot to do. Keeping the right distance behind the three aircraft ahead, checking above, below, behind, just flying the ruddy thing. I can picture my book exactly as I left it, face up on the grass. I hope the breeze won't lose my place, or anyone else pick it up.

'*Bandits! Bandits below, eleven o'clock!*'

Prior's voice, a bit higher than usual, almost squeaky. I side-slip and look down, don't see them at first. Then one, then more, then a lot, silhouetted against the Channel and the fields below.

'*Attack line astern! Stay back and cover us, Lennie.*'

Just great. I push the stick forward and follow them down at a distance. We're carving down through their upper layer of fighters. The bombers have already seen us and vanish in every direction, like minnows when you poke your finger in a pool. Down below, a bunch of Me110 fighter-bombers circling each other in tight defence. Then there's a clattering rattle, feel a couple of thuds in somewhere below like someone's punched my seat. I throw the stick over left, glimpse the Me109 hurtle past. Shit!

Group of Stukas going down in bombing formation. After them! Flip the kite over so she won't cut out, dive. Close in, pick the rear left one. Closer, closer. Set the bloody sights! Closer. Get to 300 yards. He hasn't seen me yet. Blast, he has! Bombs falling, he's straightening, coming right across my sights . . .

Give him a two-second burst as I slide past. Turn back out of the dive towards him, feel my eyes bulge, vision going black and white then grey, feel the easing, feel sick but he's still ahead of me. Throttle back, stay below, out of the rear-gunner's sights. OK, now rise and get him.

He fills the sights. So big, so close.

Bouncing in his slip-stream. Thumb wet on the red button, press, feel the plane judder and slow. Go down, damn you! Bits start coming off. Fire more. Smoke from engine. Flips on his side, starts going down. Tracer bullets from rear turret. Follow him down, he's too slow, I can dance all round him. Don't overshoot. Check tail. Not supposed to do this. *Don't follow down!* they say.

Got to get him, got to get this one, then they might promote me from tail-end. Closing again, sudden picture of my book page flipping over in the breeze, annoyance then press the button again. See the sparkle of the last tracer rounds dance around then BOOM he's blown up. Debris clattering off me, duck as some hits the screen. Now out of here! Out!

Turn for home. Take the bearing. Keep weaving, don't relax. Whatever you do, don't relax. Keep jittering. Keep looking for the specks that grow, above, to stern, below . . .

Throttle down over the fence. See the tree tips stir. Headache coming on as I touch down. Bounce, run, bounce — not very stylish. But I got him, got my first one.

'A probable, then?' our Intelligence Officer Bill Raymond asks.

'No bloody probable about it,' I say, my voice high and squeaky. 'Bastard blew up in my face. Take a look at the air-frame.'

Prior's arm round my shoulder. 'Well done, Len.' Then, quietly he adds, 'I think Bunny's bought it. Saw him go down.'

Fred Tate calls me back.

'Look at this, sir.'

Under my seat are two unexploded cannon shells. He removes them gently, like peas from a pod.

'Me109's muzzle velocity too low. Got off lightly there.'

And all I can think later as I pick up my book again, remove the leaf of grass, is: Thank God I don't have to be tail-end Charlie again.

I slid out of my chair and nearly fell over, my legs were so dead. Sergeant Farringdon smiled sympathetically and put down her recording pad.

'Another day done,' she said. 'Now it's into the night shift. Fancy going for a drink?'

I put my hand over my eyes. I was still seeing green wriggles and I was taken aback at her offer. The night-shift WAAF was taking my place already, though nothing was happening on the screen yet. I dragged my eyes away.

'I fancy lying down with a cold cloth over my eyes,' I said. 'But yes.'

★ ★ ★

Before the War I'd never have walked into a pub without a man. That had changed. All those young women suddenly living away from home, working in fields or factories, getting ideas. I'd got my ideas before the War, thanks to university and Roger.

As we waited at the bar, I thought to myself a lot was changing. In the past I'd never have exchanged more than a few words with someone proper posh like Foxy Farringdon. She was from a completely different set than me — family with a big London house, cars, a place in Buckinghamshire, all that.

'Is this encouraged in the Services, Sergeant Farringdon?' I asked. 'Fraternizing between the ranks?'

She snorted like the horse she undoubtedly had.

'We're off duty and I don't give a jot. And please call me Foxy, absolutely everyone does. But it's Sergeant in the hut, yah? We can't have the men think we're incapable of discipline.'

'Absolutely not,' I said.

She looked at me suspiciously but ordered the gins and we found a place in the corner. She began to fill me in on the rumours I'd been too busy for, how one of the RDF stations had been bombed and put out of action for a couple of hours. It was said half the people in the huts had been killed. No one knew for sure if it was true.

We glanced at each other then as we picked up our drinks again. Our hut wasn't strong at all. It should have been built underground but they were in too much a hurry.

'Looks like we're front line now, Stella,' she said.

In an odd way, that made me feel better. I felt I could look Len in the eye more when I next saw him. I liked looking him in the eye, there was some kind of steady recognition there. Not a mad throwing away like Roger. Nor a pals-gone-wrong like with Evelyn. Just a recognition and a challenge.

'Foxy, I think we're all going to be front line soon,' I replied, polished off my G & T and went up for another, doubles of course.

Walking through the village to the Post Office with Tad when we were stood down one afternoon later that week, I saw secateurs glinting in a mottled hand. Saw the early faded heads flipped onto the grass and thought of the ones who had gone down already. I wondered who would be the next. Prior, Tad, St John? Myself? But I was immortal, had to believe that.

Tad was whistling as we strolled along the street. He raised his eyebrows, smiled and bowed to two young women we were passing. Got a giggle from one, a look back from the other that made me blush. Then they stopped, we stopped. We talked — well, Tad did — for a couple of minutes, long enough to discover they weren't available for a drink later.

'Don't you ever stop? What about Maddy?' I said as we walked on.

'That was yesterday I saw her,' he replied.

'But aren't you seeing her again?'

'Yes,' he said. 'But that will be tomorrow.'

I knew then I'd never really be a true fighter pilot. I hadn't that careless capacity to live in the present, to be, as they said, *regardless*. I took it all too weightily. And that slowed me down, just a fraction.

Tad stopped outside the barber shop.

'Don't worry, Lennie. Maddy, she lives like this too. This is why I like her. I'll just be a minute, you see,' he said, and went inside.

I waited. The street was silent and hot. The blinds were down in most of the shops — the grocer, the butcher, the chemist. A bell tinkled, an old lady in a brown coat stepped out onto the street, exchanged a few last words with the people inside. Behind the hedge, a lawn mower rattled. Important to keep a neat lawn during a war.

Sleepy time, like life itself had paused in the heat. The old lady walked by on the other side of the street and stared at me. Then she smiled.

'Fine afternoon, young man.'

I nodded, still lulled by the heat and the silence. Over the poplar trees in the far distance by the coast, the RDF towers shimmered in the haze. Dust rose from the street and tickled my nose. A petrol lawn mower joined in in the distance. It got louder.

I stepped out into the empty street and scanned the sky. Four tiny specks, quite low, coming closer. They didn't sound like Merlin engines. They were twin-engine planes, heading this way. I looked and, yes, above them was a fighter escort and their wings were wrong.

Tad came out of the barber's, hand in one pocket, looking pleased.

'What good country,' he said. 'All mod cons! Should I have got you some, Lennie? I'm not knowing if you and Stella . . . '

'Never mind that — they're going for the airfield! Jesus!'

I was about to start running back but Tad gripped me by the arm.

'Too late, my friend. Better to stay here.'

We stood in the middle of the street as the bombers went over, loud now, very loud. Where the hell were the Hurris? But Blue section was on patrol, Red was stood down, Yellow was somewhere over the Channel.

The bombs began to tumble from the planes, small sticks that went down very slowly at first. They dropped out of sight behind the trees. Then there was a long pause till the sounds came back, the distant thumps. One spectacular bang. Then the whine and blare of the siren. The Me109 escort dipped down and we heard the crackle of the guns. The siren cut out.

'Jesu!' Tad muttered. 'Goering fuck. They must have got under RDF.'

The grocer stepped out of his shop, looked

at the sky over the trees, looked at the two of us. Shook his head then went back inside.

It was all over in a few minutes. Then the fighter escort came low towards the village like they might be looking for trouble. We ran from the street, dived through the door of the butcher shop. A man with big moustaches stood looking at us with a knife in his hand.

'Yes, gentlemen. Can I help you?'

Crackling and rattling in the street outside. The roar mounted, we threw ourselves face down among the sawdust.

A shattering of glass from next door. A sudden yelp, dog by the sound of it, cut off abruptly. Then it got slowly quiet. We got to our feet sheepishly, brushing down our uniforms. The butcher lowered his knife.

'I hope you've got your ration cards,' he said.

And I'm pleased to say for once even Tad was lost for words.

★　★　★

When we ran back to the airfield it was a shambles. Craters in the turf, two of the huts flattened, the dispersal hut and the control tower completely blown in. The shell of my sky-blue underside Hurri was still burning. Another two were lying on their side in their makeshift pens, wings tipped into the air. The fourth seemed completely untouched.

There were the smells of burnt rubber, high explosive, burning wood. People were emerging from slit trenches and concrete huts. Some looked dazed, others purposeful. A few were swearing loudly and steadily. There were no obvious casualties except the airfield itself.

The CO came out of the equipment hut with a rack of spades in his arms.

'Right, you lot,' he shouted. 'Get those craters filled!'

Tad and me looked at each other.

'Can he mean us?'

* * *

We put the spades aside as we heard the first drone. Merlin, unmistakable. Then two Hurris drifted in over the perimeter fence. A third came in higher and faster, did a roll over the airfield, then turned and made its approach. Had to be St John, only he and Tad did that low risky roll. He'd get a rocket from the CO.

We waited for a fourth but none turned up. It was Boy who was missing, perhaps he'd baled out. No one had seen him go down. We should know by evening. We wouldn't think about it. At least, we wouldn't talk about it. Boy had been shot down twice. Baled out each time, once into the Channel. A survivor, everyone agreed.

★ ★ ★

Late that afternoon. The runways mostly repaired, we were lying on the hot grass reading newspapers. Replacement Hurris were already on their way. Boy hadn't returned and the France pilots, especially the University Air Squadron ones, the officers who'd joined up with him, were edgy and irritable.

'Someday, in the future — ' Bo Bateson began.

'The future,' laughed the Hon. Harold Algernon St John. 'What future?' He examined the crossword in the *Daily Mail*. 'Six letters, *A following shade*. Any ideas, chaps?'

'*Shadow?*' Geoff Prior murmured.

8

Late July

Maybe I'd wanted excitement, simple as that. Expand my horizons — and what better way than this, looking down on England from 20,000 feet? When it seemed likely there was a war coming and I'd have no choice but to be in it, I remembered Dad's talk about the trenches, how they always envied the pilots up there above the mud and stink. He told me little about the Great War except how it was important to keep your feet clean and dry and keep changing your socks, but that bit about the pilots stuck. *Stay out of the trenches, son.*

He took us to an air display once. I was small and the planes were so loud. A Vic of three biplanes did acrobatics, rolls and dives, flying inverted and finally loop the loop. My mouth dropped open and my stomach flipped with the aircraft. It was the most exciting and perfect thing I'd ever seen — the rising, the flip onto the back and the engine going faint, then coming over the top and diving down and flattening out to roar level over our heads.

Tiger Moths, my dad said, looking at the programme. The two words buzzed in my head: tiger . . . moth. How could anything be both? And yet they were, these bright yellow biplanes, all delicate and light, all roar and threat.

Fact is, several years on I was bored stiff on my arse at Stafford and Meeks, drawing elevations of houses I'd never afford. Another three years and I'd have completed my apprenticeship. Another three years and I should be engaged to Christine, because that's what happened if you went to the flicks often enough and held hands and got involved in sticky kisses. It was grown up. And it was boring.

So when Eric Gilland from the office started talking about the Volunteer Reserve, how you got to fly for nothing, I went along. And though the kites were rubbish and our instructors not much better and there was far too much drill, it was exciting.

At first they had me down as a bomber navigator, what with my draughtsmanship background, then when the War got closer and it was clear they needed all the fighter pilots they could get, I stuck up my hand.

Tiger Moth, Anson, Harvard trainer. Austria absorbed into Germany. Then they took over Czechoslovakia. Finally the first Hurricane landed in the cow pasture we called our flying field. It looked like something from a new age. It looked like the future, though it still had a single blade prop and hadn't yet been metal-skinned. But it had a retractable undercarriage and it flew like the wind itself. It was so smooth and yet solid, almost thuggish.

The pilot jumped down carefully and walked towards us. He was short and slightly bow-legged and his accent was Northern and he was not an officer. This was as different as the plane, and the two fused in my mind. Together, they were the future, a future I could have.

The War came closer and at last we soloed Hurricanes. Believe me when I say it was beautiful. So fast, so manoeuvrable, so on the edge of being uncontrollable. I'd never known an adrenalin surge like it. If sex was anything like as good as this, it was worth pursuing (not that I'd get that with Christine before marriage). That morning in 1939 when I first parted company with the Earth in a Mk1 Hurri was the morning I truly fell in love with flying. And when I landed it heavily, trundled up to the huts, switched off and jumped down onto firm ground, I felt like a god come to earth.

'By God, sonnie, you fly like a pig,' Keith Symonds our trainer had said. 'Better go up and do it again.'

'Yes sir! Absolutely, sir!'

Whatever the future held, I reckoned, it was worth it for this.

The Spits were different. They came later, were even more of the future, were somehow aristocratic. Art deco, Stella called them. The art deco fighter plane. I took against them, though they were faster and more manoeuvrable, with a higher ceiling. They were too posh, too sleek. They were like overbred dogs, a total bitch to build, temperamental, unstable and easily messed up.

Then the War came, and finally the invasion of France. I was still training, volunteered to go full-time and I left the office. Awkward farewells with Christine, far too much I didn't know how to say. We wished each other good luck. Privately I hoped she'd find someone else to take her out. It was all in the arrangements we didn't make. I walked home alone, late, bumping into walls and tripping over kerbs in the blackout because I'd forgotten my torch and I was giddy with guilt and relief. Only later did it occur to me maybe she was too.

They held us back from going to France. We weren't too worried; we thought then the war in France could go on for years. Six weeks later it was all over, and we still hadn't fought. Not that I was that keen on fighting. It was flying and adventure I wanted. Something other than the day job.

I waited for peace. That's what normally happens. The leaders get together, have secret discussions and announce peace and its terms. But somehow the moment passed, somehow it didn't quite happen. Somehow we weren't ready to cave in.

And now we're in it. I realize I've really gone and done it as I switch off and jump down from my plane and look round the bombed half-repaired shambles of our air-field. If they wipe us out, there'll be an invasion, and wipe us out they could.

I never realized it would be so bloody, so close to, or so frequently dull. Terrifying. Yet when you finally give yourself away, fly above the past and future for an hour and get life back again, unexpectedly, walking in the evening on the way to the pub, you will see houses, trees, faces of your fellow citizens, all sharpened in intense relief, and realize this is what you sought all along.

Evelyn phoned me at my digs, said he'd got the number from my mother. He'd been posted as group organizer with the mysterious Civilian Repair Organisation based over at Maidenhead. If he was able to borrow a truck, could he come over and see me tonight?

I stood in the hallway with the phone pressed to my ear, thinking how good it was to hear from him, a warm familiar feeling that came from much shared. His easy confidence, his humour, his education. Quite unlike the intensity of young Len, struggling to articulate . . . And there was the vague sense of guilt I'd been left with after I'd explained that too much of me was still with Roger, and now I was joining the WAAFs I would be posted away . . . I was so touched and relieved he didn't seem to hold that against me that I said Yes. Come on over and we'll go out for a drink.

After all, my pilot is scarcely my boyfriend. We're not exactly going steady. And Evelyn is just an old friend from the past, one who's likely to have more future than Len.

I rang off and shivered as I turned to go back up the stair. Someone walking over your grave, my mother would say. Or someone else's. And I already knew, like so many others, that I might as well grab what was there even if it meant being short of sleep and easy conscience, in those days that were so crammed and uncertain and sweet.

I went upstairs, ignoring Mrs Mackenzie's curiosity and disapproval, and began to run a bath and look for my better stockings.

We came back late from The Cock, drifting in the half-light up the lanes and through the orchards. An evening of competitive line-shooting with the Spitfire glamour boys down the way. Line-shooting in reverse, we downplay everything that happens except for our fear and incompetence and luck, but still the facts are there. We shot down this, we did that.

And though the neighbouring Spitfire squadron was more famous than us, being closer to the coast and so more front line, we've both experienced the same things. We've all looked wildly round a shining empty sky suddenly filled with growing specks, our hearts thundering, super-alive, supercharged by a high-octane mix of terror and excitement. We've all pulled the plug to Boost and felt the surge as we flew into battle, leaving our daily selves behind. That's what let us talk and joke so easily, what flowed between us with the drinks — an unspoken common knowledge no one else could possess.

These were not the people I wanted to

spend all my time talking to, but it sometimes seemed they were the only ones I could talk to.

I was thinking about this as we drifted in groups through the light mist, home towards the big house that served as our barracks. Something clattered into the tree in front, then I felt a thud between my shoulder blades. I snatched a windfall apple off the ground and with St John and Tad in tight formation turned on our attackers, and we fought a battle of apples and pears in the moonlight, ducking and weaving all the way through the orchards and up the pale flinty lane to Parsonage Farm.

Evelyn turned up late but triumphant, pushing firmly up the stairs ahead of a muttering Mrs Mackenzie, who for once seemed quite abashed, perhaps because he wasn't a youth but a man, one used to being in control, whether in front of a lecture class or in charge of a CRO squad.

When I greeted him at the top of the stair he looked at me full-on, nodded briefly, smiled, put his hand lightly on my arm and kissed my cheek.

'It's good to see you again, Stella,' he said. 'You look lovely still.'

I felt the scrape from his shaving that morning. I'd forgotten how firm and steady he was — his movements, the skin over his face, his speech. And also how old he was. No, not old; *senior* was the word. He was only ten years older than me, but despite growing up in the twenties he seemed to come from a more substantial and serious age. Two of his elder brothers had died in the Great War, which linked him to a different generation in my mind. After all, that war and the silence that followed it were part of what had happened to my mother and father, not my friends.

I blushed and made an effort not to run my hand through my hair.

'It's lovely to see you, Evelyn,' I replied. 'You look well.'

He smiled. In truth he did look good, in a suit but without a tie, quite raffish. Carrying a tan overcoat, hat, full of energy and purpose. The War has that effect on some people, as though they've finally found their calling.

He hailed Mrs Mackenzie heartily as we went down the stairs, practically slapped her on the back, and I could swear that complaining old crone smiled as we went out onto the dark street.

I lay listening to Tad and Sniff Burton's breathing settle then snore, but I was much too awake. Perhaps the moonlight pouring in the curtainless window was something to do with it. Also the excitement of that day's raid. I lay in bed still seeing the fat slug bombs dripping slowly from the planes, then the gutted remains of my kite, the bomb craters across the grass runway as though some giant moles had been at work. And before that, the sleepy afternoon heat, the dazed drifting of nothing happening in an English village. The fruit fight as we came home in the moonlight . . .

I got up, pulled a dressing-gown over my pyjamas, found a cigarette and pushed the window up, lit into the cool night air. It wasn't so late, not even eleven o'clock yet, but we'd be woken by six tomorrow . . .

I stubbed out the cigarette on the brick sill, paused then lit another. Why not? It could be my last. No, that was getting morbid. These thoughts are true, but we can't afford to think them. See too clearly and we can't function. But if we don't see, we miss so much and

108

that's a waste because this time may be all we've got. That's what's odd about these blokes, these companions of mine — they're so very aware in the sky and so deliberately blind on the ground. We just chat and joke, drink and flick through light magazines.

Tad, now, he's not blind. He's just very focused on whatever he's doing, chasing women or trying to revenge his family and his vanished country. Either way it's whole-hearted. He's got a bigger picture that keeps him going.

I leaned on the windowsill and breathed deep. And had a memory flash of myself as a child, leaning on a windowsill in a summer night while our neighbour Mr Hartwell mowed his lawn. And I was calculating in a school jotter how long I'd been alive, expanding the years into months, days, hours, seconds. Then I began to calculate how many more I had to go, assuming I lived till seventy. And as the mower clicked, revved down, turned, it struck into me that the time I took to do this calculation would have to be subtracted from that total, and the time it took to do that subtraction would be as well. And I'd seen for the first time how our time is running away, and I'd stopped mid-calculation and just stared into that long dusk with my childish heart hammering, appalled.

I watched the fire crawl down my cigarette as I looked into the dark and yearned for Stella to help me see right. I waited till the red circle closed in on my lips then threw it away, trailing sparks. I pulled down the window and went to my bed, and this time slept till tea was brought at dawn.

9

End of July

A good deal of the myth is true. It was a summer seen through heat haze. There were a very young men who flew and fought, killed and died over the Channel or the English countryside, and those who were not killed were back in the pubs that evening. They were seldom serious; serious was not their style.

It was a time of rumour of Fifth Columnists and paratroopers, of elderly Local Defence Volunteers drilling with pitchforks or one rifle between them. It was a time of ARP wardens, the Observer Corps, Land Girls and Naval VADs, Auxiliary Fire Service and WVS, WAAFs and Wrens. Mobilizing the entire adult population, Britain had gone overboard on acronyms. The unions had made a deal with the wartime government and men and women were working ten-hour days, six or seven days a week in the factories.

It was a time of uncertainty, fatigue and excitement. There were lots of parties and dances and the pre-war sexual morality was vanishing like the dew on those hot mornings.

For the pilots that summer was a time of the head turning, turning, tuned to the little things, the specks that grow. A blur coming out of nowhere to fill a rear-view mirror, and then the army motorcyclist overtakes. The wooden handle of a trowel in a village garden, abandoned among flowers. Spent matches on the grass around the chairs by the dispersal hut, untold numbers of dog-ends flipped out of windows, ground white flecks into new concrete runways. Pale knuckles gripping the *Daily Mail* that just a year before had urged appeasement. Intricate stitching round the badge '*Poland*' as it's sewn onto a uniform sleeve, sun flashing off the needle as it works. These tiny details they live and die by.

That's how it was. The many untruths are more subtle.

By the end of July the pilots in Len's squadron were complaining they were being held back. Supply convoys and Channel ports were still being attacked, but now the emphasis seemed to be shifting to airfields. Formations of fifty or more bombers, with Me109s as fighter escort — but only a handful of planes were being sent up against them, enough to disrupt but not to knock out.

'Never you mind,' drawled St John. 'The point is, if we can't knock them out, the same applies the other way round, see?'

Silence as they tried to digest this. Everyone knew St John had a hot line to Fighter Command because his cousin was a high-up there, and they were getting a rare glimpse of HQ strategy. Mostly they just relied on guesswork and rumour like everyone else.

Len lay in a deck chair in the hot sun with the *Picture Post* across his knee. His friend Tadeusz was reading an indecipherable newspaper entitled *Wiadomosci ze Swiata*. To his right, on a low table Johnny Staples was writing a letter, and Billy (Shortarse) Madden was playing Ludo with Dusty Miller. The CO strolled out with a photographer from the Ministry, who took some pics of them then asked if they minded setting out a chess board, it being more ... appropriate. The photo was taken, with the two men leaning forward, studying the pieces (which meant nothing to them) intently. It remains yet, still reproduced from time to time in books about that summer, another small untruth, a joke among the vanishing few who were there.

The photographer thanked them, the chess pieces were replaced by Ludo, the CO went back inside and Dusty and Shortarse resumed their titanic struggle. Another morning at the height of that summer. All the young men occupied or pretending to be, trying to make out they're not hooked, like fish on a line, to the Tannoy's click. Waiting, waiting, letting the hours go by.

'I don't care for all this high strategy,' Prior complained again. 'I'm just saying it's time we got up in numbers and took 'em on.'

St John patiently explained they weren't even front line. They were near the rear of their sector and so would never be first choice to get up and dance.

'But not to worry, laddie,' he added. 'Your chance will come soon enough, believe me.'

Again a few ears twitched, wondering if this was St John's guess or information coming from Intelligence. He reached over and flicked the magazine from Len and began skimming the pages.

Tad grunted and threw down his paper. He sat scowling at the grass, his right knee jumping, his fingers drumming on his thigh.

'Not good news?' Len asked.

'Very bad news from home,' Tad said. 'German bastards and Russian bastards. Terrible things have happened, you know.'

'Remind me who's in charge there now you've surrendered, old boy,' Dusty asked casually.

'Surrendered? We have never surrendered! Never!' Tad glared at Dusty.

'Sorry, old chap,' Dusty said, trying to keep a straight face for he pulled this routine most days and Tad never failed to rise to it.

'Where did you get the paper?' Len asked. He felt embarrassed by both Dusty and Tad.

'Newspaper of Polish Air Force,' Tad muttered. 'It means 'News of the World' but not like yours. It is serious.'

'Serious?' Dusty said as he rolled the dice. 'This is no time for that sort of thing.'

Len closed his eyes as the bickering went on. Far as he was concerned, this inaction suited him fine. He had a date for that evening and wanted to be able to make it. He wondered drowsily if the War was a side-show for romance or the other way round, and how was he ever to become *regardless* at either.

I took my time off from the console, borrowed a cigarette and went to the door of the hut. Smoking gave me something to do in the breaks. It was something to look forward to, the lighting up then that harsh sweetness passing through my throat and nose. My mother would be horrified, thinking only very fast women smoked.

I lit up and stared out at the bright morning. Rubbed my eyes and blinked a few times, trying to rub away the green blips. Trying to wake up a bit. Trying to think about Evelyn, about Len.

Instead I stood in the open doorway and looked down the hill till the sound of wind in the trees was like running water and I was back there again, behind the childhood waterfall. Someone was coming up the river towards me. I saw the pale flash of his skin, felt that mixture of resentment and relief at being found. He was in the distance, water flowing over his arms, his back. His skin was so white, hair dark or maybe just wet as he came my way. Working steadily upstream like a returning salmon to join me.

'Quiet this morning, Corporal!'

I just nodded, not sure if Major Henley was referring to me or business on the screen. In any case it was too late. My rescuer, the only secret sharer of my childhood solitude, had gone. He never came close enough to identify anyway.

I flicked away my cigarette and prepared to receive the Major's gallantry.

Hot in the sun, asleep among the buzz of voices, I'm young again. I'm leaning in pyjamas on my bedroom windowsill, watching our neighbour from the cottage next door mowing his rough lawn in summer twilight. My body feels smaller, lighter, cleaner. I've just finished calculating how many seconds I have to live. I feel the seconds drain away like water between my fingers.

The thought makes my chest heavy and achy. It makes the evening more special and more painful. Even as Mr Hartwell wheels and turns at the end of a strip, the seconds are draining away and there's nothing I can do about it.

Then I'm in the outer porch. Dad has accused me of lying, which I haven't in this case. It was my sister that did it, and I've been clouted across the ear and smacked again on the bum for insisting I didn't do it. Oddly, I'm more angry at my father than my sister.

I'm looking through blurry tears at a row of jam jars, each crowded with drowned and half-drowned wasps. Some of the wasps are well down, motionless, hung preserved in the depths. Others are still trying to escape, lifting spindly legs through the sugary solution. They haven't yet accepted what's coming to them. I can almost hear the buzz, and below that the tiny frantic screams. But there is calm in the depths, no motion.

Scramble! Scramble! Red section scramble!

I'm upright and running. Get to my plane and realize I've forgotten my parachute. Run back, pick it up, climb into the cockpit as Tate waits to strap me in.

'Hey, Len!'

I turn and our adjutant takes a picture. It's his new enthusiasm. I give him the fingers and begin to roll.

The photo exists yet — a young man grinning in his cockpit, apologetic in his way, still waking up and hair all over the place, so present and alive.

Climbing into light cloud then above, he's still yawning. He clamps the oxygen mask to his face and gives himself a quick blast from the bottle. Better. They climb to their given height then add on 2,000 feet for luck and fly on.

The interception has already been made. Way ahead and at a variety of heights, dots are spread out and moving lazily round each other. For a moment he's looking at a collection of wasps drowning in a sticky solution, dying in heaps in the vast sticky sky. For a moment he sees clearly that's what's happening. Then he's right in among it, aiming himself at a group of Dorniers.

★ ★ ★

The action is fast, a blur of reflex actions. Later he will sort it out for the Intelligence Officer at the debriefing and state, 'We engaged a group of Dornier bombers circling in defensive formation,' but really it is not like that. It's a frantic, jolting, shambles of split-second decisions and reactions. It's a world where someone is too old at twenty-seven. It's like trying to stand upright on a rolling log and shoot flying ducks while navigating the rapids.

Does the Intelligence Officer know he is not getting the reality as he tries to slow down the torrent of excited young men jabbering and gesturing? Bill Raymond tries to sort out the stories and put them together again into something coherent, a narrative that will tell what really happened. He needs to settle on the likely figures: How many aircraft went down? Of what make were they?

At times he guesses the same aircraft is being shot down by everyone whose path it crosses. Everyone knocks bits off it, everyone is quite positive they destroyed it. They groan and become vehement as he works through their stories, cutting down the numbers. We were there, mate! We know what happened! But he knows well enough that if their initial claims were correct, the German air force would have ceased to exist.

At the same time, he is under some pressure to produce good figures, the kind that will cheer in the evening papers. Unlike the German figures, the losses given will be accurate, but the kills will be nearly as inflated, by two or three times.

It seems in any battle there are phantom aircraft, phantom tanks and troops — those the protagonists saw being blown up, destroyed, bayoneted, yet somehow weren't. So it is with Len as he's debriefed in turn. He tells of the phantom probable Dornier whose right-hand engine he saw blow up, the Me109 he gave a two-second blast as it slid past, saw smoke billow from the nose, a probable at the very least. Then he emptied the last of his ammo into the nose cone of another Dornier, saw the aircraft tilt, then another squadron's Spit moved in.

He says nothing about the range at which he opened fire. Altering the synchronization of a plane's guns to converge at any distance other than that determined by the Air Ministry is still a court martial offence. Seeing Tad's successes, more and more of the pilots are doing it but none talk about it.

Bill Raymond hesitates then notes down *Half probable Do.? Check*. Then calls on the next, Sniff Burton. Who openly and cheerfully admits he can't remember a thing about the action, though he'll wake during the night shouting out from dreams of it with wide, unseeing eyes.

Though the pilots are stood down, they will linger a long time by the dispersal hut, drinking tea and devouring cigarettes and waxing indignant, putting together an alternative story, their story, their phantom story. After all, they were there, they did it, they saw it all! And the more they talk, the more they convince themselves, the more their story is set and coherent. And the further it moves from what in their hearts they know to be true: two minutes of blurred intensity, incoherent as a waking dream.

The lorry comes, they climb on, some wearily and others still jittering with adrenalin. The afternoon sun shines hotly on the grass, their uniforms, their burned faces, until their voices fade. Their replacement stand-by flight ease into deck chairs, pick up magazines and cards and newspapers and settle down to wait.

Phantom aircraft sizzle and drop below the surface of the Channel as the real ones limp home in a horror of smashed glass, running wounds, dead men and the staring, pale-faced living.

Such a fuss in the years after the War when the true figures of enemy aircraft shot down were compiled. Squadrons and their aces saw their kills cut by two-thirds. They protest yet, the few who remain. It cannot be. They were there.

They were there but even they couldn't see the true losses.

I sit in my swivel chair and stare into the screen at the little falling blips, and for the first time wonder if there is a young Fräulein on the other side of the Channel looking into a similar screen. Our lecturers said we had to assume the other side had some form of radio wave location, though probably not the same as ours otherwise they would have targeted the masts from the outset.

In the empty hours I wonder about her. I catch a glimpse of her face in the glimmer reflection off the screen. She looks very like me but turned-around. Her straggly hair like mine is always threatening to bounce away from its perm, she too grins sardonically at nothing, she also rubs the two vertical lines above her nose when she worries.

What does she worry about? She worries about the blips she sees coming her way — not as many as I see, but enough to be concerned. She worries about her boyfriend who's a pilot or maybe, worse, one of a bomber crew. Perhaps the rear-gunner of a Stuka, or the navigator/bomb-aimer lying belly-down in the glass coffin nose-cone of a

Heinkel. If so, she really does have something to worry about.

She could as well be my pal or my sister, this woman. We face each other across the miles as we watch our screens, trying to guide or forewarn our lovers so they will meet, and when they meet both of us cannot be happy.

Fräulein: my twin, my sister, my mirror. My enemy who is not my enemy. I lean closer to the screen and stare into the hollow discs that are her eyes, trying to see what they may see.

10

Beginning of August

As I sit at the door of the receiver hut at the end of a fairly quiet day — just the one big build-up — trying to find the energy to cycle home, there's finally time to think about Evelyn last night and Len tonight.

Why should I feel guilty? It was good to spend the evening with Evelyn in a corner seat, drinking gin and talking about literature, art, theatre, the new films — all that stuff that is, hah, a closed book to Len. Or at least, not a wide-open one whose every page he's read. It was so good to have something to talk about other than the damn War all the time, and even when we did we were considering it from a different angle.

He seemed to have forgiven me for breaking it off — though of course I never put it like that — because I wasn't in love with him as I had been with Roger (I didn't exactly put it like that either). And that made me feel so relieved and warm towards him. That he could be so mature. That he still wanted to see me because he liked me. And of course that made me be more likeable.

In fact I showed off and flirted and thoroughly enjoyed myself. So it wasn't his fault that I took his arm as we felt our way up the black road. Nor was it his fault that his lips lingered on my cheek as we said good night at my door. And I can't blame him that he looked down at me from under the deeper darkness of his hat brim and started to speak seriously, sincerely, of how he felt about me.

I put my hand to his chest.

'I'm touched, honestly,' I said. 'But this isn't fair on any of us.'

'Any of us?' he said.

'I'm . . . seeing someone else. He's a pilot and a bit younger than me.' (In fact, only two years younger, but I feel safer when I lean on the difference a bit.)

'Of course,' he said. 'Thank you for telling me.'

He sounded so understanding and sad without making a fuss about it, that I had to open my mouth and say what was also true.

'But we can still meet once in a while. I've so enjoyed talking with you.'

He hugged me carefully then made his way by torchlight over to the truck he'd borrowed. I saw a faint wave, then the pale glimmer of his face, then he drove away. I hesitated then went inside, quietly up the stair.

And as I thoughtfully peeled off my stockings, I realized with a shock he really does love me. *Me*, for who I am, not what he gets from me, and with slight shiver knew this would always be rare in my or anyone's life.

★　★　★

I get up stiffly from the doorway of the hut, collect my bike round the back and set off slowly home, thinking of the man I'm going to see this evening, assuming he's lived that long.

Up to this point, the air fighting had been limited and sporadic if intense. Both sides had been probing and responding to each other's strengths and weaknesses. The decisive conflict was about to start as August began with some cloudy days. The invasion barges for Operation Sea Lion were assembled in the Low Countries; as the RAF frantically dug more land lines for their communications network and honed the lessons of their RDF ground control of fighters' experiences, the *Luftwaffe* got three gigantic air fleets into place in an arc stretching from western France to Norway.

In English villages that weekend, the anti-landing obstacles were dragged off the squares and cricket matches were played, albeit by scratch B teams plus local available servicemen. The Local Defence Volunteers drilled and patrolled, shot at some harmless motorists, hopelessly lost since the removal of all signposts and place names. There was a consuming fear of Fifth Columnists (and indeed a few were landed, farcically ill-prepared for their missions), and any parachutist dropping out of the sky was assumed to be German. Many a British pilot got to his feet with relief at being alive to find himself menaced with a pitchfork or an ancient rifle. Worse still if the pilot happened to be Polish or Czech. Lovers in haystacks and parked cars in country lanes were in more danger from the LDV than bombs.

The mood was at once anxious and business-as-usual. In the factories working 8.00 till 7.00, seven days a week, was becoming normal, with longer hours for special rush jobs. People were falling asleep in canteens and at kitchen tables with the wireless on. The greatest effort was directed at the production and repair of fighter aircraft as it became more and more apparent that the survival of the country lay with them.

The first evacuees began to drift back from the country as the mass bombing raids hadn't materialized. Sleep and having a good time were becoming the topmost priorities. Cinemas and dance halls were crowded, and lovers lay, it seemed, under every hedge in England, as people sought to take pleasure in the days that were left.

So we met as arranged in the High Street. It was a warm evening and I was sweating inside my uniform as I got down off the bus and saw her. Auburn hair piled up in the fashion, some strands escaping already as she studied her feet. Out of uniform in a pale grey skirt and jacket, light raincoat over her arm, she was pretty, but something had subtly altered and she didn't quite look like I'd expected or remembered.

I pushed aside any disappointment, checked once again it really was her, then crossed the road to greet her.

*　*　*

I knew it was him, of course. I'd seen him coming down the bus stairs then felt unaccountably shy or embarrassed. So I kept looking down, giving him my best profile. Trouble was, even in that glimpse he wasn't quite what I remembered, as if the special-ness, the glow, had been stripped away and left just an ordinary young man pressed into a grey-blue uniform. The memory of last night still hung about me, and interfered with my smile as I raised my face to greet him.

* * *

We went to the flicks, something by the Marx Brothers. I wasn't really in the mood for it but she seemed keen and anyway it was what one did on a date. It let us sit close together in the warm dark and not talk. Though I wanted to talk, the words were log-jammed in my throat when I saw her. So it was easier to go to the pictures instead.

The newsreel gave the scores for that week. Apparently we were downing them at a rate of two to one. Even if that was true, which I doubted, we could still lose simply by running out of planes or pilots, or if they started hitting RDF stations and airfields on a regular basis. It was a mystery to everyone why they hadn't. Maybe all this was just a preparatory phase, though it had cost some of our best pilots, and the real onslaught was yet to come.

I shivered, tried to put it all out of my mind. Then the news cut to a bunch of lads scrambling, all keenness and grins and neat partings as though they were running onto the pitch for the old school. Taking part with laughter on their lips . . . Far as I could recall, we weren't laughing as we ran.

Half of them didn't have their parachutes or Mae Wests, and as they leapt onto the wings of their Spits — of course it had to be Spits — I noticed they were the old single-blade prop jobs, so the whole thing was a put-up job for the cameras anyhow. It made me wonder just what I could believe these days. Then there was a clip of Mr Churchill talking, and I did believe him because he was saying things were bad, right bad, and we were really up against it, which of course we were. I took her hand or she took mine when he started saying we would win through in the end if we stuck to it and gave everything, but it was going to be hard. Yes, I thought, I believe that, and we gave each other a quick smile in the near-dark and our hands squeezed a little tighter.

★ ★ ★

The fighter pilots dashed across the sunlit field and it was all rather heart-warming though Len muttered under his breath. I told myself that was what the man next to me really did, and they (and presumably the Navy) were all that stood between us and invasion. Meanwhile he was trying to explain something about parachutes and propellers

134

then the person next to him told him to shush, and he looked embarrassed and contrite, not like a bold and valiant defender at all.

I tried to soothe him and explain it was just a picture, just a propaganda image like the German ones but made by our side. Then the old man with the big cigar came on, hamming it madly but as always it gripped you by the throat as he gave us the bad news then the good, and everyone in that crowded picture house stopped talking and smooching, and for a moment we were all joined together in the dark.

★   ★   ★

It may have been my mood but the main film didn't amuse me. It was too far away from what was on my mind.

I studied her face out of the corner of my eye. She looked serious, attentive, just the corner of her mouth twitching once in a while, folding the tiny mole near her upper lip away into a little valley. As I watched her, looked at those moving lips, she gradually began to grow clearer. She began to glow. She laughed, her teeth glimmered, she glanced at me, realized I'd been watching and withdrew into herself. Then I was annoyed at the film, annoyed we'd wasted time by going to see it, irritated because it was the kind of thing I'd done with Christine, for no better reason other than it was what was done. I shifted and scowled at the screen. What had once seemed fast and wild now looked pointless and laboured. I wished Harpo would stop pulling faces at the camera and pretending he couldn't speak. I was sick of pretending.

I glanced again at Stella. She seemed withdrawn, utterly absorbed in the film, smiling slightly as she followed its silliness.

★　★　★

I'd seen the film before, with Evelyn as it happens. We'd pulled it apart then and it didn't improve on second viewing. It was one of their poorer efforts. Still, it was obviously the kind of thing Len liked so I made an effort to seem interested.

Finally, during one of the slapstick routines, I yawned. One of those huge jaw-locking yawns. I covered my mouth and tried to look as if I was convulsed with laughter but it was too late. Len was on his feet, hanked me by the hand and practically dragged me up the ramp and out into the foyer.

'You were bored!' he said.

'No, not really. It was a bit warm in there and it's been a tiring day.'

He laughed curtly like I was speaking nonsense, and I wondered if he was really angry, if he was in fact short-tempered. I didn't need a short-tempered man.

'That's a relief,' he said. 'This isn't what I want to do.'

We were leaning against the poster at the side of the foyer. One or two people were drifting in and out.

'What do you want to do?'

He stared back at me.

'This,' he said. Then he began kissing me, so hungrily my mouth opened and I forgot all thought of yawning and the fact we were in a public place. My heart was drumming the advance as we finally separated.

'Golly!' I said. 'If that's what you want to do, we'd better go somewhere else.'

We caught the bus back to my billet.

'What about Mrs Mackenzie?' Len asked.

I said something very rude about Mrs Mackenzie and we went inside and quickly up the stairs.

* * *

'This is my room,' she said.

'So I see,' I replied.

137

It was a change to see her more ill at ease than me, not knowing where to put herself. There wasn't much to the room — a single bed, a seat, a table and chair, cupboard. A few photos, some books, a gramophone and a stack of records on the floor. I looked through them while she made tea in a tiny curtained-off alcove. A mixture of jazz — Ellington, Basie — and popular songs, plus a lot of classical music that meant nothing to me, symphonies and quartets and the like. A spare box of needles sat by the gramophone.

'Would you like to listen to some music?' she asked.

She was standing in the alcove holding two cups and saucers, and as I looked at her there was a glow around her outline and an amount of light coming from her lips and hands and eyes. She looked like the only good thing I'd set my eyes on for months. Indeed it was surprising I wasn't dragged towards her across the carpet, given the force of attraction operating.

'Yes,' I said, and sat down on the end of the bed.

She put the cups on the bedside cabinet then knelt down to the pile of gramophone records.

'Jazz?' she said.

'Yes please.'

It was hard not to start giggling, there was so much glee in that little room.

She wound the gramophone then set a pile of records on the floor beside it, put the first one on the spindle. That was promising. She put on the bedside lamp then switched off the main light, hesitated then came and sat beside me. She looked down at her hands then turned her head my way and smiled as Duke Ellington launched into 'Mood Indigo' and the light streamed from her eyes.

* * *

I hadn't kissed or been kissed like that for ages. The kind where your heart is in your mouth. The kind I never shared with Evelyn, however nice it was.

My lips got swollen. Every so often I took a break to wind the gramophone and turn over the records. So we played the same selection over and over. From that night I would never hear *Rhapsody in Blue* without living again that shabby little room, those kisses, his scratchy blue uniform and my hammering heart pressed up against it.

I unbuttoned his uniform jacket. I untied his tie and put my hand on his throat.

'One more time?' I asked.

His skin was hot, his eyes were very bright and close. I made no attempt to stop him touching me and going as far as modesty and common sense would permit.

Honestly, if it wasn't for the dread of getting pregnant, I think I'd be a fast lot.

★　★　★

I walked home through the dark town and into the countryside, then with my torch took the short cut across the fields where cows stood pale and glimmering in the moon's light and the dew soaked my shoes and socks. It was very late; I'd have to take a good blast of oxygen tomorrow to get fully awake, though adrenalin did a lot of that for you.

I walked on through the long grass and thistles and cowpats towards the distant mass of the pile we'd commandeered as our barracks. My thoughts were as if I was very drunk, though I wasn't. Everything normal seemed to have stopped, slipped away somewhere, and all that was left was the cool mystery of the night, my humming, and some high-flying thoughts. *Everything we have, we lose.* So to want something, anything, someone, is the beginning of tragedy.

And yet, and yet.

I jumped over the last fence and crunched

up the gravel path towards our billet, and narrowly avoided being shot by our guard who had Fifth Columnists and German paratroopers on the brain.

* * *

I straightened the crumpled bed covers, washed and got into bed. Though dog-tired I lay awake a long time with the moonlight coming pale between the curtains and striking the silent gramophone and the end of the bed where we had sat.

The night before with Evelyn seemed an age away and everything had changed. I was in it now. I pictured the slogan that was everywhere these days: GO TO IT. Len's youth and vulnerability and kisses had dragged the heart out of me, and it lay so open I wondered it couldn't be seen beating in the moonlight. And yet this was such a bad idea, not because he wasn't a good man, I'd wager anything he was, but because there was a strong likelihood he'd die and that would kill me if I let him grow more important.

I lay awake a long time, 'Mood Indigo' running through and through my head, my body singing softly to itself.

11

Early August

His letter is still in its small, faded envelope. Typed little sheets, the folds darkened and paper yellowing. Smudged with the sweat of sixty years back. A faint whiff of grass, plus hair or engine oil. That summer! His hands closed this, hers opened it.

Inside, pale pages like opaque windows, showing dimly through to his world.

Dear Stella,

Had a bit of a shaky do yesterday — but no flap, don't worry, I'm fine, near as dammit. Yesterday we scrambled to bust up a swarm of bombers over ███. When we got there the Spits had already engaged the fighters above, so we went in line astern, real copybook stuff (they want to throw that book away — like a lot of things, it's gone out of date fast). A case of Tally-ho bambambam, a cross between the hunting field and the school playground. Still, got to admit some of these

142

university types have guts, flying in to 10 to 1 against, and we just have to follow.

Hellofagoodshow as Billy Madden would say, totally wiz. More just hell and leave it at that, I say. Johnny Staples got an He111 then baled out, Tad and Coco Cadbury shared another, I added another probable (Me110, seeing you ask). Then more 109s bounced us from above, total shambles all round, glare through the glass, chaps squalling on the headphones, hot metal breakfasts whizzing about the sky.

I'm sorry to say Geoff Prior's had it, saw him blow up, a shame because he was a good leader and, I think, a good man. And one of our new blokes, can't remember his name, went down in a flamer. Then I spotted Tim Baker with one of the bastards ('scuse) on his tail roughing him up, and I went down to put my oar in — got him, I think, but of course can't prove it — and must have stopped looking behind in the excitement and one of the opposition must have gone down to look after his mate because this banging starts. Then he nails me good and proper. Starboard wing starts to fold, nose goes down and there's a bonfire blowing through by my hands (thank God I wore Mum's leather gloves) and my kite is definitely on the way down and out. Trouble was, she wanted to take me with her. I switched everything off, got out of the harness but the cockpit hood jammed and I was stuck in there and things got a bit hot and bothered till I suddenly fell out. Banged my arm on the way. Dropped a while then remembered to pull the cord and I'm floating down towards Merrie England, beating out the last of the flames round my legs, missing a shoe but the foot's still there so I ain't complaining!

So I landed smack in a plum orchard somewhere near Wateringbury and I'm dangling up a tree with half a dozen giggling Land Girls trying to decide what to do about it when this wrinkly old fella comes along, takes a look then shouts up, 'Just dropped in for a cuppa, then?' and nearly ends himself laughing. I was lost for a reply, so confined myself to a simple gesture.

So that was that. I got down then woke up on a ride to hospital where they've looked after me and where I'm sending this under the eagle eye of Matron (God rot her!). I'm all right, really. A wonky wrist, something funny with my elbow, and for the rest a bit like your toast the other night — a little burned, a little scraped, but sound enough underneath.

The good news is, I've a week's leave till I'm fully operational again (they want to keep me from writing off more expensive machinery), and I've an Immodest Proposal. Could you, would you, care to spend a couple of days at an aunt's cottage out Ludlow way (minus aunt, who's with another sister in Wales). It's in a valley by the river, real quiet place, guaranteed no air-raid sirens.

So can you? No strings attached. You know. But nice to revisit 'Mood Indigo' a few more times, especially the crackly bits. It would be good to spend more than a few hours together — sun, cider, sweet nothings. Can do?

Love, Len

PS Like the typing? Hand temporarily SNAFU.

The truth? The truth is more in his diary. Those pale pencilwritten (neat at first, a draughtsman's hand) battered pages.

He was slow that morning, even a blast from his oxygen bottle before taking off couldn't make him alert. Their flight went up early, round 7 a.m. From the start he was struggling to stay in formation as they climbed (Geoff Prior insisted on a tight V till the end, which this morning turned out to be for him). His snap decision to go down after Tim Baker was a mistake. Just before scramble they'd been talking about their families over a mug of tea in the dispersal hut, and he'd briefly felt connected with him, so when it happened he had to follow him down.

And when the bullets and cannon shells started hitting home, he was so astounded he did nothing for a couple of seconds. And when he did, he was flustered. Then terror-struck. Going down in a flamer was the flyer's biggest dread. Hammering on the canopy as the plane went spinning down, he was trying to twist away from the flames blowing into that tiny space. Lord knows how he got out, for *he* doesn't.

Whatever he typed laboriously and one-handed in the cool, near-empty hospital ward, the reality had charred him deeply, and from then on he notes nightmares of falling and burning. His hopeful proposal to Stella, which he didn't think very likely she would take up, may well have been a way of keeping his thoughts trained forward onto one good thing.

'I *am* excited,' I admitted to Maddy. 'I didn't think I'd get leave but Foxy Farringdon offered to stand in.'

'She sounds all right for a toff,' Maddy agreed.

'I'm starting to warm to her,' I said. 'But now I can see Len and me going away to live together for a few days, I'm a bit nervous.'

'Not half as nervous as Len, I'll bet,' Maddy said. 'Stands to reason.'

'How's that?'

Maddy laughed her deep, gurgling laugh and drained her glass.

'I'll bet you next week's chocolate coupon it's his first time and it's not yours.'

I thought about it. I removed a lemon pip from my mouth, all yellow-white and slippery, and wondered why I didn't feel more embarrassed. Maybe because she thought sex was natural and funny. Hard to remember, but in those days women friends didn't even admit to having their period.

'I don't gamble with something serious like chocolate,' I said.

She laughed, loud and free and slightly

drunk. A couple of middle-aged men at the bar turned and stared at us. We stared back at them till they looked away.

'Seducing the young and innocent,' she said. 'I don't know what your mother would say.'

'I know exactly what my mother would say,' I replied. 'But that's a different generation. As long as I can keep it from my father. For all his casual ways, he wouldn't be happy about it.'

'So what's the invisible *but?*' Maddy asked.

I looked into the last of her gin and picked out the lemon.

'It's a terrible thing to say,' I said, 'but when I got that letter I almost hoped . . . ' I sucked the lemon, made a face and looked away, blinking. Maddy put a hand on mine and waited. Sometimes she knew when to wait.

' . . . Hoped he'd been injured seriously enough to get him out,' I said quickly. 'I want him alive.'

'Then you've chosen someone with the wrong occupation,' Maddy said quietly. 'Better keep it light, or go back with Evelyn.'

As Maddy went up to the bar, ignoring some of the looks she was getting, I sat frowning as I drew with my little finger in a pool dripping from the lemon. I doodled a circle, put a line through it, then a stick man. Out of the stick man's (or woman's?) mouth came a speech bubble. I hesitated then entered a question mark, frowned down at it, then made four blobby asterisks and added an exclamation mark just in time to look up smiling as the drinks came.

'Still,' I said, 'might as well live for the day. Everyone else is. By the way, what's SNAFU, Maddy?'

She threw back her head and laughed and laughed. She looked at me and shook her head like I was a sweet but silly child. Then she leaned closer and said it in my ear.

' 'Situation Normal, All Fucked Up', love. The Yanks use it.'

'Oh,' I said. 'Of course. How very useful.' Then to cover my embarrassment, I added, 'So who have you been flaming it with this week, Maddy?'

'I been out with a sweet sailor boy I was looking after for a while,' she said. Then she propped her arm up on her elbow so her sleeve slipped down. On her wrist were four bangles, blue-green with rosy lights, and a chain of tiny fish carved round them. Not my taste but looked expensive.

'Golly!' I said. 'You must have looked after him well.'

'Oh!' she said. 'I did, believe me.'

She laughed and shook her wrist and the bangles rattled together. She never said what happened to her 'sweet sailor boy' but she wore those bangles pretty much all the time, and their light clacking followed her wherever she went, and became one of the sounds of that summer.

Our trains crawled westward through that day, but I didn't care that we had to stand. The carriages were packed with soldiers, a few sailors, evacuees, some exhausted pale-faced people coming back from long shifts in the factories and workshops. I'd left my RAF uniform behind and got a few curious, a few hostile looks.

As we waited in a bombed siding for another train to pass, she leaned against me where we stood. The weight and warmth of her body pressed into mine, and I felt for the first time the real ache of tenderness. I felt for her tired feet, the heavy, sleepy lean of her head against my chest. I put my arm round her back to hold her up and looking down over her auburn head I saw some curls escaped to swing like bells against her white skin at the nape of her neck, and I felt faint with the near-certainty that tonight I would know her.

She sighed, her head shifted against my jacket as the train jerked and I held her more tightly with my unbandaged arm. At her feet was her small blue suitcase and next to it, mine. Also a large basket of food queued for and bought with ration book in hand. I had a newspaper and a book by James Thurber — a present for her that I hoped she'd approve of — in my coat pocket.

I shifted on my feet, felt patient, at peace with time in a way I hadn't been since that evening in childhood I calculated how long I had to live and felt the precious seconds trickling away even as I wasted time calculating them. Some unseen shutter clicked as I was looking down at her case, and I knew that stray moment would stay, labelled *On Holiday, August 1940*. The blue case, her new brown shoes, the way the sunlight fell across them both, confirming them precious.

A long day and my feet were killing me in too-small shoes I'd bought in the hope of making myself look dainty. We stood by the window, shamelessly letting our bodies melt together through coats and jackets. I was thinking how we didn't know each other yet but very soon we would, and wondering how I felt about that. Nervous, mostly. Not at the thing itself but at how much I wanted it.

In mid-afternoon, on the second train, someone offered me a seat. I peeled myself away from Len and took it gratefully. Towards evening the crowd thinned out and we got a seat together and sat hand in hand heading west into a golden pool of light I'd have happily drowned in.

Finally we got out at the tiny station in nowhere and looked for a taxi. The stationmaster seemed to find this very funny. A taxi, here?

'So,' I said to my guiding light, 'how far is it to walk?'

He shrugged, looked a bit shifty I thought.

'About three miles.' Pause. 'Maybe four. And . . . there's some uphill in it.'

I silently cursed my shoes and my vanity. He took the two cases, I carried the food, and we set off.

* * *

If the cottage was in a valley, it was one near the top of a hill. The road went up and up. It began to rain lightly, then not so lightly. A wind got up and drove the rain through my light coat and plastered my suit and stockings to my legs.

He apologized several times for the weather and the gradient. I said he might have arranged it better. He apologized again. I said that it must be tough carrying the responsibility for the world on his shoulders.

He put down the cases, grimaced, flexed his unbandaged hand. 'It certainly is,' he said. 'It's not far now,' he added.

'You've said that so often, one time it must be true.'

He strode out in front, humming tunelessly. When I recognized it was 'Tipperary' I had to kick him.

'Ouch!' said my fearless fighting man. 'That's sore.'

The rain got heavier and we sheltered behind a tree for a while.

'Thought you was once a bit of a tomboy,'

155

he said. 'Outdoor activities and that.'

'Was was a long time ago,' I replied.

Still the thought cheered me and I tried to look on it as an adventure as we set off again. Eventually we came to a track that branched off to the right. It was downhill, which was good, and muddy from an undrained stream, which wasn't. We carried on through the mud. I didn't like those brown shoes that much anyway, and what's another pair of stockings?

And finally we were there.

'Well done,' he said. 'Sorry it was a bit of a hike.'

'Oh, did you think so?' I said carelessly.

The cottage was half-way down a hollow, a sort of gutter, with trees on both sides. It was built of old brick, with a slate roof and little diamond-shaped panes in the windows. Across the lane was a small orchard and a stream at the far side made watery sounds in the dimness. The rain had stopped, the wind dropped and there was a glow in the western sky and I had to admit it was all rather pretty.

He went round the back into a shed, came back with a key and let us in. It was a bit unused-smelling, cool but dry. We opened a few windows, he lit the fire, I started heating the main meal I'd brought. It was an adventure, and felt vaguely naughty, like playing grown-ups. I kept expecting someone to come in and tell us to go to bed.

Which, come to think of it, wasn't half a bad idea.

★ ★ ★

After we'd finished eating, we stood a while in the doorway, looking down the valley and listening to the last sleepy birds calling in the woods. The few clouds were high and pink, the breeze had dropped. A dog barked somewhere in the distance, a sheep responded faintly. I leaned into him, felt his arm come round me all lean and young.

'You must have a very understanding aunt,' I said.

'I do,' he replied. 'And yes, I did tell her about you.'

'And what did she say?'

'*Enjoy yourselves*. She didn't add 'while you can' but she might as well have. I hope that's all right?'

'Fine,' I said. 'I like to be acknowledged, even if it's as a loose woman.'

'There's nothing loose about you,' he protested. With some conviction, I thought.

'Oh yes? Take me upstairs and find out.'

We went up the creaky narrow stairs. First room was his aunt's bedroom, all faded

157

chintz and a few books and photos. Second was a little side room, a narrow-looking single bed, a lovely but curtainless casement window looking out over the darkened woods, a chest of drawers, a chair.

I went over and opened the window and heard the water sounds from the stream. He stood awkwardly in the doorway.

'It's perfect,' I said. 'I'll always remember.'

'Remember what?' he asked.

'That we've been happy here,' I said, and held out my arms to him.

12

Early to mid-August

I'll never forget this yellow room. The narrow curved mattress that rolls us into each other as we sleep. The curtainless diamond panes and the window that rattles in the wind till we prop it open and sleep with the breeze on our faces, that air full of summer night and owls and water and the odd shriek as some small animal meets its end in the woods.

I love it all. How we can lie in bed at night and watch the constellations rise through the trees, wake and measure how the night goes by their position. The smooth, creaking, ancient floorboards, cool under my naked foot. The vague sweet smell of wood smoke throughout the house.

And above all she who lies sleeping on my arm as the morning light calls in. She is asleep, face smooth, untroubled, distant. The weight of her head, her thick hair, lies full on my upper arm — how it will tingle when she wakes!

Her eyes open, she looks into mine. Her eyes fill up as she takes in where she is.

'Well hello, lover,' she says in her best film-star voice, and the day begins again.

In a while I will pad downstairs and make tea in the quiet kitchen, throw open the window and hear the thrush that haunts the garden shed. I'll bring the tea upstairs and we'll drink it, propped on the pillows. And later, if I am lucky — if she is lucky! — because we are young and new, we will start again, returning with more attention to the places we have been.

'Finest summer I remember,' Old George our nearest neighbour said without irony, re-caning his hollyhocks.

Right enough, I thought, it's mostly been sun day after day and nowhere to hide in the sky. The way men become wavering black sticks against the glare. And those soft distant thuds day and night as we walk through the orchards. Lovers giggling in the lanes as we do, my finger lifted to his puffed lips . . .

There was a wireless in the cottage, and we listened only to the Light Programme. Most of the time Len didn't seem to think about the War or going back to it. But I noticed how he fixed on little things, the thin, high drone of a single-engined plane in the sky one morning. Or the way a wasp crawled from the plum he picked, but it was too groggy with heat to fly or sting, and I too felt drugged with heavy juice as I leaned to flick it from his arm.

'Well, keep out of mischief, young 'uns.' Old George leered, then hee-hawed as he shuffled off, leaving me with fingers clenched round a windfall apple, still fizzling at the edges of my last bite. I slung it away into the undergrowth, looped my arm in Len's and we set off before the heat went out of the day.

* * *

We stretched out on the short cropped turf of the high moorland, looking across into Wales.

'We'll go there someday when we have a car,' I said. 'We can take a good look around Tintern Abbey and do some walking. By the way, can you drive?'

'Nope,' he said. 'But if I can fly, I can surely learn to drive. And one day find the money to buy a car.'

I stretched and yawned, and reached for another sandwich as if there were plenty time.

* * *

After lunch, in a low hollow out of wind and sight, one touch led to a kiss led to a caress led to making love. We were in a hurry, so only the bare minimum of clothes removed. It was grabbing at experience, so we could say we'd done it outside. This wasn't said but it hung over us like a cloud of midges, sorrow on account of the greed on account of the anxiety.

Still, it was an experience, new to us both,

and worth it for the feel of the breeze, cool where wind hadn't been for years.

'We can get a house in the country and grow a thick hedge round the garden,' he said. 'Then we can do it outside whenever we want.'

'When it's not raining and the children are away at school,' I replied, and then there was a long pause. I think we wondered if we'd gone too far too fast.

'Don't babies sleep in the afternoon?' he murmured. 'Well, then.'

I'm walking at noon along a forestry track back to the cottage. The sun is hot, my plimsolls are white on the earth-brown track, the oak and beech on either side are strong dark green. I sweat happily and hum, stripped down to a shirt with the sleeves rolled up, carrying my jacket over one arm. Across my shoulder in an old duffel bag are the few extra foodstuffs from the village shop for our meal tonight. There are two hawthorns by the side of the track, and wild strawberries sharp and near-ripe along the drainage ditch to my right.

I'm thinking about cold beer from the pantry when I get back to the cottage. I wonder if the weather will hold for tomorrow and the picnic expedition we've been talking about. In truth, I don't really care. If it rains, we'll stay in, which is fine by me.

I'm thinking how after that first heart-thumping moment when I reached out for her, sex is more pleasurable and interesting than I'd ever imagined, and less scary. *Almost better than flying*, I told her afterwards. *Oh, I don't know*, she said. She's sharp.

Then I found myself whispering into her throat *I love you*. Perhaps that was bed-talk, true in its moment. She pressed my head harder against her neck and we said no more about it.

What we do in bed (and once on the moor) is lovely to do, embarrassing to think about. When I think about it, I see it from the outside. But how it feels from the inside is the point.

I must remember that before time does some hand-tinting to these pictures in my head. Remember that and the smooth-soft texture of her skin, near-white in private places. If I get to be old, I want to have that memory still. But more pressing for now is this sense of coming to myself on the track through the green trees, and the way the wild strawberries are scattered only on the south-facing side of the ditch, and the gummy smell of the woods.

Now I'm not thinking. There is only the earth-coloured track before me and the green around me and the white gym shoes moving and sweat tickling down the runnel of my back.

I'm so grateful for my senses. The ground is dry and warm, I'm getting a blister on my big toe and the skin itches under the bandage on my right hand, the air under the trees is pale green, and there's a web stretched against the sky between two branches. Now coming round a corner, the river runs slow and glittering through the valley below.

Then I see the bone, just off the centre of the path. I stop and pick it up. It's light and smooth. And clean, the way things that have no life left in them are clean. I run my thumb round the curved groove at the broad end. Pale grey, so thin its edges are near transparent. Scapula, I think, from a hare. Or a lamb. Anatomy isn't my strong point. I rub my thumb along the bone and see the knuckles rise under my skin. Some day this hand too will rot.

I turn and look behind: the track snaking back through the trees. I look forward. No one there either, only more track and more trees and the river valley below. Yet I feel . . . noticed.

I'm looking down on myself from a great height.

I see myself, the reddening arms and neck, white shirt and the shadow of the duffel bag moving slightly as I breathe, and the world surrounding me.

Now I see myself as the sun does, see the white gym shoes motionless on the track and the head staring down at what's in my hand, see the clothes on the skin on the skeleton around the soft organs. There is light everywhere. The trees are breathing out and I'm breathing in and the flowers turn towards the sun.

And then it's gone, and everything's normal again. I flip the little piece of bone into the trees and start walking towards food and drink, shade and a woman.

Across the river in a green field, quivering slightly in the heat, two men and a dog are working sheep. For a moment I'm out of myself again. I see that they're the centre of the world, as I am. I cup my hand and shout. The men do not move, perhaps the dog's head jerks, then the echo comes back faintly.

I'm walking again empty of thought but noticing everything — these yellow flowers turned towards the sun, the hidden pigeon calling in the wood, my own shadow jerking alongside, these fingers uncurled in the breeze, a twinge in my right knee, the slight sweaty pleasing sway of the body that is mine. Young. Alive. Now.

The track ends and I duck into the coolness of the narrow path under the trees. Then I'm coming down through the thistle field above the cottage, and Stella is perched like a red-crested heron on the gatepost outside. I whistle and she looks up, waves. And I smile because it's much better than being a dry bone as I hurry towards her through the last of the thistle field.

'Did you get everything?' she calls.

Her eyes are wide open, her arm is strong and smoothskinned on the gate, but I'm not quite ready to touch her. I see the white bones under her wrist, so many, so intricately connected.

'I got the lot,' I say.

Then she jumps down from the post and puts an arm round my waist, and it feels natural and right that a body should meet a body, coming through the thistle field and all.

He has nightmares. So old a child, so young a man to have bad dreams. It isn't right.

I woke in the night to find him struggling, his body giving off terrific heat. He tried to free his arms but the sheet was tight around him. A whimper started low in his throat. As it grew I put my arms round him then shook him awake, cut off the yell by jerking him from that world into this, and for a moment I wonder if it's what dying is. Jerking from one world into another.

'Flames,' he muttered into my armpit. 'Was going down in flames.' And then he said quite clearly: 'Strangers have taken over the airfield.'

'What?' I said.

'What?' he replied.

'What did you say?'

'Can't remember,' he said. 'Glad you woke me.'

He threw off the covers and I could have sworn his slim body was steaming in the moonlight. He lay for a long time rigidly looking up at the moon through our window, lay till I felt his skin start to goose-flesh.

'Think I'll take a walk,' he said.

'What — at four in the morning? You're crazy!'

He looked right at me.

'Not necessarily,' he said. 'Want to come?'

★ ★ ★

Outside it's like the blackout but worse. It's so dark here in the country. He takes me by the hand and starts to lead me down the hill. He seems to have cat's eyes and moves quite easily as I stumble along. The moon comes out from behind the cloud and I'm beginning to see a bit, then the faint path we're following goes in under the trees and it's black again.

It's years since I was in the country at night. I'm almost afraid, and shiver to think how it was when there were bears and wolves. Eventually he pauses, then leads me uphill to the left, going slower now. His head presses close against mine.

'Quiet now,' he whispers. 'We're nearly there.'

Nearly where? I wonder, but don't say it. Possibly my love has gone completely barmy. Yet I've never seen him so assured.

He pushes me gently against a big tree. I

can see the pale glimmer of his hand as he points ahead.

Nothing there, at least not that I can see. What are we looking for — Fifth Columnists? It's a small clearing, a patch of moonlight, some undergrowth and a couple more big dark trunks. I start to think I see significant shapes, then blink and realize I see nothing. Then I understand we're waiting.

With nothing to see, I start to hear the sounds. I'd thought it as silent as it seemed dark, but neither is true. There's water sound, clear as anything. And light wind in trees. And a faint scuffing sound in the leaves and grass near by. His hand tightens on my arm.

And they're there. As though just materialized, a low dark shape something between a dog and a small boar, pale stripe up its forehead, standing frozen in the moonlight, one leg poised. By its side, two, no three, small ones like piglets. As they root among leaves, I feel I'm looking into a different world, one with its own laws, nothing to do with us. My breath catches, my right foot comes down on dry leaves — a scuffle and they're gone. Never saw them going, they're just gone.

I hear his breath come out, then he takes my arm and leads me silently back down the slope to the path.

★ ★ ★

'I saw the den the other day,' he said on the way back across the field. 'Wondered if they'd be about by night. Have you seen badgers before?'

'No,' I said. 'Never. Thanks so much.'

Behind his head I could see dawn was coming. He seemed lighter, unburdened, and I was touched he'd shown me not just the badgers but what they meant to him. Something unsaid, unspeakable maybe, but I could feel relief coming off his loose, tired, springy body.

'Thanks for coming along,' he said. 'Now I really feel like some breakfast.'

Hand in hand we started wandering up the path, hungry, towards the dawn, his nightmares forgotten for a while.

It was time out of this world, time we should have been asleep in bed, time rescued. Looking back, it was so strange and unconnected to anything else, I sometimes wonder if it happened at all or if it was a curious, overheated dream, a spurious imagining of another world, a world to come or that might have been, where we were lovers and the world was innocent.

13

Mid-August

On our second-to-last evening we walked up through the thistle field and down the lane to the pub. Len was set on going trout fishing in a nearby lake or reservoir, talked about it most of the way, outlining the essentials he'd have to borrow, the challenges and delights of high-summer angling. But when we enquired at the pub, we were told fishing had ended on account of the War. No boats available, no permits. A short man with a drinker's face said that he was sorry but there it was.

We sat at the window with the evening light flooding in.

'Shame about that,' I said. In fact I wasn't displeased; I thought there were better things to do with our last day than pursue small, slithery cold-blooded animals.

'Mm,' he said. 'Excuse a minute.'

He was gone more like five. Most of it spent up at the bar, talking to the red-faced man. I thought he was trying to buy cigarettes and taking a long time about it. I sipped my cider and wondered how my mother was getting on with my dad away most nights as an ARP warden. Maybe it would be a relief for them both, no longer having to pretend they were much of a couple.

Len bounced back to our table.

'Fixed,' he said. He sat down and drank from his pint, a big grin escaping the corner of his mouth.

'What?'

'We're fishing tomorrow. Getting a lift with Mr Mannion there, he's lending us his gear. Water bailiff.'

'How did you fix that?'

He wiped the corner of his mouth, looked right at me and grinned again. He had the body of a man but looked so like a boy who'd managed to get off with something. He looked at me like that sometimes, so natural and thoughtless, and when he did my heart turned over.

'Gamekeepers' union,' he said. 'He knows of my dad, they've some mates in common. So . . . '

'So you bent the rules a bit?'

'There's no rules,' he said, 'because of the War. This is more by way of a favour. Wild brown trout!'

'Do you really want me to come along?'

He looked so astonished I forgave him. And anyway, an inner voice reminded me, this might be his last chance to fish, it would be mean to deprive him.

* * *

It was a hot sunny morning, our last day. Sandwiches and a Thermos, then up to the top of the lane in time for Mr Mannion in an old Wolseley. He had a petrol allowance for his job, and he drove us for some miles along half-buried country roads till we came to a long, narrow, glittering lake with small islands and slim trees, like a Chinese painting.

He gave us the key to the boat shed, told us we'd find the gear in there, gave us a pick-up time then drove off.

'Well, OK,' Len said as I stared after the disappearing car. 'He's not a thing of beauty but he's doing us a big favour. A smile for him would be nice.'

'I can't help it, I don't like drinkers,' I said. 'It reminds me too much of my father. It makes people so careless with everything around them.'

But I cheered up when he opened the boat shed and we pulled out a surprisingly new rowing boat. I'd expected to be standing admiringly on the bank getting eaten by insects for hours on end. A boat was different. So we heaved it down to the water, piled in lunch and life jackets, oars and fishing gear. I got in, he pushed and jumped in, took the oars and started pulling out for the islands.

The day was hot. There was a slight breeze out in the middle, enough to keep insects away. I told him I was happy to leave the fishing to him and stretched out on my coat; fingers trailing in the cool water, sun in my eyes.

They were long and dreamy, the hours we spent there. I was hypnotized with the easy, rhythmic way he cast, something between a swing and a jerk of the arm and the line flew out behind his head, snap of the wrist, arm straightened again, and the cast whipped out ahead then dropped so lightly into the shining water. I like watching anyone good at what they do, like I'd fallen for Roger during his fluent, devastating analyses of later Jacobean dramatists, and Len was clearly good at this. He seemed in place, for once at ease with himself and the world. He told me some of what he was doing, casting ahead of the few rises there were, into the anticipated path of the fish.

He took one, all shining and muscular. I felt bad looking at it lying in the bottom of the boat, but knew I'd be keen enough to eat it. Two more he threw back and I was happy to see them jerk back into life, flicker then vanish. A second chance, I thought vaguely. I'm glad I'm not God having to play God. Having to decide which airman, which bombed civilian lives and which dies. There's no reason for it. It's not on account of virtue, nor always skill. Luck is small and Fate too big a word for it. It's what happens.

I watched him, his tanned arm moving rhythmically back and forward, at once frowning and smiling into the stretch of water off to the side. Serious play, I thought. He's playing but taking it seriously, as a child does. The way we make love. It's a game and we can smile and laugh, but we don't take it casually. That would be insulting. There's things to be learned here.

He rowed in close to the bank and we drifted along it in the light breeze. I lay back, smoked a cigarette and looked at the sky, the few white clouds puffed up like pigeons' breasts. I heard him grunt, then his arm whipped back and forward again. I sat up in time to see his wrist strike back, saw his whole face flare as the rod bent.

He played it in, I had the net ready. A big one, I could see that. I was praying for his sake it wouldn't drop off the hook. I decided if the hook stayed in and we got this fish, he'd survive.

It got closer and closer to the boat, then pulled away again. He worked it back in, looking tense now. I stretched out as far as I could, had a couple of passes with the landing net but missed. The rod was bent at a ridiculous angle. He brought the fish in close again, I leant and swooped, got the net under it and lifted it on board.

A big one, absolutely beautiful. I had such mixed feelings as it flapped round my ankles. Then he caught it and bashed it just before I had time and wit to ask him not to, to tell him that in some way the fish's fate was bound up with his. Silly idea. He washed the blood off his hands and looked up at me.

'Thought we might have lunch on one of the islands,' he said.

'A fine and private place,' I said and smiled to myself, knowing he wouldn't get the quotation, then felt bad for my cheap superiority. Did he feel superior because he could catch a fish like this but I couldn't? I cursed my vanity or insecurity, whichever it was.

He grinned back at me, full of youth and openness. 'Too bad I forgot the French letters,' he said. 'Still we can be Adam and Eve behind those trees.'

'We can be more than that,' I said, then felt

around in my coat and produced the packet I'd lifted from the bedside table.

⋆　⋆　⋆

We lay naked on our clothes in the broken shade. I idly stroked the few black hairs around his nipples, he flicked away the flies that tried to land on me. I thought this was as perfect and far away as we could get.

Then he murmured, 'I wonder how the lads are doing.'

I lay very still, wondering at the stab of anger I felt. Something close to jealousy.

'I'm sorry,' he said eventually. 'I'm so pleased to be here but I can't help wondering.'

'Wonder to yourself,' I said. 'No, that's not fair.'

'It reminds me of school summer holidays,' he said. 'I didn't want it to end but at the same time I sometimes used to look forward to getting back and catching up with everyone again. Being part of it.'

'I didn't realize you felt part of it,' I said.

'Nor did I.'

I propped myself upon an elbow and studied him. Long straight nose, wide mouth, eyebrows arched high like he was permanently surprised. Brown eyes with flecks of

179

hazel. My man. A complete stranger. Beside me and 150 miles away.

'Len, what are you doing this for?'

He frowned slightly and seemed to give it serious consideration.

'Sex,' he said. 'The sex is terrific.'

I thumped his chest.

'No, stupid! The RAF, this whole fighter pilot bit. You didn't have to do it. It's much too . . . dangerous. And don't make a joke about it or I'll squeeze your bad hand.'

He grinned and took away his bandaged hand, put it away behind his head.

'The flying,' he said. 'I love flying — did I forget to mention that? There's nothing like it, the moment you feel yourself lifting into the air. Or when I'm cruising at ten thousand, looking down on cloud mountains and canyons, or way down onto hedges and rivers and houses and fields. It's calm and yet exciting. I feel so . . . The world from up there looks . . . ' He paused then shrugged. 'Well anyway, it's kept me out of the trenches.'

'But there are no trenches in this war.'

He giggled. 'I know, my dad got that wrong. He thought this war would be like the last one — completely pointless and bogged down in trenches.'

'But it isn't, is it?'

A long pause lay between us, the sunny afternoon suddenly grown serious.

'No,' he said. 'It isn't, is it. It has to be done and we can't duck it.'

He sat up and looked around.

'What, no applause?' he said. 'I thought we were Olympic standard! Let's go in for a swim.'

'Like this?'

'Why not? There's no one around. Even if there was, as my mother used to say, you'll never see them again.'

'I wish *my* mother would say things like that.'

Then as I swam in smooth circles round his thrashing and splashing, I thought again of what he'd said about flying. How it was calm and exciting at once. And I thought of my childhood fantasy of the cave behind the waterfall. If that's what flying was for him, little wonder his voice changed when he talked of it. Little wonder he was reluctant to speak of it at all. I could understand it — one doesn't wish to spoil something special by talking tosh about it.

Still, we hadn't got to the bottom of it. After all, if he'd wanted to stay out of the Army, he could have volunteered for RAF ground crew. And if I'd wanted security, I could have stayed with Evelyn.

I blew all the air out of my lungs, took a last look around and jack-knifed then swam down, and with my outstretched arm briefly touched the bottom, soft oozy mud, before striking up again for the surface and the light of day.

Light on water, water on light, I wished I could stay and stare at them for days. But, ridiculously, I was aching to be back. Back at the dispersal hut with the merrie men, however irritating they were. Back with the card games, playing 'Up the River' for penny stakes, back in the Mess eating burned bacon and hardened eggs with loads of bread and butter while the light broke outside, back with the silly jokes and edgy remarks and stomach jumping when the Tannoy clicked.

I wondered what was wrong with me, that only the promise of death and killing and sex could excite me now. I'd been at it too long and it had scarcely begun. That's why I wanted the fishing, to get back to an innocence. And it worked, for a while. But once I'd caught the fish and we'd made love, the restlessness rose up again.

Absurd, because at the same time I knew myself dreading the prospect of being back at the airfield again, and I would have stayed there with her for ever.

★　★　★

Mr Mannion's Wolseley came as we were hauling the boat back up to the shed. For a moment his stout figure was caught against the falling sun and he stood charred and wavering against the glare like it was eating him.

I shook my head to chase it away, shook hands and got in.

We didn't say much on the drive back, both sleepy with air and sunshine and light on water. He dropped us off at the top of the lane. We waved goodbye to the water bailiff we'd never see again, and wandered down the lane to the now familiar cottage.

The key under the plant pot, the smell of wood smoke, the dripping tap in the back kitchen. Upstairs we lay on the narrow bed and fell asleep for a while. I woke abruptly, looking up at the wallpaper, at the blue birds frozen in flight. The light was starting to go. Stella's head was turned away and she was whiffling in her sleep.

I put my hand on her breathing ribs, felt the rise and fall beneath her shirt. The birds were perfect, unmoving, but we were imperfect and alive. And I was hungry. I slipped away to prepare the fish and left her to sleep awhile though it was the last evening of our leave and like as not we'd never come this way again.

The train back took most of the day, crawling along with long delays, packed out. At least this time we had seats. We read the Thurber together and laughed at men and women going through ridiculous but recognizable rituals.

His hand was itching under the new light dressing I'd put on that morning. A good sign, I reckoned. Sign of healing. He flexed his fingers, they seemed in full working order. Good enough to make love. Good enough to fly and press the red killing button.

He fell asleep, head on my shoulder, in a siding by a bombed bridge. I looked out at it, the arch into thin air. It didn't look possible.

I turned more pages of my book, but my attention was gone. The seat was uncomfortable, the train was packed, mostly with soldiers. Sometimes it seems the whole country is on the move, I thought. Nothing will be the same again. The War isn't something fought by somebody else. It's ours now — the Home Guard, the air-raid wardens, the people running this train and working the armaments factories and farming the land.

I looked round the train at the weary faces, the pale and the sunburned, the sleeping, the waiting and the animated. Land Girls, evacuees, troops and administrators. It was then I saw there had surely been too much upheaval for everyone to return to their places once it was over. Up till now I'd thought of the War as an interruption of normal life. But it wouldn't resume the same.

Some kind of landslide was going on; it destroyed some things and created others. It was, if nothing else, an eventful time.

Len's head slid down my shoulder. He grunted, his head came up and eyes opened, completely blank. Then he saw me, and smiled as if it was good what he saw, then went back to sleep again.

How can we love anyone in wartime? I thought. It's too stupid. Then I looked round the train again and saw that everyone on it was going to die, sooner or later. How can we love in the face of that? Then again, how can we not?

Wartime is like real life but more so.

I got back to barracks late and dog-tired. I came into the Mess and saw the bar was busy and Sniff Burton was playing rags on the battered piano. But no other face did I recognize, not even the ones shouting around the ping-pong table. There were lots of them and they were mostly young. It had happened: the airfield had been taken over by strangers.

'Hi, Lenny,' Sniff said. He looked older, tired. 'It's been a wild time since you've been gone.'

My heart thumped up into my neck.

'Tad OK?' I asked.

'Tad? Sure,' Sniff said. He paused, rubbed his nose on his sleeve. 'But most of the old guard have gone west and we've been bombed to hell three times. Have a good time?'

I looked over at all the new fresh faces messing around at the bar. At that moment I couldn't picture Stella at all; they got in the way.

'Yes,' I said. 'I had that.'

14

Mid-August

Shaken awake in the dark, mug of tea, sign the chit. Wool, cotton, sheepskin, leather — I pull on animal layers, feeling mechanical. Breakfast, the truck, first light, mist below the tips of trees, grass glittering with wet. Cold metal, dew-streaked under my bandaged hand. The world grey as me, entering the machine.

Whiff of oxygen to wake up as we climb — me, Tim Baker, and a Sergeant Mackay, one of the new boys. Three weeks training since he soloed. It was a year in my time. The boy's struggling to fly this thing at all. At least Tim is fairly casual about formation and we fly in a loose Vic of three as we gain height.

Standing patrol over the estuary, protecting the ports and forward airfields. As my kite slides about in thin air I think of Stella sleeping. What use is thought? It can't touch. Touch is what we need, I have learned that much.

Lord, it's cold up here. Everything glazed, nothing doing, patrolling the coast at 15,000 feet. See the sunlight start to spread over the water below. How come the sun keeps rising through slaughter? Goes to show we're not much, which is just as well. If the world were batted round by the likes of us, it would bounce like a ping-pong ball between heaven and hell till it was cracked as we are.

I'd got a brief update last night. The enemy had changed tactics and stepped up several notches while I was gone, were attacking the sector airfields in numbers. The whole atmosphere on the base had changed, darkened. All the joshing was gone and it felt like our crisis was coming.

The CO was dead, also Johnny Staples. And aristocratic St John, who I'd come to like though we never talked that much about anything that mattered, killed taking off in an air raid that also did for cheery Fred Tate and four other ground crew. That hurt, I'd felt a warmth for Fred who'd never harmed anyone. Then Shortarse bought it over Portsmouth, same day as Bo Bateson near Dover. I know now how the survivors of France felt — old, isolated, surrounded by people who never knew the faces that have gone.

We've been looking and looking and trying to instruct Mackay in the basics, but we've met with nothing but light. And now throttle down over familiar trees, thinking of bacon as the appetite finally awakes. Touching down, the earth reaches up and murmurs beneath me, like Stella when I returned to bed two mornings and a thousand years ago. I feel myself lit up, confirmed, as I slide from the cockpit to the ground.

The screen that morning was crowded with blips, dipping and falling and rising again like green mobile stalactites. I was slow and clumsy at first, as though I'd forgotten it all in a few days. Then it became automatic, mechanical. Bearing, range, height, number, Tizzy angle for interception.

I read them off and heard in my ear the controller sending them up, knowing full well from Len that the pilots would always add on a couple of thousand feet if they could. There'd been high-level arguments about that because controllers liked to be in control, they didn't like pilots making decisions for themselves.

I was glad not to be covering Len's sector. I definitely didn't want to follow my lover's blip across the screen. It was bad enough hearing the pilots' voices (their language in battle was hair-raising), getting higher, shouting then screaming *Look out! Look out!* and then the scream, cut off suddenly, mercifully, as the IFF blip vanished from the screen.

The controller had asked us if we'd like to

be relieved during battle so we didn't have to hear the language. Language! I thought. We hear much worse than language. We hear screams. We said: no need. We'd heard it all before.

'If we were ever sensitive plants,' I muttered to Jessie Walker beside me, 'we're not any more.'

★ ★ ★

I took my mid-morning changeover, and smoked a cigarette sitting outside the hut in the morning sunshine. I thought about Len, wanting and not wanting to picture what he might be doing at that time. Almost certainly he'd be fighting today: the skies were very busy. He could be dead already and I'd not know it till the evening when the phone went in Mrs Mackenzie's and by arrangement one of his friends gave me the news.

I shook myself and drew more deeply on the cigarette. I made myself picture an island in a lake, lying naked in the hot sun, or the shock of cool water on my skin everywhere as I went in. And I smiled, because they couldn't take that away from me. I'd had that, and nothing would ever make me regret it.

I stubbed out the cigarette on the concrete

and went back inside into the dim. Jean Finlay showed me the blips as she slid out of the chair: very close, due to pass virtually overhead. Then we'd lose them, for the RDF masts only pointed forward. Jean went outside for a smoke and a call came in from the Observation post — a group of Me110 bombers plus Stukas with fighter escort were heading this way. Unusual, I thought. Enemy aircraft didn't normally use this as a flight path.

Then we heard the rumble of engines. Major Henley wheeled in his chair, head cocked, eyebrows raised, listening. Then a curious howling wail. Then the screen went blank, the floor rose and the walls leaned in and I was already sliding under the table. I saw the Major lift from the ground and fly across the room. Then the air imploded and I was deaf and soundlessly saw the room turn grey with smoke and dust. I felt another thud in my chest like a great fist thumping, the table rocked. Then I was pushed across the floor and banged my head on a metal cabinet. It was really sore. I crawled back under the table and clung to a leg. The room rocked again and my head squeezed till it felt as if my eyes would pop out.

Then silence. The dust settled as the smoke began to drift out the missing wall. Someone was kneeling over the crumpled shape of Major Henley. It was Jessie and she was weeping.

I crawled from under the table then pushed myself onto my knees. I stood up and went slowly to where the door had been, stepped into the dazzling sunlight. I tripped and nearly fell, then looked down. Saw the WAAF uniform, the long splayed black hair of Jean Finlay. Her legs were lying on the other side of the road. I blinked, then turned away but I'd already seen. Figures were climbing from the slit trenches, somewhere there was sobbing and near by someone cursed fiercely, continuously.

'What's the matter?' I heard someone say. 'Haven't you seen a dead body before?'

I do not have to see this, I thought. I know about it, but I don't have to see it.

I sat down on the ground and took out a cigarette. There were running feet and people moving about, coming out of the slit trench by the masts, tearing at the caved-in walls of No. 3 hut. I'd better help, I thought. At least check my screen. Can't have any more of the bastards getting through.

I threw away the cigarette and got to my feet.

We were stood down for a couple of hours after the morning patrol. I didn't feel like talking to anyone, so walked across the airstrip and in under the trees. I took out my penknife and began to carefully carve my name on a large beech tree. Under the grey bark was pale green then off-white, the colour of the bandage on my hand. The new CO had apologized for putting me straight onto active service.

'You can see how it is, Len. We're scraping the barrel here now they're onto our RDF.'

'Thanks a bunch,' I said.

He'd laughed and promised me a beer later, then told me I was flying dawn patrol next morning. Nice man. Polite.

I worked slowly and carefully on the carving, made sure I cut right through all the layers of bark so it would last. I wanted to be able to come back when this was all over and find it. Come back with my children and show them even as they yawned and pulled to be away. Wood pigeons were calling above my head, rabbits scuttered in the undergrowth. For half an hour I was happily lost — or perhaps *found* — in what I was doing.

LEN WESTBOURNE
AUG 1940

Then I sat down at the edge of the wood, lit a cigarette, felt at ease. Then what the CO had said when we were being stood down came back to me and suddenly meant something. *They're onto our RDF.*

Christ! I thought. Damn to hell.

I got to my feet and hurried back through the trees and over the burnt-out grass towards the huts, for once desperate to get back into the air.

★ ★ ★

We were called. I almost sprinted towards my Hurri, in so far as one can sprint with a parachute pack banging against your thighs. I couldn't stop thinking about attacks on the RDF stations. I knew just ten miles away Stella was working in a wooden hut at the base of the masts, there hadn't been time to build proper shelters. I wanted to find enemy bombers, any enemy bombers, blow them out of the sky.

Then as we climbed, the red light on my oil

gauge came on. I banged it a few times but it stayed that way, and the engine temperature was going off the clock. I cursed and radioed I was heading back for base, made it in a long glide and pulled off a decent landing.

As I touched down, a new Hurri was being delivered. It had been promised to me. A small figure jumped down as I approached it. She grinned at me and I tried not to look dumbfounded.

'Do you know what the guns are set for?' I asked.

'Six fifty, I think,' she said. 'No oxygen bottle, but she's a beauty. I, ah, put her through her paces on the way over.'

I waved over an armourer and asked him to synchronize the guns at 300 and get someone to fit oxygen. Then I walked back across the grass with this unexpected pilot. She was delivering planes, mostly repaired by the CRO. I remembered that's who Stella's former boyfriend worked with.

'Do you fly Spits too?' I asked.

'You bet,' she said. 'They're the best!'

I was impressed. Of all the planes in the Air Force, they were the hardest to fly, to land, especially to take off.

'That's a matter of opinion,' I said. 'Too highly strung, if you ask me.'

She glanced at me.

'Have you ever flown one?' she asked. 'Really put it through its paces?'

'I was hoping you wouldn't ask that,' I replied.

She laughed and I joined in. It was pilots' talk, same the world over. Presumably the enemy argued over the comparative merits of the Me109 and the 110, though I knew which I'd rather fly and fight in.

We were quickly mobbed when we got to the dispersal hut. Or rather she was. I stood outside till Tad returned with Blue section. I was relieved to see him. He did a slow roll at ground level across the airfield, which was difficult and dangerous and forbidden, but as he only did it when he'd made a kill, he seemed to get off with it. Then one of the new chaps, wobbling uncertainly over the boundary fence. He bounced hard, went into the air then back down again.

'Still,' a quiet voice said by my side, 'the Hurri is tough and stable, I'll grant you. A Spit might have flipped, being landed like that.'

Then she held out her hand.

'Use it well,' she said, and was gone with her lift from our eager adjutant. If I hadn't been in love already, I'd have been in love.

15

Mid-August

After an hour or so, someone got the power back on and the screen came alive again. Mostly I was seeing mush from a build-up beyond my range. They were learning, starting to put together big raids well across the Channel, and making feints to keep us guessing. A few more attacks like the last one and we'd be out of action. Not so much because of the masts, they seemed hard to damage and I suppose the blast went right through them, but because the huts, as I'd just learned, were almost entirely unprotected.

There were nineteen dead and ten injured from the raid, most of them while sheltering in a slit trench that a bomb happened to find. It was the slit trench I was supposed to be in. I thought on the whole I'd stick with my table. Some of the men were still in a deep shelter and refusing to come out. I couldn't blame them.

But I was angry, mad, call it what you will. At last I'd tasted what bombers could do, what was starting to happen to people in the towns, what had happened to soldiers and civilians across the continent. I couldn't forget the mess that had been Jean Finlay, her stockinged legs lying neatly across the other side of the road.

I stared through my thumping headache at the screen, began turning the dial as the bouncing green lines came into focus. The assistant controller was reading off figures passed to him by the first-day trainee at my side. We were working again for the same reason Len had to run awkwardly to his plane and take off.

For the first time I didn't think of Len's flying as a nuisance that got in the way of us seeing each other. He was doing what needed to be done, and I hoped he did it well. I think I prayed he survived, yes I must have, but that day I prayed he and his friends downed bombers and the people in them, even at the cost of my Fräulein's tears.

I took a couple more aspirin and carried on.

Outside the dispersal hut Tim Baker, Tad and I were talking to the new man Mackay, trying to impress on him the basic rules of combat: watch the sun, never fly level for more than two seconds, keep your head moving, get close before you shoot. Make your second attack on bombers from below, to keep well under the rear-gunner.

He looked at us, nodding earnestly. I don't know what he saw or thought; he kept his opinions to himself did Sergeant Mackay. I liked him for his earnestness. He didn't pretend this was some game fought on a playing field. He wanted to win and he knew he was badly under-trained. So he asked questions and listened hard.

We were just going for lunch (since the last raid, we were all sharing the same Mess and about time too) when the scramble came for everyone. I hesitated, cursed, then pictured Stella at her console and bombers closing in. So I put down my knife and fork and started running, hollow in my stomach. At the other end of the airfield the new Spitfire squadron were going up too, and we had Blue section in behind us, Tad leading it and Sniff Burton as wingman. They were singing 'Banks of the Ohio'. I reckoned they were made for each other. We rose into the air, tucked in our wheels and started climbing. I felt confident in behind Tim. He was a very competent pilot, not in a hurry for death or glory. And there'd been a bond between us since the day I followed him down and took an Me109 off his tail. I knew he'd do the same for me.

They sent us to Dover. We could hear from the squawking on the R/T there was a big show going on up there. We arrived pretty much at the height of it, the Spits way above going for the fighters. They were welcome to them, for I didn't reckon myself a match for a good flier in an Me109.

There were stacks of bombers already hitting the port, the town, the boats. Tim gave the old *Tally-ho!* for form's sake and we went in line astern. Ripped right through the bomber formation like scissors through silk. Fired a bit, hit nothing, wondered if the synchronization had been done properly. Then we turned and came back through them from below, Sniff somewhere up behind me still warbling in my ears *Then only say that you'll be mi-ine.* He'd said he sang when he was frightened. He was singing very loud so I assumed he was very frightened.

Me I was thinking of these planes bombing RDF stations and I closed right in on a Me110, waited till it filled my sights and then some, pressed the red button and . . . Nothing. A very brief rattle then not a sausage, not a solitary tracer. I cursed and sheered off, furious with the armourers. I turned away and saw Sergeant Mackay's Hurri closing head-on with a bomber. I watched them, shouted on him to turn aside, and the shout caught in my throat as both planes sheered away at the last minute but turned in the same direction and flew straight into each other. For a moment they hung there, then there was a terrific yellow-red whoosh and they dropped earthwards as one.

I turned for base, head still frantically swivelling as I cursed and cursed. I'd liked the man. I'd thought we might be friends.

Then I spotted a lone Me110 below me. Heading for home with smoke trailing from the port engine. I thought: get this one. Checked my guns again but still nothing. Damn. Still I peeled down and closed in for a closer look.

The rear turret looked badly shot up, the gun didn't swivel towards me so I reckoned the gunner must be dead. So I flew across its bows, keeping well away from the forward-facing guns. Let the pilot have a good look at me. Maybe I could intimidate him into going down.

I made another pass, this time so close I could see him looking up. I gestured for him to go down, turned and came back at him. The plane was really in bad shape, wonder it was still flying at all. Parts of the wing gone, rudder badly shot up. As a pilot I admired the man's courage and determination to get home. He held his course. They were a brave bunch, no mistake.

I flipped my kite on its back and over again. Pressed the red button and this time it worked. I came in again, determined to stop this one getting home. Let him have it the length of the fuselage, saw bits fly off. The plane staggered, then turned and lost height. One of the crew jumped, then another, I saw their chutes open and was pleased.

But this bloody pilot was still heading out for the Channel. Now I was furious. Right, I thought, I'll have you.

I closed, gave him another burst. The other engine began to suffer, saw oil pouring from it. The plane lost more height and finally turned inland. Good. I followed him down, waiting for the pilot to bale out while he still could but he didn't. Maybe he had an injured crewman on board. In any case, they were now too low to jump.

Wooded countryside, a couple of fields, a hill beyond them. He was really low now, staggering about the sky. And I was urging him on, willing him to keep it steady. I sighed with relief as he just cleared the trees, this same man I'd been determined to kill a minute before. He prepared to crash land, I tensed as he began to overshoot the field.

The plane hit the ground, I saw earth fly up and it skidded sideways then stopped. I turned, flew back over. Saw the pilot opening his cockpit hatch as three men began to run across the field, and felt relieved.

Then I turned away and flew for home, wondering what the hell I was about.

★ ★ ★

I landed and told Fred Tate's replacement my guns had been jamming and would he have it fixed pronto. I hung around and five minutes later Tad came dropping down over the boundary fence. His tailplane looked a bit shot up but still he flipped his kite over on its back and did a slow roll over the airfield. I thought his plane staggered a bit but somehow he flipped out of the roll, very low, then circled and landed.

He walked over to me, his dark eyes jubilant. He'd added another definite Me110 to his total, plus a probable Heinkel.

'I saw Mr Baker go down,' he added, 'but he baled out. I saw his chute open, so no problem, you know.'

I felt bad because I'd lost Tim in the fight. I was supposed to stay with him, but it wasn't always possible.

Then he asked about Mackay. I told him. He put his hand up to his face and nodded earnestly as Mackay had.

'Head-on attack is only for very good pilots or crazy people,' he said. 'It is far too blooming dangerous. Crazy is not so good.'

Someone waved us from the dispersal hut. We went inside and found everyone clustered round the wireless.

'Listen to this!' the adjutant shouted. 'You lads have been on live!'

And so we were. I stood there, suddenly very tired, and heard the reporter standing somewhere in Dover describing the fighting, all the different levels, the dive bombers coming in low, the Me110s higher, and all the fighters still mixing it. He sounded very excited, like it was an amazing show. He was calling it Hellfire Corner. No doubt it was. I wondered if he'd seen and reported young Mackay's end.

I glanced at Tad but he seemed distant. It was the strangest thing, our war was now being observed and reported even as it happened. If I'd had a wireless with me in the plane, I could have been doing it and listening to the commentary. It made me feel odd and divided from myself.

I shook my head and went off to get some lunch. Tad came running after me, put an arm round my shoulder. I was astonished to see he had tears in his eyes.

'Sorry about Mr Mackay,' he said. 'He seemed a good chap, you know.'

I stuck at it most of the afternoon till my replacement for the evening shift came in. I pressed my knuckles to my eyes, swivelled away from the console, stood up then promptly fell down. I was lying on the floor, which struck me as needing a good sweeping. Someone was tugging at my sleeve, I tried to co-operate so they wouldn't tear my shirt, and got to my knees.

Then I was standing with some help. Arms round my shoulders, and it seemed I was getting a lift back to my billet. I protested about my bike and it was placed in the boot of the staff car. I sat in the front and was driven by our adjutant on some mission he had to do first. We went through endless crescents and avenues, and I sat saucer-eyed in the back looking on all the *Daily Mail* streets I'd always seen as so banal. But now that clattering lawn mower seemed defiant, those garden gnomes oddly touching, that family mutt worth preserving. I thought the few people in the street, the ration-card queue out into the road, the Auxiliary Fire Service swarming round a burning house, all equally brave and necessary.

Then again, looking back on it, I was a bit concussed.

The adj finally dropped me at my place, even rang the bell. Mrs Mackenzie came to the door. Even she seemed kind in her way. The adj told her about the bombing.

'Oh, I know,' she said. 'It's terrible the damage they do. A bomb dropped in the street round the corner. The mess! There ought to be a law against it, I say.'

She took me into her kitchen and put the kettle on, then produced a dark, dusty bottle from the cupboard. She put out two glasses on the table.

'Sloe gin,' she said conspiratorially. 'I'm told it's very good for shocks. I think we'd better have one apiece, don't you? Oh, your mother phoned.'

I tore my gaze away from her white and yellow roses out in the garden.

'My mother?' I said stupidly. 'What for?'

'I don't know, but she left this number to ring. It's a neighbour's, apparently.'

I drained the glass, puzzled. My mother had never phoned me here. Mr Jenkinson across the road had a phone but she'd never bring herself to ask to use it because she didn't like being beholden.

I dialled and got Mr Jenkinson. He told me

to wait while he got my mother. He sounded flustered and concerned, almost embarrassed. Eventually I heard a door close in the background then my mother came to the phone.

'It's about your father, dear,' she said.

'Sergeant Polarczyk!'

The CO stood in the door of the dispersal hut, silhouetted against the glare. Tad sleepily put down his newspaper, that week's 'News of the World'.

'Yes?'

'Yes, *sir*, sergeant.'

Tad said nothing, just looked up at him. The CO came into the hut and stood there waving his curved pipe, which was a bad sign. He was pale with anger.

'So,' he said, 'what do you do it for? To show off? To be clever?'

Tad slowly stood up. He blinked a few times. For once he didn't salute or click his heels.

'Sir, not knowing what you meaning. Not show? Off?'

The CO jabbed his pipe at him.

'Don't give me that no-speak-English stuff, Polarczyk! I'm talking about the victory roll over my airfield. You know I've forbidden it. Now today is the second time! It won't do.'

Tad looked at him innocently.

'Three times, three victories, sir. You prefer

I not shoot anything?'

Our new CO was a mild man but now he began to froth slightly.

'I prefer you obey my orders! They're for a damn good reason. If you have anything — *anything* — wrong with your aircraft, like a wonky rudder, holes in the wings, dodgy flaps, and you try that at ground level, you've a bloody good chance of killing yourself. I'll not have it!'

He jabbed his pipe another couple of times at Tad then stuck it in his mouth and swung away to look out the window.

'A friend of mine was killed that way at the end of France,' he said more quietly. 'Good man, great fighter pilot. Bull Durham — you'll have heard of him? He tried a slow roll and ploughed in. I had to help bury him. I'll not have it again — understood?'

He turned his head and looked full at Tad, who nodded, seemed contrite.

'Understanding, sir, I think. No slow roll low.'

The CO looked at him suspiciously. Took his pipe from his mouth then stuffed it back in again.

'Good,' he said. 'Oh, and Command in its infinite wisdom has finally agreed guns can be synchronized at closer range, so you can all stop pretending you haven't done so already.'

With that he stomped out the door. Someone whistled the opening of 'Stardust', Sniff giggled in the armchair. Tad slowly sat down and picked up his newspaper again.

'Durham was a very good pilot,' he said quietly. 'But maybe he tried the roll too low.'

★　★　★

It was late that afternoon, as we were flying back from a non-encounter over Gravesend. The enemy had feinted and the real attack knocked the hell out of RAF Manston, so we weren't feeling very clever. I was flying tucked in close to Sniff, then I became aware of another plane sliding into position on the other side. I looked then looked again.

'Down beside where the waters flow . . . ' I heard the accented warble on my headphones, then Sniff's near-hysterical laughter. For there was Tad, calmly flying his plane upside down, with a pipe stuck in his mouth that looked remarkably like the CO's.

The way I saw it, my dad had always suited himself. He was, in his easy-going way, at once the most amiable and most selfish person I'd ever known. He did absolutely nothing he didn't want to do, and even at this late hour, as I sat in the back of Mr Mackenzie's little Ford as we trundled screamingly slowly towards the hospital, I couldn't decide if this was reasonable or unforgivable.

He'd inherited some money from my granddad who'd survived the Great War then promptly died in the flu epidemic after it. Dad always lived cheaply, so he only worked when he had to. He mostly built and repaired small boats. Sailing was his passion so it was a nice enjoyable way to get by. But he married a woman who worried and worked to plans, so whenever the planning or the worrying got too much he simply moved out. He had a daughter (who from the start he alternately indulged and neglected), then foresaw how much having a child could limit his freedom of movement and had no more. At least, I supposed that was the reason. It was not the

214

kind of thing I could ask my mother. He was also rather fond of women.

When I was a child and still living at home, he spent most of his evenings in the workshop or out drinking in company. He had an endless supply of good humour, jokes and tall stories, was a dab hand at finding creative solutions to little mechanical problems around the house and people's cars and garages and sheds. He was often intoxicated but seldom drunk. He was one of those people who just wanted everyone to be having a good time and couldn't see why they weren't. An ordinary, unusual man. My father.

Then the War came. We were all sitting in the kitchen, listening to the broadcast. At the end of Chamberlain's announcement my mum got up, tut-tutting, switched over to the Light Programme and started cooking. I sat on in a daze, wondering how this was going to affect me and whether I was for or against it. I had signed the Peace Pledge after all, was meant to be a pacifist.

I gradually became aware my dad was still sitting in his easy chair, unusually silent. In fact he was gazing across the kitchen as though the other wall were a long way off, as though he were watching something sail off into the distance. Then he lifted his clasped hands towards his chin, cracked his knuckles as he did before starting a job.

'About bleeding time,' he said.

I looked at him, startled by something unusual in his voice. And he looked back at me, and I've puzzled for a long time what I saw in his eyes.

Then he picked up his jacket and grinned. 'Just going out for a couple before tea, May,' he said, and was off.

He came back home and announced he'd joined the ARP. He nearly succeeded in making himself unpopular during the phoney war, zealously enforcing the blackout. Now the bombing had started on the coastal towns, the ARPs were seen as heroes instead of pains in the neck. I gathered he spent nights patrolling the streets, or ducking into shelters during sporadic raids then emerging soon as the all clear howled. He worked days and nights among the rubble, the ripped-apart warehouses and factories, sorting out gas mains and water and electricity. No one was as useful and quick-witted at propping up walls, opening up cellars, locating mains, comforting and joking with those whose lives had suddenly disintegrated.

He had little time for pubs, lost weight but kept on singing and talking. Very quickly he was put in charge of the squad. The few times

I'd seen him in the last months, he seemed the same man but leaner and somehow focused, as if he'd finally found a purpose for his talents. For the first time since I'd ceased to be a child, I respected him. And the atmosphere was better at home — now that Mum had something real to worry about, she worried less. (Also Mum and Dad were seldom awake and in the house at the same time, which I reckoned might be something to do with it.)

The car drove slowly through darkening streets. People were making their way home or to shelters, wondering what the night would bring. I wondered at how already I was summing up his life to myself. I held my head in my hands, as though it was a fractured, aching globe that might split in two.

Mr Mackenzie began to speak quietly as he drove on towards the centre of town. He told me what he'd been told by his younger brother who was in my dad's squad.

The raid had been one of the spasmodic ones on an aircraft construction factory. First by day, then using the flames as guides when they came back at night. There was a bad oil fire, and the water supply kept cutting out. Four firemen were killed as a diesel tank exploded. Nearly a hundred workers had been killed on the day shift.

Jim Gardam's unit had just been thankful they weren't sent to clear the factory. Instead they were sent to the streets behind the gutted factory. They took cover as more bombs came down, then emerged again. A couple of stray bombs had demolished the house opposite, left only one wall standing above a pile of rubble. Under that wall, a neighbour said, was the entrance to the cellar where the family went when there was a raid.

They started shifting rubble with crowbars, pickaxes and bare hands. One of the squad levered up some bricks below the wall and saw the dull gleam of a large bomb. He lowered the bricks gently and backed away on suddenly weak legs. An unexploded bomb on a time fuse could go off any time.

While they waited for the bomb squad, a faint sound rose from the rubble. A scratching then the faintest cry. A whimper. Again. It sounded like a baby's cry.

'We'd best get them out,' my father said, stepped over the UXB and began levering up some planks.

After a short pause, three other men followed him. They tore away at the rubble, very aware of the bomb six feet behind them. They opened up a hole, Jim Gardam propping it open as they went. They got down into the cellar and eventually managed to force the door open. Jim crawled in, disappeared then emerged holding a small dog. There'd been nothing else there. He stood among the rubble with a big grin on his blackened face and the dog in his arms, prepared to walk back over the bomb.

Then the wall above him collapsed.

★   ★   ★

Mr Mackenzie drew up at the darkened hospital. I took his arm as he helped me out, and together we groped for the front door and went inside.

16

Mid- to late August

I sat for a long time before I could look at him properly. My eyes kept jumping off him. His face was still smeared with dust and oil, but he looked quite calm. Unsmiling for once.

The damage was to his back and his chest. The doctor admitted his back was broken and his ribs had caved in. Even if he lived, he'd be paralysed. How I hung from that 'if', like a butterfly from its pin.

So many jokes, so many yarns, so much sliding away from anything difficult. So many boats and yards and rivers messed about in. So many pints of beer between those parted lips. A mistaken marriage, but I existed because of it, and most of the time I was very glad for that.

How to sum up the shape and meaning of a life? Then his eyes opened and he looked at me, blank at first then as though he was coming part-way back from a long way off. I could feel he was there again. Saying nothing, just looking at me.

'You had an accident, Dad,' I said. 'A wall fell on you. You're in hospital. Mum's coming back soon.'

He nodded slowly. His lips opened.

'Good,' he said, so hoarse I could scarcely make him out. A pause, then he spoke again. '*It's good.*' Then he closed his eyes again and went away again.

Good? I thought. What was good — that the wall had fallen, that he was in hospital, that Mum was coming? Life itself or his life, that affair of jokes and drinks and ingenious solutions and good company?

Mum arrived. Now the worst had happened, she was calm and sensible, not bitter or hysterical. She took his hand and looked at him for a long time. There was so much I wanted to ask about their marriage but couldn't. Even if I had and she'd told me — like whether she loved him, and how she felt about his other girlfriends, what she thought of him — I still wouldn't have really understood it. Sitting in the chair looking at them both, I felt that a marriage was a mystery that could never be adequately grasped from outside, not even by one who had lived near it for most of her life. Good? Bad? Awful? I didn't know.

He died that night while I was asleep in the chair. She woke me up and told me he'd gone, which was very like her. He looked just the same, foreign in his unsmiling dignity, very far away from me. Internal bleeding, the doctor said, nothing to be done.

I took his hand. Perhaps I imagined it was cooling already. I leaned forward and kissed his forehead like I'd seen in films. The doctor and nurses busied around, they needed the bed, I suppose.

At the door we both stopped and looked back. I don't know what she saw but I saw a grave stranger, a man who used to be my father and had become, like so many, changed by the War. Had he found himself in those last few months? Had he found a cause to give meaning to his weak, enjoyable life, or had it just been his last and most spectacular lark?

I took my mother's arm and we left the building. Outside, as we waited for our lift in the summer dark before dawn, she turned to me.

'It's as well,' she said firmly. 'He'd have *hated* being paralysed.'

I wasn't sure of her mood. I wasn't at all sure of my own. I was numb yet curiously wide awake, felt the next seconds and minutes of my life were crucial.

'I imagine so,' I said cautiously. 'I expect he'd have been a terrible patient.'

'Terrible!' she said, and she began to laugh at the sound of her voice and I did too, and we were both still laughing as her neighbour pulled up in the car.

Only when we got home and I lay once again in my own childhood bed did it get through. He was gone for ever. It was the fault of those bombers. I fixed on that so hard I could hear my teeth grinding. For a moment I saw Jean Findlay, a broken doll with her head at an impossible angle and her long black hair flowing out and her legs not there.

I truly think I'm learning to hate as much as to love.

You'd think the faded diary a window, so clearly does it show through to the dispersal hut. They're sitting fully kitted up. It's hot, the door's wide open and they sweat under their Mae Wests. One plays cat's cradle, his hands flickering obsessively. Sniff Burton and Tadeusz are playing 'Up the River' and fleecing two officers. Two more kip in deck chairs. The kettle boils continuously. There's the occasional flick of a magazine page.

Len sits at a small table, writing his diary, his left hand thrust knuckle-deep in his hair. His ankles are locked, his right elbow is held at an awkward angle. The draughtsman's point wears down to dull and broad at the foot of the page. He writes:

First: Forget the jousting, all that 'chivalry of the air' guff. All that went out with France. The meek inherit the earth all right — six feet down in bloody no time. The seaplanes the enemy have for picking up their air crew can be considered legitimate targets — they're using them for reconnaissance. Ignore the hospital crosses, right? Yes, it's come to that.

Second: We hit bombers, 109s are out. Got it? Leave 'em to the Spits. Just dodge them and get back to the bombers. Break up the formation, have a squirt, then piss off home. It's not magnificent, but it's war.

Third: This is ambush, not duelling. Whenever possible we go in with height and sun on our side. Pick the straggler, get in close, nail him, get the hell out. And forget the fancy acrobatics, and the tight formations that went down well with the brass hats and the ladies. The Display days are over.

Fourth: The WAAFs on this base are strictly off-limits, and that's official. So: paws off!

Fifth: Stay alive. If we're still flying, we're not defeated and that's all that's being asked of us. This comes from Fighter HQ; that's the way they look at it. Drink if you must. Sleep when you can. And to the new boys: get through the first week and you're in with a chance.

Sixth: This round's on me. What'll yours be — watered Scotch or potato-and-oats-flavoured beer?

The new CO goes through the same pep talk whenever new boys arrive, and they come and go quite fast now. I've got it off by heart.

He's right, of course. The odds we can do nothing about, so cold method must be part of our madness. Calculating, measured, unheroic.

I'm so tired. My bad elbow aches. Four sorties already today. Everyone's touchy. Worse, everyone's trying to be polite in case our last words to someone are angry ones.

I wish to be in a room with no curtains and sharp little panes and the morning light across her face. That would be good.

Dated 18 August, the day of another huge attack. The 15th had been the biggest single effort the *Luftwaffe* made during the Battle, but this one was nearly on the same scale, one the RAF couldn't and didn't attempt to match. Dowding's strategy remained one of limited engagement, conserving his precious pilots.

The sky was clear and attacks started early and went on into the evening. More aircraft factories were gutted. Front-line airfields were bombed again until at one the air crew refused to leave the deep shelters. An over-enthusiastic officer was only just prevented from firing into the shelters to flush them out.

Flying this number of sorties from vulnerable airfields, the pilots were becoming exhausted and ratty. They disagreed with their Controllers, disputed the tactics coming from Fighter Command HQ, wondered why they were always so outnumbered, and argued with each other. After the fifth sortie of the day, Tad's Hurricane landed safely, but when it taxied to a halt he didn't get out of the cockpit. The air crew ran to it, fearing the worst. They found him head down on the controls, fast asleep.

Len made it through that day though he was too tired at the end of it to write up his diary, too weary even to take a walk in the woods. Instead he took the lift back to barracks, ate some food then stared at a pint of beer. He became aware of a ripple of disturbance in the far corner. He looked and saw Tad in an armchair openly weeping.

Len went over and sat awkwardly on the arm of the chair. No one else dared go near. Tears were not part of the form.

'What's up, Tad?'

Tad lifted his hand from his face. There was a soggy note in it.

'My cousin Ludwik,' he said. 'Boyhood friend, you know.'

Then he carried on weeping noisily. Len hesitated then went to the bar and got a double whisky, brought it back and put it in Tad's hand. Tad looked at it, at Len, drank it in one.

'Like another?' Len asked.

Tad shook his head.

'Flying early,' he said. 'I must be clear.' He straightened up, rubbed his hand across his face. 'I'll take a walk now.'

He got up and walked past the silent pilots, out of the door and into the night. After a pause Len went back to his pint, drank it quickly then swayed to bed and fell asleep face down, fully clothed.

I jumped down from the adjutant's staff car, waved as it drove away. I crossed the street in the dusk and waited a moment outside the familiar door. It wasn't a moment I wanted to hurry. For the last days I'd been living for nothing else. I breathed in the thick roses, the more homely wallflowers and honeysuckle up against the trellis by the front door. Somewhere across the street, 'I'll Be Seeing You' was playing from a wireless, and the tune or the words thickened in my throat.

I felt nervous but pretty well. Well because several cloudy days on the trot had given us a break and a chance to rest. Odd how even in our incredibly modern war we were still dictated to by such a thin thing as cloud. And my new skin was growing back, smooth and pink. Nervous because I hadn't seen her since her father's death. We'd spoken on the phone, I couldn't get away to see her or go to the funeral. That felt so wrong.

Now I felt like the first time I flew solo and wasn't at all sure if I could bring her back to ground safely but there was no one else around who would.

I rang the bell. Mrs Mackenzie answered, full of *Poor child* and *Dreadful news* and how they'd suffered a power cut all afternoon just when she was cooking, which was all pretty gruesome but at least let me escape past her up the stairs.

Stella put her arms round me, didn't kiss me but leaned herself in to me as though all her bones had been removed. We held each other a long time, standing swaying on the threshold. I was just remembering the feel and smell of her, the hair springing free from its clip, the slimness of her back and the solidity of her hips.

'Want to go to the pictures?' I asked eventually. 'Or go for a drink?'

'Don't feel like going out,' she muttered to my neck. 'Tea and music?'

And that's how we spent the whole evening. She made some fancy tea, then she put on something classical with a clarinet. We lay on the bed together and she began to talk about her dad. I noticed she now had a small picture of him on the bedside table, sailing a boat and grinning like crazy at the camera. She talked of her childhood memories of him, how much fun he was when he was around, how as an adolescent she'd realized his shortcomings, how she'd largely cut off from both of them when she went to university and the remorse she felt about that.

She talked and talked in my arms as the clarinet unfolded its patterns. When the piece ended I asked what she wanted.

'Same again,' she said, so I wound the gramophone, changed the needle and we began again. She lay squeezing a button on my shirt as she told me about his last call-out, the UXB and the collapsing wall, the wait in hospital. There was talk of him being awarded the George Medal, which would be good but she'd prefer he was still alive.

Then she was silent and we both listened to the music being melancholy and beautiful for a while. Then she tried to tell me how angry she was, how she wanted me to kill the people who dropped bombs, and I told her about Mackay and the other dead new boys whose names I'd forgotten already. And I admitted it sometimes seemed the only time I got excited these days was when I thumbed the red button and my plane juddered and slowed from the recoil, and the tracer bullets began to dance across a fuselage.

She held me tighter then and we held on to each other.

'What are we becoming?' she murmured.

I knew what she meant, and in that at least we were close. Then it was natural to kiss her. And she kissed me back, quite fierce, and when I was ready she climbed on top of me and took what she needed.

When she lay in the silence with her sweating head against my shoulder, I felt moisture in the pool of my neck, and held her more tightly with my heart so open and aching they could have done surgery to try and fix it right there, and I wouldn't have resisted.

'What was that music?' I asked as we put ourselves together again.

'Mozart's clarinet concerto in E flat,' she said. 'I'll educate you yet. Oh, Len.'

17

Late August

He was mine, no doubt about it. A lumbering Do17, the 'flying pencil', too low to dive, too slow to run. I'd followed down a Me109 against orders and common sense, but he'd outrun me and pissed off back to France with a whiff of smoke coming from his engine nacelle. But now here was this bomber, heading home. He wouldn't drop any more bombs on anyone's dad, I decided that.

I checked my tail one more time then went in. Got in close before taking out the rear-gunner. Then I could take my time. I checked again and closed.

My first burst shattered the canopy. Then the pilot was sitting there, his shoulders and head twisting towards me to look. As he turned, my second burst caught him and blew his head off.

Believe me, I was very close and saw perfectly well.

I saw how the slipstream caught the neck, the stub of the neck, and as the blood kept pumping out, smeared it back along the fuselage in ragged streams — like raindrops across the windows of a train, I thought. Bright red on grey, right back to the tail, then flecked across the cross.

It flew on straight and true for a full thirty seconds, then slowly dipped and entered the sea. I thought, the plane's so stable, why have pilots at all? Stay on the ground and guide them. In the future, we will not be necessary.

Then I turned and, feeling kind of numb but hungry, turned and flew home for lunch. Number four. I am one hell of a fellow.

What have I done?

Nothing. Nothing at all.

So I was back at work the day after the funeral. My headaches had stopped, just the occasional ringing in my ears. This time I didn't sit at the console like a nervous daydreamer, hoping not to make a mistake and waiting for my shift to end. Instead I read the screen actively, leaned forward to it like I was attacking the planes myself. When I saw the IFF blips that signalled our side, I silently cheered them on.

For maybe the first time in my life apart from university, which is a study in detachment anyway, I was fully engaged. I wasn't standing back out of it being ironic or just observing.

Fact was, I thought even as I read out the details of the approaching hostiles, I joined up because of a vague dislike of bullying and because it was the thing to do. I'd hoped it might be more exciting than a job like teaching. That would come in time. Like Len's mates, I was embarrassed to talk about great causes, probably because I didn't at heart have one. I disliked what had happened to Poland and Czechoslovakia then the Low

Countries and France. I disapproved of it but essentially it was nothing to do with me. I'd joined the Peace Pledge when I was eighteen because peace seemed a good idea to someone who wanted to be left in it.

Even this later stage of the War, the blips and all, had made me meet Len (good) then got in the way of me seeing him as often as I'd like (bad). But it was essentially not to do with me because other people themselves were not to do with me.

I stopped, hand on the calibration dial, appalled at what I'd let myself think. Then as I reeled off bearing and height, distance and approximate numbers, I knew it *had* been true and I knew that it had ceased to be. Something to do with being bombed personally, and Jean Finlay's death and then my father's, had connected me to other people. Even the ones I didn't particularly take to were connected to me, just by being alive and on our side.

I stared at the screen and wondered about the ghostly Fräulein looking back at me from the other side. My pale sister, my opposite number. I didn't know if I was connected with her. I didn't know if I could afford to be, or if I could afford not to be. That was the dilemma, wasn't it? Be a poor fighter or a poor human being.

For a while I tracked a group heading south-west. Then they straightened and came our way. Directly our way. I'd been here before and passed on the warning. I was prepared to sit there to keep tracking all that came behind, that felt like my duty and my personal desire, but the new major ordered us all out when the force got within a mile or two.

As we ran out of the door I looked up and saw them, the small buzzing fighters first, then the deeper drone of the bombers, and felt that deep clutch in my belly. Then Major Astley pushed me into the slit trench along with the others, and I huddled down, desperately trying to strap on my tin hat. That was the worst bit, waiting with my face pressed against the cold earth as if I was already in my grave. Last time I'd seen, before I turned away, what happened when a bomb fell in a slit trench, and I was terrified of having my body mangled. It was all I had.

Then the earth began to shake and the noise began. First off to the left, by the masts, a series of huge blasts. Then directly behind, thudding earth into my back. Someone's hand was clutching my sleeve. The major lay partly on top of me and kept apologizing as he struggled to crawl away. I elbowed him in some kind of a panic.

I glanced up from my private terror and saw Foxy Farringdon looking back at me. She grinned in the oddest way, raised her eyebrows at once rueful and mock-rueful. Then her face altered as there was a particularly big bang and the earth began to slide. It stopped and she was staring down, all whitefaced and her teeth clenched. And suddenly I wasn't so scared because I was out of my private terror. I was connected. There was a bunch of us in a trench, all scared, all hoping and struggling to survive. I wasn't alone. We were the same.

Two more sets of explosions, the rattle of machine-gun fire from above, a scream somewhere suddenly cut off. Then the sound level dropped and the engines began to fade. I lay face-down in the earth, almost comfortable, still trying to understand what had just happened to me. Something big had, for sure. I could feel the difference somewhere in under my ribs. It was almost like falling in love, as subtle, as undeniable, as irreversible.

Then Major Astley got off my shoulder and I sat up and looked out. Incredibly, the masts were still there, all six of them. One of the huts was leaning badly, the aerial had been blown off ours and two of the windows had disappeared. A bicycle, not my own, lay twisted at an extraordinary angle. Someone was already being carried out of the next trench along.

I pushed down on the rim of the trench and climbed out. Staggered slightly on my feet then steadied again.

'Are you all right, Corporal?' Major Astley asked.

I looked down at myself, then back at Foxy and the adjutant and a secretary I exchanged cigarettes with, all crawling out of the trench.

'Yes, sir,' I said.

Bastards have ruined my stockings, I thought. Then we all started walking back to the hut to check over the equipment.

There was a lot of glass on the floor, some embedded in the wall, but amazingly the console was still working. I could see fresh blips building up across the Channel, so I pulled on the headphones and got back to work, still holding on to this rare and precious feeling. I felt it pass through the hut, this sense of connectedness, as someone swept out the glass. Jessie Walker took up her pad beside me, Foxy Farringdon settled down with her latest pupil, Major Astley struggled to get through on the phone and the adjutant brewed up tea for us all. It passed through like the life-giving shock wave of a tender bomb, and I thought at least something positive has come out of this, like me and Len on a wider scale.

I hope I don't forget it, I thought. I hope I never lose it. I hope we don't die before we can share it.

An hour later I was sitting outside having a cigarette while my replacement, a new quiet woman called Millie, was on. It was a fine morning, slightly hazed. A Vic of Spitfires swept by low, chasing bandits to the north, and when I waved up the nearside wingman waggled his wings. I thought of Len, and wished him well and good hunting.

At last I was able to visit Tim Baker in hospital. He was a little pale, but what else could I expect. He thanked me for bringing cigarettes and wanted to book 'a slow smoochie with the poppet', which I took to mean a dance with Stella. Said he'd be a little stiff, but maybe she could help with that. Winked. Swine!

'I'm fighting to protect my girl from hogs like you,' I said.

'Any excuse, old boy,' he replied, 'any excuse will do' — then that inward smile, quite at odds with his posh drawl and that preposterous moustache.

We stood at a window in the dark, smoking as the bombers went over. His hand shook on his stick and I helped him to a chair. His hip was worse than I'd realized: he'll not fly again.

'Well out of it,' I said.

Silence. I'm a fool. We've flown a hatful of sorties together. In a way I love the man. There was the far-off thud of Bofors guns — shooting in the dark, but you have to put up some kind of a show, like me and Tad with

241

those darts so long ago.

He shook his head, lit up another, never said a word.

I left with the all clear, got a lift from the CO's batman, who'd been visiting his son. We didn't talk much. The night was clear, there were many stars like so often on these blackout nights. I thought: not all the faint ones are far away, nor all the bright ones near. Some are planets, that fuzzy thing's a galaxy.

It seemed important, I hung on to it while the bitter smoke of Gold Flake stung my eyes.

'Bloke next to Eddie died in the night,' the batman said. 'Spare a cig?'

We hit something in the road.

'What was that?'

'Dunno,' he said. 'Something small.' We didn't stop. 'Well out of it, I reckon.'

I shook my head, lit up for two, passed one over.

⋆   ⋆   ⋆

Into the shelter, here come the planes. They are silver and have no wings. They drop their load. Nothing explodes. A sound like footballs bouncing.

I look out from the shelter and the airstrip is thick with severed heads, like turnips or huge brown hailstones.

One rolls at my feet. It is for me, personally. I lift it up. The hair grips my fingers so I cannot put it down. I know I'm going to recognize this and it will be too frightful to bear. The face starts to swing round —

* ⋆ ⋆ ⋆ *

I woke screaming, trying to beat the blanket off my face. I apologized to the others as I got dressed and went outside for a cigarette. It was right dark out, no moon but cool enough to chill the sweat along my skin. I kept my eyes wide open, fixed on the pale blur of my hand as it rose to my lips. I didn't want to see anything else.

I thought of my fierce excitement just before I killed, and my numbness once I had, and then like Stella I said out loud, '*What are we becoming?*' The night made no answer but an owl's low hoot. I dragged the lit tip left to right across my face, then into my lips with the good end and dragged the harshness deep into my lungs.

18

Beginning of September

We went to a dance, the four of us: me and Len with Tad and Maddy. It was an Observer Corps do and almost everyone was in uniform. The dance hall was a long wooden hut with painted walls and a raised stage where a small but determined swing band was giving its all to some Glenn Miller numbers. There were a few streamers and balloons and somehow the whole thing was infinitely touching to me, this desire to share some fun and laughter in the middle of a war. Though we didn't know it, this was the crisis week when we came nearest to cracking.

My slit-trench vision of things had faded a bit — as these things do, I was beginning to realize — but it was still there and I felt unusually well disposed towards my fellow mortals. I was particularly well disposed towards my paramour and positively hung on his arm, which I knew made him feel good.

So we had a few drinks, then Maddy and Tad disappeared outside for a while and Len and I had some dances, mostly quicksteps and foxtrots. As we danced, we caught up with each other. I told him about the bombings, keeping it light as possible, and he held me that bit tighter. He seemed older, as though the tiredness had sunk inside like water. He told me he'd finally visited his friend Tim in hospital but didn't enlarge much on it, and I was torn between accepting his privacy and trying to stop distance growing between us.

We drank and danced some more and grew warm and closer on the turns. We kissed a while in the corner, in the shadows off to the side of the stage. Maddy and Tad reappeared looking tousled and flushed. I told Maddy to at least pick the grass from her dress and what a tart she was. She laughed and told me I wasn't exactly being demure, hanging on that man like I was begging for a bit of him and she knew exactly which bit.

I said, 'In that case I'll have a dance with yours,' so I grabbed a rather surprised-looking Tad and dragged him onto the now crowded floor.

He was a great dancer. Rhythmical and, well, witty. Prepared to lead and give me some of his beat, but without being bossy. Shorter and wider than Len, he turned on a sixpence.

'If you fly like you dance, you must be very good,' I said.

He made a face.

'I like the flying well enough,' he said. 'It's the shooting at me I don't like.'

I started laughing and couldn't stop. That seemed to me so funny and truthful and modest. It was the first time we'd talked properly.

'You were bombed, I hear,' he said. 'That must be so frightening, you know.'

'Yes,' I said. 'The worst part is just waiting and being helpless.'

He nodded as we foxtrotted in and out of a tight space. He somehow steered me through without bumping anyone. He must be very good in the sky, I thought.

'Yes,' he said. 'Helpless I hate, too. Things happen to my family, my country, and I am here and cannot stop them.'

He looked so desolate then there was nothing I could say that wasn't foolish. I imagined what it was like, no longer having a home one could go back to or run away from. It didn't feel nice. I held him a bit tighter.

The dance ended. I looked around, couldn't see Len and Maddy. The band launched into 'Night and Day', Tad bowed, asked if I'd dance with him again. He kissed my hand when I said Yes and looked at me with open pleasure. I began to see why he and his fellow Poles in other squadrons did so well with women. Len might be an exception, but with other members of his squadron one couldn't help sensing they wished they were back in the Mess with male company.

Then to my surprise in the following dance I found myself talking about my dad and how he died, and the hating, how it was inevitable and bad for us. And he listened and didn't laugh. He said that Len thought if you believe in what you're fighting for, you can do it without hatred or anger, just do it because it has to be done. Maybe this was true, but he himself needed the hatred.

He looked at me hard. His big dark eyebrows and strong nose like a hawk's beak. He was rather impressive, I decided.

'It is not a question of flying but of shooting,' he said. 'For me, shooting is best when hating. It is like fuel. Perhaps when it is finished, I crash.' Then he shrugged and smiled. 'But this is shooting line, yes? I prefer dancing with lovely ladies, you see.'

I looked at him with new interest. Then as 'I've Got You Under My Skin' ended I was telling him I'd heard the man with the big cigar talking about them — the fliers — some days back, saying how much was owed by so many to so few.

'He must be thinking our Mess bills,' Tad said. 'I owe so much.'

We were still laughing as Len came by with Maddy draped over him like ivy. He looked a bit embarrassed, bless him, so I extricated him by taking her to the Ladies.

'Tad's a wonderful dancer,' I said.

'He's pretty good at lots of things,' she replied and giggled as she reapplied her lipstick, her bangles clacking away. She glanced sideways at me.

'I like Len,' she said. 'He's kind of serious, then suddenly he's like a kid again.'

'I know,' I said. 'It's rather sweet.' I plucked the lipstick, which was mine anyway, out of her hand and leaned towards the mirror to make my mouth yet more irresistible. 'I'm quite serious about him.'

I was surprised at the way it came out. She looked at me again.

'Quite serious,' I repeated.

'Good,' she said. She put her hand on my arm. 'I think that's very brave of you.'

⋆ ⋆ ⋆

We went back into the hall and up the far end to the bar. I spotted Len's head, the slightly too long brown hair. There was a knot of people around him and I smelled trouble like

248

it came out of sweat glands. A big hefty man in Observer Corps uniform was jabbing his finger into Tad's chest. I couldn't hear what he was saying. Tad's face was stiff and pale but he wasn't responding.

I pushed in closer, Maddy in behind me. I saw two men backing up the tall one and another trying to play the peacemaker. Len was trying to explain something but his fist was clenched.

The tall man jabbed Tad again.

'You bloody foreigners think you own the place! And our women! Why don't you go home and keep your nose out of it?'

Tad grinned a quick, tight smile.

'I have no home but here,' he said. 'I don't think anyone owns Madeleine.' Then he added 'Least of all you, my friend.'

Then the big man's fist was coming up and Len was cutting across between him and Tad. He caught the blow right on his temple. He staggered sideways then came back and jumped for the man's throat with both hands. Then Tad joined in and so did hefty's two mates and I got pushed backwards out of the mêlée. I'd never seen grown men fight before and it was horrible. Maddy screeched and waved over two more pilots from the squadron, and they joined in. Then some more Observer Corps showed up.

It was like Len said about their dog fights: a shambles. Blows to the face, arms round throats, kicking and flailing, people falling down, slipping. It was the violence of it, the fury that had suddenly erupted, that's what was shocking. As was my inability to do anything about it.

It wasn't like in the films. It wasn't heroic or funny or even clean-cut. I saw Len fold as he took an elbow in the gut, then I was pushing to try to get in to the circle to pull him out. I saw him get off his knees then with a horrible shout he threw himself at the red-faced tubby man who'd hit him, and started trying to pull the man's head off. They both fell backward on the floor, the tubby man on top. Tad was in the centre of a thrash of fists and shoulders. The band was still playing 'Smoke Gets in Your Eyes' but the dancing had stopped.

Then the military police burst in and broke everything up and in seconds the whole thing ended. Men were clutching their wounds or drifting sheepishly back to the bar. Len had been arm-locked by a military policeman. I didn't know their exact powers but I had a strong feeling they could arrest anyone in uniform and this meant trouble. With a bit of luck, it meant non-flying. I was pleased to see Tad had been secured too, though it took

250

three to hold him.

Then the CO from the squadron was in there talking to the MPs. He took them aside and whispered in their ear. Next thing was our men were being released with just a minor bollocking (as they put it so tastefully) all round and we took them outside.

'What was all that about?' Maddy asked.

'You, mostly,' Len replied. He seemed angry and I couldn't decide if it was because of his loss of control or that he didn't do better in the fight.

'I think not,' Tad said. 'Those boys don't like my accent, that is all.' He put his arm round Maddy then looked up at the dark sky and laughed. 'Whoee! Maybe we are letting off some steam.'

'What did the CO say to you?' I asked Len.

He massaged his eye.

'We're to report to him in the morning. Oh, and he said next time try not to get outnumbered.' He shrugged and laughed quietly. 'Well, they're not going to ground us at this stage in the game. Experienced pilots are worth roughly their weight in gold right now.'

'So you can get into fights?'

He looked at me for a long time while Tad and Maddy canoodled at the other end of the porch.

'Yes,' he said finally. 'We can get into fights. But I tried to stop it till that bloke insulted Tad about being foreign. The man's risking his life being over here, Stella.'

I knew I should leave it but I couldn't. I was still shocked by that physical violence so near to me. The sheer *anger* of it, so close and so personal, much more so than bullets and bombs all released at a distance. I wasn't sure if that made it better or worse.

'So is he fighting because the cause is right or because he likes flying and fighting? And what about you?' I asked.

A long silence, then I looked up at his face, side-lit by the light that spilled from the hall as another couple stumbled out. He looked tired and drawn but rather fine. His right eye was already swelling up.

'I don't know,' he said at last. 'But right now, does it matter? When it's serious, I'm not sure how much motives matter. Maybe only what you do counts, not why. Maybe *Why?* is just a game you play at university.'

I thought then of Roger, his beautiful elegant way with an argument. The way he used to dispatch causes like a bullfighter did away with bulls. Roger was now on the North American convoys and somewhere way in the back of my mind or heart the anxiety was always there. Had he put *Why?* behind him

252

like a childish toy of our student days, or having come to his own conclusions, did he not need to think of it any more? Then I admitted that more important to me was whether he'd put me, us, behind him. That mattered to me more than these high-flown speculations. Simple ego as usual. Me, me, me.

I drew Len to the other side of the porch and clung on to him. We kissed lots, which is often better than thinking.

★　★　★

We got our lift back sometime after midnight. The night was clear and soft. As we sat on the men's knees in the back, someone wound the window down and the night air blew over our faces. Behind me Tad started singing quietly *'I'll be seeing you in all the old, familiar places/that this heart of mine embraces all day through'*, and Maddy joined in. I could feel Len's face pressed into my back, felt the wind on my face and saw a handful of stars in the northern sky, and for a long moment felt I was travelling home through the night with a mixed bunch, like I'd always wanted.

May we learn to take without anxiety the days that are left.

19

Early September

Shaken awake in the half-light, mug of tea into my hand, sign the chit. My right eye throbbing and swollen as I looked out on the dawn through a slit. Not the best way to prepare for another day staying alive.

Tad was sitting beside me on the truck to the airfield. He was looking cheerful, shaved and neat and whistling. The word had got round about last night's doings and we took some flak about it but the general feeling was we'd stood up for the squadron's honour. Me, I was less sure. I still felt the rush of murderous rage that had gone through me like a corn-field fire. I had wanted to tear that man's head off. Then I shivered at the picture.

I quietly told Tad I was sorry for what the man had said about his being a foreigner over here. I said we were all bucked that he and many others thought it right to come over and join in. Everyone knew the new Polish 303 squadron had downed another six aircraft the other day;

they were great fighters.

He put his arm round my shoulder, which I still wasn't used to, and he laughed.

'Thanks, my friend,' he said. 'I should know Maddy would get me into trouble, spreading herself around like that. But she's a great girl, great!'

He blew on his fingertips — his hands were surprisingly small — then crunched the apple he'd picked up and with a whoop hurled it into the poplar trees as we sped by.

'Say, Tad,' Dusty Miller called, 'how come you haven't joined 303 squadron, be with the other Poles?'

Tad stared at him, then broke into a big smile.

'And leave you lot blind without me?'

And there was laughter because it was true. Like other Polish pilots we'd heard of, Tad had phenomenal eyesight and, not having trained on RDF ground control, had always relied on it. Time and again he was the first to spot aircraft.

Now we drove past hop orchards dark-wet with dew that was getting heavier as the month wore on. We bumped down the track in a plume of pale dust, and I thought about how much I loved these morning rides, just as I hated the growing sick, heavy feeling in my stomach as we got closer to the airfield. I loved the onrush, the clear, cool morning blown into my face and waking me up, the undemanding company of friends. I'd have been happy if we'd never arrived, just kept on bumping for ever down the pale flinty tracks of southern England.

★   ★   ★

Someone must have messed up or else the enemy was getting smarter. We were hearing how Biggin Hill had been given another pasting when we became aware of a buzz on the horizon, low over the trees. Getting louder. Wrong sort of engine. Then we were all running towards our planes, preferring to take our chances in the air to getting caught helplessly on the ground.

I was being strapped in as the first plane appeared over the boundary fence. My engine caught, the chocks were dragged away and I began to trundle. It all happened too slow, the bomber closing in and me gradually picking up speed. I glanced to my left and saw Sniff Burton's tail wheel come up. Then to my right where Tad was leaning forward in his cockpit as though it could make him go faster. Then my kite was starting to get unstuck even as I saw the first flashes from the bomber's nose and then the fat slug bombs dripping from below it.

A hell of a bang and my windscreen was covered in earth. Then the plane flipped and I was on my back with a terrific roar and jolting. I cut the ignition and prayed the cockpit cover would hold up, for only it was stopping my head from getting ripped off by the ground we were skidding over. I tried to hang on and squeeze myself small as possible. I think I was sobbing *No, no,* when there was a great jolt and my head slammed into the instrument panel and that was it.

★ ★ ★

It was quiet but rocking when I came to. Someone was pushing the wing up and down, as if that would help. I had a very strong desire to get out of the plane but could see no way of doing it, not with the hood pinned to the ground by the weight of the Hurri. I felt the tickle and taste of blood running from my nose down over my cheek and forehead. It was very uncomfortable being upside down. I felt my head was starting to swell up and panic wasn't far away.

There was a rapping at the canopy beside my head. I turned and saw Evans squatting and looking anxiously through at me. Then he gave me the thumbs up and something oddly like a quick grin. He seemed almost amused. His mouth moved but the glass was thick and my ears were still ringing.

It must have been half an hour before I was freed, slithering sideways out of the cockpit. I lay on the grass, snatching for breath and feeling my head pulse. I didn't want to move ever again.

Tad sat me up, arms round my shoulders as I tried to fall back again.

'Did you get off?' I asked.

He grinned savagely.

'Depends how far you call off,' he said. He pointed, and over the hedge on the west perimeter I saw a Hurri's wing, canted up towards the sky.

'And Sniff?'

'He got away all right. Trouble is the 109s got him.' Tad nodded over towards the trees. Behind them a black twist of smoke rose lazily into the still air. 'I know he is killed. The Spits all got shot up to hell at the far end.'

I shook my head and tried to stand up. The ground was making like we were at sea. I kept noticing how quiet it was, the kind of silence that follows much noise.

'Think I'd better sit down for a while,' I said.

★   ★   ★

So I sat down for an hour or two, feeling very strange. Then the CO talked to me. He didn't seem to make much sense but told me to stand down for the rest of the day, which was fine as I felt quite tired.

I lay down in the long grass away from the huts but couldn't sleep, kept slipping back into that roar around my head. I was thinking about Sniff, how I couldn't remember much about him apart from his name and his sniffing from hay fever which drove everyone crazy and how he rattled away at the Mess piano, and a delighted quiff of fair hair that jumped up from his forehead, and there he was, suddenly past tense. Gone. He must have had parents, brothers and sisters maybe, a girlfriend. Just like whoever had shot him down. Who we must kill in turn.

I got up, slipped through the perimeter fence and went for a walk through the woods. It was cool and green in there. I found the tree where I'd carved my name but it looked too much like a tombstone so I took ten minutes to carve a thumbs up fist below it then wandered on my way.

I had a hell of a headache and felt edgy and snappy. I stopped at the edge of the field, cracked a dry branch and suddenly was close to tears. Then I went on to the village, sat down in the tea shop to get a decent cup of tea and some cake. The woman behind the counter told me she'd heard that the RAF had sunk barges full of German troops and the Channel was awash with bodies. Surely the invasion would be soon — did I know anything? I assured her I knew absolutely sweet Fanny Adams and concentrated on my cake.

I found myself back at the airfield — it seems I can't stay away. I've nothing else to do, nowhere else to go. I sat in a chair in the sunlight, wondering. We're all desperate for this to end but what else are we fit for now? We're like elastic that has been stretched way beyond its size so when the pressure's off it won't spring back again. That's what the War does and nobody told us. Our dads could have told us but they didn't want to talk about it.

I looked around at the lads. I looked at them playing cards, flicking through magazines, arguing over tactics and pubs, places to go in London, snoozing in the sun or brewing up inside the hut, waiting for Blue and Yellow sections to putter down over the boundary. They used to look so relaxed to me. Now I could see the tension that came off them like a heat haze. They were pretty bloody scared. It was in the little things — matches cracked across knuckles, a tuneless whistling from Tad as he turned another page of his Polish Air Force newspaper, the edgy irritated corner of the mouth of the man next to him whose name I didn't even know, the misdeal in the game of cards, the shock that jerked through everyone when the Tannoy clicked. It came to me: these are doomed men and they know it.

Then I thought: so are we all. It's just that in wartime it's speeded up a bit.

I sat there in the sun, dazed with heat, without any answers, just feeling a half-formed question go through me like another nausea attack. Only Coco Cadbury seemed genuinely at ease, smoking a pipe and reading a book as though he had a lifetime to spare. What was his secret? Was he just very stupid? He didn't seem stupid, the few times I'd talked with him.

A plane came droning down over the trees. Then a pair more. Then another, weaving drunkenly and shot up round the tailplane. That left two more to come. There was a long pause. Everyone was counting but no one was speaking about it. They went back to their papers and cards and fitful dozing.

Then the CO came over, with a medic of some sort, a man with very light eyes and a quiet voice. He drove me back to barracks, asked me some questions about what had happened to me that morning, and shone a light in my eyes. He tapped various parts of me, looked in my ears with something cold, asked the date (which I got wrong), the day of the week (right), the name of the Prime Minister.

'Tommy Handley,' I said. 'Only joking,' I added. 'It's really Ernest Bevin.'

He hesitated then smiled. Sort of. He asked about my headache, if I'd ringing in my ears, if I was feeling normal.

Normal! I told him if this was normal, the world had gone mad. Nothing had been normal all summer. Would he call this normal? If I felt normal, there was something wrong with me.

'Take it easy, old chap,' he said. 'I have to ask these questions.'

Then I felt suddenly very close to tears. I think he saw that, and he asked when I'd last had leave. I told him: after my last accident (that was the word I used, stupid really). I said I'd gone off for a few days with my girlfriend but I really couldn't remember when that was.

He nodded then asked a bit more, about how I was sleeping and that. Then he shook my hand, stood up and said he had to get on. He was going to see more pilots. He told me to get some rest because I had concussion. I probably wouldn't fly for a few days. Then he went off. I'd a feeling he was quite senior.

* * *

I was sitting in the Mess, swallowing aspirin and catching up my diary when the news came through. We were to be withdrawn for a spell, to Scotland, somewhere near Aberdeen. I reckoned the medic chap had something to do with it, and he was right. It wasn't just me, the squadron was in pretty bad shape. Too many pals had come and gone. Everyone was shattered, and at least a couple of the lads had been breaking off early from combat and flying home. They were brave enough men, they were just too tired to feel up to it.

I'd a few days leave for my concussion, and I hoped to see Stella then go and visit my parents. Something needed to be said, I didn't know what. Then I'd go north to join the squadron and have a damned good rest.

I wrote a quick note to Stella, sealed and addressed it. I slumped in the old leather chair in the corner of the Mess. For once there were no high jinks going on at the bar, just quiet steady drinking as the news went round of our posting. I looked up as someone called my name, grinned and slipped the letter into my uniform pocket. Then, despite the strange high ringing in my head, I got up to join them at the bar, sip a pint of thin wartime beer, and be in the company of men who for the first time felt maybe they were going to survive this.

★ ★ ★

When I stumbled into our room last thing, I found Tad packing up his gear. He was, I think, in a worse state than me. He never drank heavily before early flying, but now he could relax and a steady stream of vodka had gone down his throat that evening.

'Off to Northolt to see Polish friends at 303 squadron,' he said. 'Tell them they are not all so hot. Then we will go into London, to the 400 Club for some night life. Lots of Poles, lots of women, lots of laughing and lies.'

'Sounds good,' I said. 'Home from home.'

He pulled tight the drawstring of his kitbag and sat down heavily.

'We do our best,' he said, 'and General Sikorski is a fine leader. But really we have no home, and I think perhaps we will never return to Poland.'

With that he flopped back on the bed, closed his eyes and was away.

I pulled his bag against the wall and noticed a pair of brown shoes under the third bed. Everything else of Sniff Burton's had already been gathered up. This was the scuffy old pair he never shone because he claimed he was allergic to shoe polish. Well, we wouldn't have his maddening sniff keeping us awake any more.

I picked up the shoes and put them out in the corridor and closed the door carefully. Then I brushed my teeth, my head swimming and my eyes watery. I managed to get undressed though it took all the concentration I had, lay down and was gone.

I've told Maddy so it's official: I'm very late. I doubt I've ever been this late. Len and I had been a bit careless, which is crazy for intelligent people. We're trying so hard not to conceive, but at the same time another part of us is devilling away trying to upset all our plans and make more life.

Maybe that's what all this wartime fornication is about. People have not just much more opportunity, but also more motivation. In the midst of this destruction, we want to make life.

But that's not part of my plans. I veer between panic and a kind of silly pride, a vision of growing large and round as if I were the world itself, round and whole. I think of telling Len but I fear his response, whatever it might be, and then I think no point worrying him unnecessarily. So I wake early each morning, looking for that familiar ache but it's not there. Instead I lie confronting that other ache. I miss my dad so much, in a way I never did while he was alive.

So what would it be like to suffer the loss of someone you know you love while they're alive, and miss while they're still there to be missed? Under the bedclothes, I shiver and feel myself withdraw a little. I'm not very brave.

★　★　★

I get up and dress for work in the early light. Hands on his hips, jacket open and a big grin on his face, from his photo my father looks out at the world like it was a lark. As if there was a song or a joke somewhere just out of sight but he could hear it. On mornings like this, I don't hear it.

Len's letter is waiting on the mat. I read it quickly and feel ashamed. Ashamed at my own invisible withdrawal. Then I am angry — what gives him the right to be so candid and open? It's not fair for I'm not like that. I veer like a weather-hen. I love and I don't. I want a child and I'm terrified of it. At times I think of Evelyn, who asks so much less of me. And way behind that, I think of Roger Whitticombe, smarty-pants, intolerably good-looking, wit and cynic, my first lover, at this moment ploughing the grey seas somewhere in the Atlantic.

Then Len says he's being withdrawn and tears come to my eyes. Tears of relief, I hope, and not that I'm not going to see him for however long. Grant me one unselfish thought. I picture him sliding on his back at a hundred miles an hour with only the cockpit hood sheltering him from a quick but horrid death and the idea makes a twist right down in my stomach, a sharp pain that makes me think after all we are connected or that my period has come.

Which it has. I'm not going to add to the world's population. Ninety per cent relief and ten per cent disappointment. We must, must be more careful.

Then I cycle to work down the back roads, feeling all kinds of mixed things, contemplating seeing my slightly loopy darling tonight and my mum at the weekend to help fill the dreadful silence of that house. I notice the leaves are turning floppy, dark and dusty. Not even wars halt seasons, and that helps shrink this calamity.

I prop my bike up against the hut in the broken shadow of the transmission masts. Inside they're taking bets whether we'll get bombed today. Fact is we're stretched to snapping point. The Chain Home and Chain High networks have both been holed several times, though already repaired. It looks like they're targeting us and the airfields that are meant to protect us, especially the sector airfields that direct operations.

It looks very bad but I briefly notice the morning is beautiful even as I sit down inside the hut. If the War wasn't on we could enjoy it, but then again we wouldn't notice as much. We wouldn't ache so.

I can't square all these things, but am comforted to feel the rustle of his letter as I loosen my uniform jacket and lean in towards the screen.

So we had one more night of kissing on the bed, waiting for the moment when she'd look down on me with her face soft and pupils all enlarged, and she'd smile, sit up on the edge of the bed and start to unbutton her blouse. And I'd lie there feeling like heaven's gate was opening.

No one has ever been that good to me. It makes me quite tearful, this tearing feeling in my chest as I try to give her what she gives me.

And she reaches out, lifts the needle once again from the inside of the record back to the outside again, and then the crackle and the opening and we return to our own melody.

Even when this war is over and we're sitting after supper in the sleepiness of another evening of married life, the kids finally in bed and asleep, I know I'll never be able to hear that clarinet concerto and not see it all again. The night is warm, so is the little room, so even with the window open we easily lie naked on the bed. And all the while as our hands move and then I move, slowly and gently so as to give no sound to Mrs Mackenzie downstairs, our mouths keep whispering goodnesses to each other as the music unwinds — melancholy, joyous and unstoppable.

⋆ ⋆ ⋆

There was just time to bury Sniff before our squadron left. I was among the ones who carried him. When we lifted the coffin onto our shoulders, we staggered a moment. It was heavy, very heavy. But Sniff Burton had been a light, wiry man. As I stared straight ahead and we tried to walk a straight line from the church to the grave, I heard a faint rattle through the wood pressed to my ear.

It dawned on me. There must have been so little of him left in the burnt-out wreck. So they'd added stones so we'd feel we were carrying more than some charred bone and teeth, and someone had overdone it. Another fake, like the game of Ludo becoming chess. And I felt sick because it made me picture what was really in the box we were carrying.

Lies and fakes have that effect — they make the truth grimmer.

20

Early September

I got off the country bus, hoisted the kitbag over my shoulder and walked down the lane between the fences, noticing the little signs — a fence sagging here, verges run wild there, too many rabbits running about. According to Mum, even with the Land Girls the estate was still short-handed. It was short of cash and the slide had started in the Great War when two of the sons died and old man Wycliffe lost heart. From the windows of the bus I'd seen the empty cottages and the ones stuffed with evacuees.

I crossed the little footbridge over the stream, shifted my bag to the other shoulder and came up the back way through the trees. A fair breeze was blowing and it flipped the poplar leaves from green to silver over the rusting swing where my sister used to sit for hours in a yellow dress, not letting me have a go. Washing was blowing on the line but there was no sign of Mum out and about, so I put down my bag and sat carefully on the swing seat. It creaked but held.

I pushed with my feet and swung gently. There was a squeaking, groaning sound. These days Lily lived near the workshop where they assembled radar and R/T sets. She was working all the hours God sends according to Mum and was too busy to write. I'd had a card from a weekend she'd spent in Brighton with her Joe ('my Joe', she wrote several times, and I wondered if she was as possessive about him as she had been with the swing).

I let the swing come to a halt and sat there with my feet trailing the ground, feeling low and lost and as if everything was broken. My childhood seemed very far off, as if nothing good had replaced it except Stella, who was far away. My head still ached dully. I wanted to sleep for an awfully long time. Already the palms of my hands were stained with rust and flakes of green paint.

'Leonard! What are you doing there?'

And here comes my mother, small and round, smiling and tired-looking, hurrying towards me past the currant bushes with her apron flapping. She hugs me and for a moment something is restored, something feels secure and unchanging, then I notice the grey as I bend to kiss the top of her head.

★　★　★

I'd forgotten the smell of the house, and it almost made me weep. The medic had warned me of mood swings and told me not to take them too seriously. The pantry and the kitchen both had the same smell. Under the cooking and furniture polish was that damp whiff of countryside. It was something I'd longed to escape from yet yearned to return to.

For a moment I'd a flash of living with Stella in the new suburbs, coming home from the draughtsman's office in the evening, putting on old trousers and going out into the garden. That's what I wanted, wide acres of normality but our normality, not my parents'. Something newer, with more said. We'd have more honesty, more obvious love. That's what I wanted for our children. That, to be honest, is what I wanted for myself.

I asked about Dad. Apparently he was still asleep in the back room, making up sleep on his one day off a week. There was another rush job on at the factory, there always was. Did I know he'd switched to aeroplane parts? Then he came in, yawning and unshaven in his old pyjamas. We shook hands, one brief clasp and then release. He turned aside as if embarrassed, put the kettle on the stove.

I sat down. He sat down. We didn't know what to say. He was my father, we had so much to talk about and I didn't know how to start.

'So,' he said, 'how's the flying going?'

'All right,' I said. 'Pretty busy, you know. Shot down another bomber last week.'

For a moment, our eyes met. His were pale blue. I don't know what he saw. I saw my father in late middle age. I couldn't see him any other way. I couldn't see him as a young man going into the Army, into the trenches, shit scared or full of patriotic fervour. I couldn't see him not knowing who he was going to marry or where he'd live or how many children he'd have or that I'd be one of them. That was the young man I needed to know about and I couldn't make myself start. Not in the dim kitchen as he scratched his chin and yawned over his tea and my mother fussed about and made him toast.

'So you're enjoying yourself,' he said.

'Oh yes,' I said. 'It's great fun. Wizard. Time of my life.'

He looked away then and there was a pause before my mother broke in to tell me how the strawberries had been early this year but the currants and everything else were small with lack of water. And then the conversation moved on to small catchings-up until we had lunch outside, waving wasps off the salad as we talked about local news and nothings either changed or unaltered by the War.

★ ★ ★

In the evening Mum sent us both down to the pub. We went on Dad's motorbike that he used for getting in to work. At first I clung on to his jacket, then he yelled to put my arms round his waist. Which I did, feeling pleased and awkward. But it was fun, leaning together into the corners through the late light, feeling the flies and insects ping off my hands and jacket. The sudden warmth as we went by a stone wall, the moist coolness as we went past trees.

He pulled up in the courtyard and switched off. He glanced at me, nodded, almost smiled then averted his head and we went in.

★ ★ ★

We talked cricket and footballers, then crops and weather. I went to get the second pints. He looked up as I came back.

'Your mother tells me you've got a new girl,' he said.

I nodded eagerly, wanting to tell him all about Stella.

'That's right, Dad. She's — '

276

'Saw Christine the other day. She's still working for the Council. She didn't seem very happy to see me and she didn't ask about you. Pity, I thought, she's a good 'un.'

I lowered my head and drank off the top of my beer.

That's what he did. Every time there was a chance of us actually talking, he found a way of heading it off. At last I got fed up with it and made a head-on attempt.

'Dad. You know when you were in the trenches — '

'Right waste of time,' he said abruptly. 'We did all that and twenty-odd years later you're having to do it all over again. Only difference is, everyone's in it this time.'

His voice was thickened and bitter. He was talking as much to himself as me.

'But surely the cause is good,' I protested.

'That's what we thought then and all,' he said. He kept staring down at the table. 'A lot of people died, son,' he said eventually. 'It's best not thinking about it. Best just get on with it.'

So we got on with it. We had three pints, which left him one up, as usual. Perhaps he's right, I thought. Perhaps we should just get on with it and not want to think or talk much about it. That's what that generation did.

I hope if I have a son we'll do it differently

but like as not we won't. I briefly pictured myself at Dad's age, sitting here sipping beer alongside my boy with the War, my war, coming between us. I realized how hard it would be for me all those years later to say anything useful about it. By that time it would be a distant, unlikely experience, though it had set up everything that followed. Maybe I should just give him my diary and let him know how it was, though even it doubtless had dodges and half-truths in it. If I was anything like my dad, I'd only let him have the journal after I was dead and it was too late to say anything of the love that was between us.

I snickered to myself, to the imagined offspring sitting on the bench beside us. Doubtless the beer was having its effect. Doubtless I should accept my father as he was. If he didn't want to talk about it, what right had I to make him? *Because I'm his son and he's my dad*, part of me silently insisted. I thought of Stella and her dad, all the things she regretted having not said or asked. I opened my mouth.

'Right!' he said. 'Best be off, then.'

He stood up and looked down at me.

'Right,' I said. 'OK, Dad. On our bike, eh?'

I lay on the bed in my childhood bedroom. My mother was in her room next door with the radio on for company, and through the wall came the steady muttering of the Home Service. At least, I thought, she's had some practice, with Dad being away a lot over the years. In the old days Mum used to play music, now she just listens to the friendly voices. I think she's shocked at how much she misses him. I am. There's a difference between someone being away a lot and them being dead.

I crossed my arms across my chest and looked up at the ceiling. At times like this, missing someone isn't a sweet ache. It's devouring.

I traced the fine lines of cracks on the ceiling and watched my thoughts branch and spread. I imagine Len being gone for ever, then I recoil from it, get angry. Nothing should hurt me like this. I must learn to live, as my mother is learning, for myself again. I can go off into my own little bubble, to that cave behind the waterfall where no one can find me. Then I don't have to think about

279

him. Sometimes on the phone I've nothing much to say, he complains I sound distant. Well, I am, and I really can't help it.

At other times I can see him so clearly it's as though he's present and we're connected again.

I put my hands behind my head, rolled my head to loosen my neck. After all these years of being much the same, my mother had changed. I didn't know if it was because of the War or Dad's death. But earlier that evening I'd been talking, cautiously, about myself and Len. I'd been hinting we were doing it, having sexual intercourse.

'You must do what you think is right, dear,' she'd said. Not the usual line about what the neighbours might think, what other people do. I was astonished. One of these days, if things went on like this, Mum wouldn't vote Conservative.

I smoked a cigarette leaning out the window, watching my breath rise and vanish in the cool night air, wondering where Len was right at that moment, and if he'd spoken with his parents as he'd said he wished to. I hoped so. After all, I thought as I exhaled into the night, you only have two of them, and I miss one of mine more than I ever thought likely or possible. I miss Len too, when my heart is open enough to allow it, as it does now. Trouble is, I can forewarn and guide him but I can't protect him. The best we can do is look out for each other.

I stubbed the cigarette out into the pebble-dash, hid the butt in among the ivy, but stayed leaning on the windowsill, looking out at nothing visible till the shivers rose along my arms and I came back in.

Another medic checked me out, shone lights in my eyes till I was half blind. Then said I could rejoin the squadron but I shouldn't fly just yet. So I said goodbye to Mum and Dad — or at least Mum, Dad being already off to work in the components factory — and caught a series of trains north.

The journey took two days, the trains packed and stopping lots. On the second day the rumour went round that the invasion had started. So each train delay made everyone very jumpy, and the lady beside me kept looking anxiously at the sky for paratroopers. I'd noticed that rumour, along with death, is the principal product of war. It was impossible to know what to believe, so mostly we believed nothing except what was right before us. I saw a pair of eagles near Carnoustie but no paratroopers, and that was good enough for me.

I arrived at our new station north of Aberdeen on the evening of the second day. Our CO, George Davies, now known as Uncle George because we'd decided he was all right really, picked me up in his car at the station. He told me through his pipe-reek that, yes, in places the expected invasion had been signalled, there'd been bonfires lit by the Home Guard, and church bells rung all over the country to warn us. But nothing had turned up yet. London had taken a pasting, in retaliation for our bombers' raid on Berlin. Bombed all day and most of the night, docklands on fire, big show, hell of a mess. And more today. Huge numbers of bombers.

But Fighter Command were in seventh heaven and even Stuffy Dowding himself had raised a smile, because the RDF stations and our sector airfields were being left alone just at the point they were about to break. If the enemy kept hitting London, we could remain operational and do our best. The units Dowding had held back were being thrown into it now, another Polish and a Czech squadron were operational and running up the scores. The question was: could the city take it? Exciting times, and we were missing it. Uncle George seemed genuinely regretful. Can't say I was.

It was near dark as he turned up a drive and stopped outside a big Victorian pile. Loads of turrets and twiddly bits.

'Built by some tobacco manufacturers,' he said, 'but for now it's all ours. Said to be haunted, great snooker room. Wizard, eh?'

I got out of the car and breathed the cool, foreign air. Very thin and earthy and a stink of bracken. There was no background light at all, and the stars were coming out all over the shop. The sound of a piano came over the gravel, someone stumbling through a lugubrious 'My Funny Valentine'. Sounded like Tad's playing, heavily accented and eccentric as his speech. Then I thought of Sniff Burton, his light touch on the piano, and I heard again the stones in his coffin rattle by my ear. And I thought of Stella and how at least she wasn't being bombed at work.

'Wizard,' I said. 'Just ace, sir.'

21

Mid-September

The diary as always is written in pencil. Steadier than before, the tip kept to a draughtsman's point. But it's heavily smudged in places with what seems like earth or plant stains. And now the entries are longer and more detailed.

This was his one time out in the helter-skelter weeks of that summer, his time to think and see his position, if he could bring himself to do so. But there is little of that. Most of it is absorbed in recording what he did. It seems to have been important to him, the physical detail, as if it were a handhold he was holding on to, above a drop too great to contemplate.

Through the neat but smudged pages, the map references that hold good yet, the dog-eared corners and the grease stains, it isn't hard to see him as he walks alone into the Cairngorm mountains.

★ ★ ★

He walked quickly along the rough track from Linn of Dee towards Forest Lodge. It was late afternoon and the clouds were low. Rolls of mist tangled with the lower slopes and cut off the tops of the hills up ahead. Even with map and compass, a less than ideal day for heading into the wilderness.

He walked on, gradually getting in a rhythm as the track drifted on uphill. The big army backpack, stuffed with clothes, cooking gear, food, sleeping bag, notebook and maps, cut into his shoulders and slumped in at the small of his back. He began to sweat and increased his pace.

After an hour or so, the path sloped down to Forest Lodge, which turned out to be a closed-up shooting lodge surrounded by a broken stand of Scots pines, their red trunks glowing in the diffused light. He dumped his pack, lay face-down by the river and drank.

The mist parted, a breeze blew away the midges. He propped his pack against a boulder and sat back against it with the sun in his face. After a while he reached into his breast pocket, took out a new packet of ten bought in Braemar and lit one, cupping his hand against the breeze.

The coldness of the water, the harsh, sweet smoke, the sun filling in the bags around his eyes, all present and immediate. The clamour in his head that had kept him muttering all the way up the track had started to die down a little. He wanted more of that, more silence.

He got to his feet, filled the battered metal water bottle, pulled on the pack and set off again.

The way became smoother, with fewer loose stones. Mostly it was dry earth and mud. He took satisfaction in the way his body propelled along, and the haze of yellowish dust that blew from his feet towards the lowering sun. It was good to feel his body do its stuff without being strapped into a machine.

He wondered if Dusty Miller was back to their billet yet in his car. He'd offered to come along, seemed quite keen, but Len wanted this for himself. He'd spent a few days with the squadron, sleeping and resting off and going to Aberdeen for a couple of riotous nights, the village being dry. Now the word was they'd be recalled to front-line duties soon, for the bomber fleets were still streaming into London. Some of the lads had borrowed shotguns and gone to take advantage of an offer of some grouse shooting. He knew he'd killed enough and straight away asked permission to go off for three days in the hills. Granted, but that was all the time he could have.

He crossed a river, noting how low it was from the dry summer, jumping from boulder to boulder, then carried on as the path steepened. His ankles were tiring and the soles of his feet were hot, and his mind was still as full and burdensome as his backpack. The sun was sinking into a cleft in the mountains as he rounded the corner and the path split in two. He took out the map and checked it to see if he was where he thought he was and which way ahead to take.

He found the river he'd crossed, the rising contours then the parting of the ways. Yes, this was the glen, a long follow-up beside a stream and there was Corrour Bothy marked on the left-hand side. The path went right by it and even in the dusk he shouldn't miss it.

He put the map away then paused. It was very quiet, just the brief *Go back! Go back!* of a grouse, the faint stir of the breeze over the heathery ground. There was no distant droning aeroplane and not a person in sight. He hoped the bothy would be empty. He looked up the glen, took a deep breath and straightened his back, then he put one foot in front of the other and kept doing that till he arrived.

★ ★ ★

He hadn't remembered it taking so long. He slung down his pack at the door, lifted the catch and went in. Good, it was empty. A tin of dried milk, some firewood by the open hearth, a solitary sock hung on the makeshift drying-line.

Memory leaves out the drudgery, he thought. Anyway, I was with Leslie and we'd come singing most of the way and talking the rest, exchanging teenage certainties. I'd spoken passionately in favour of the Peace Pledge. Les was going to join the army and get abroad, out East he hoped. How young that all seems now.

He went outside and stood for a couple of minutes, listening to the burn and getting the feel of the place. Isolation is safety and there are no bears or wolves now. The only thing to be scared of round here is himself.

As if movement could brush away the memory of a head blown off its shoulders, he quickly picked up his pack and went inside.

He found the torch and made the place his. Spread out the sleeping bag on the dirt floor, made a pillow from his spare sweater, put his diary and pencil beside it. He unpacked the stove, filled the little tin reservoir from his bottle and lit the meths. The flames were yellow and directionless and cast his shadow huge on the wall.

He filled the kettle from his water bottle and put it on to heat. He hesitated then went down to the little river and squatted down to refill the bottle. For a moment he saw himself there, small in the throat of the glen, squatting patiently by a stream with head bowed, so small as to be scarcely there at all. But there, just the same.

He came back to the bothy and pulled the door shut behind him. He laid out his food supplies, found his twist of tea and added some to the hissing kettle. He took off his boots, folded his trousers under the head of the sleeping bag then got inside, more for comfort than necessity. He experimented with propping the torch up on his boot until he got the right angle, then he lay on his side, opened the diary and began to write up his walk.

He finally wrote *One cannot be the same again — Killing — Perhaps we deserve to die.* Then he lay for a while on his back, watching the torchlight make faces on the ceiling as the hard dirt floor pushed into his hip bones. He thought of what Stella had said in her last letter, how the more you care, the more you lose. It was hard to argue with that. But what's the alternative? The alternative is closing yourself off, and you die anyway. What's so great about that?

Johnny Staples, Shortarse, St John, Bo Bateson and the handsome, gentle Geoff Prior. Bunny, Junior Johnstone, Sniff, the old CO. All gone. Sergeant Mackay taking the wrong option on his third sortie and flying straight into a bomber. They seemed to have been dead for ages. They'd be dead for ages more. Not 'gone west', just gone. To their families their deaths must still be fresh as his own name carved into the tree, and like it would be gradually obscured and then finally blown over and that would be an end to it. Forgotten for ever on this earth.

He switched off the torch. He let go. He slept.

★　★　★

The morning came in grey and cold. His hips were aching as he turned over on the floor. He rolled over, groped for matches and lit the stove, put on the kettle. Then he stood up, let the sleeping bag drop off him, and padded over to the door. Opened it into a grey wall.

The mist had come in overnight. He could only just see the stream. Not the cleverest day for the hills. He considered jacking it in, walking back out and hitching back to base. Possibly only pride or some kind of stubbornness kept him from deciding to do that. Certainly he was tempted to get back to warmth and company, the company of his own kind, beer and laughter or a good penny dreadful novel, whatever it took.

Instead he had a pee against the wall, came inside and got back into his bag and began to grope around for porridge oats.

An hour or so later he was ready for the off. Thermos, sandwiches, map, compass, spare sweater — at least the pack was a lot lighter today. He looked closely at the map and identified the small stream that came down the bit of slope he could see. He could use that as a guide, looked like it went up nearly onto the plateau then petered out. He'd have to make a decision then whether he could navigate to the first summit, Angel's Peak. Fair enough. Give it a go.

He stuck the map back in the pocket of his waxed jacket, pulled the hat — damp already, brimmed with little droplets of water — down tighter, then put his feet to the slope.

★　★　★

Some immeasurable time later, for he'd been fully absorbed in his increasing heart-speed and in placing each foot on the rough ground, he scrambled up the last of the slope and came out onto the plateau. The wind was stronger and colder up here. The mist moved in solid blocks with thinner wispy bits strung between them. At first the visibility seemed better, then it didn't.

He stood for several minutes, getting colder, examining his map for features to navigate by but really there weren't any. The plateau he'd remembered with Leslie as being great walking ground, firm and open, was the end of the world. All he could do was take a map bearing on the summit and trust it. He could roughly keep the rim of the plateau on his right, that would be some kind of a guide.

He took the bearing and, holding the compass in his fist, set off over ground that, like the future itself, only appeared when he got there. There were a lot of minor contours that weren't on the map, and various peat hags, all of which tended to make him deviate from his course. He tried fixing on something on the line of the bearing, like a particular tuft of grass, but as he got closer he tended to lose it. So instead he orientated his body to the general compass direction and tried to follow that.

Distance was hugely magnified in this blanked-out world, and time went different, just as it did in combat, both stretched-out and very brief. He wished he'd checked his watch at the edge of the plateau, so he'd have some idea how long he'd been on this course. He looked now then sometime later realized he'd forgotten it. At least, he wasn't sure if the time he remembered was right, and without anyone else to check with, he realized there was no way of knowing.

He was quite occupied with this for a while and was trying to work out a system of noting down the time, or inventing a movable dial on a watch or compass by which one could mark the last time one had looked at the watch. Would that work? But what if one doubted *where* one had last looked at it?

The fact was, to hang on to some degree of certainty and sanity, it was necessary to either be very sure of yourself and have no doubts at all, or else have someone else with whom one could cross-check, and at worst end up lost together. And what was the point in writing a diary if not a way of marking things down so they weren't misremembered later?

He noticed the ground was beginning to fall off steeply to his right and he could just make out scree instead of steep turf. He checked the map. Either this was the last slope up to the summit, or . . . or it wasn't, and he'd gone right past it.

He vectored in a bit from the edge and hurried up the slope, feeling the clutch of anxiety in his breathing. If he wasn't where he thought he was, he had no idea where he was. Then out of the mist came a darker looming, and the looming turned into a heap of stones. A summit cairn. He had to assume that was Angel's Peak. If it wasn't, he'd gone badly wrong.

He leaned against the cairn, reassured by its solidity, and had half a flask-top of tea. The view was non-existent. Whatever the purpose of this trip, it wasn't for the views.

Next stop: The Devil's Point. From one extreme to the other, he thought. He took the bearing and set off into nothingness.

★   ★   ★

This section was a trickier piece of navigation. The side-slope kept trying to push him off the bearing, and there was no plateau rim to fall back on. This was right across the humping wilderness of the plateau. Under normal conditions, a pleasant, simple, joyful stroll. But these were not normal conditions. In fact, he was virtually blind.

This time he checked his watch before starting, kept repeating the time to himself. He'd estimated the distance from the map and calculated the likely time to Devil's Point under these conditions. All he could do was keep going as he was and hold to his trust in the map and whatever faith he had in himself.

He must have been walking more quickly on account of anxiety, for as he checked his watch one more time and reckoned he should be about there in five minutes, he saw the bulk of a sheep off to his left. Then it turned into a short man. He was about to wave then it turned into a stubby cairn. He hurried over to it and touched its top. 'Thank you,' he whispered aloud to whatever, and his voice sounded queer and unpractised.

Now assuming this was Devil's Point — great view, thanks very much — things got a bit simpler. A bearing near due west on a little lochan in a dip. If he hit that lochan, he knew where he was for certain because there was no other on this part of the plateau. From there he'd have a choice between following the stream down off the plateau, or carrying on up to the third summit, Monadh Mor.

This time he didn't stop for a drink or snack. He was too keen to find that lochan, he clung to the idea of it, arriving at its stony shore and knowing for certain where he really was. He took the bearing and hurried off.

★   ★   ★

The slope was long and undulating and he went fast on the downhill bits, trying not to panic.

As he peered into shifting mist, looking for the least sign of anything, his right foot caught, his weight carried him on and he fell full-length and awkwardly. He lay winded, feeling shaken and foolish. Then he carefully extracted his foot from the rabbit hole, got to his knees and tried to stand up.

His ankle held. He took a couple of steps, felt a pain but it was fading. Very, very lucky. If he turned or broke an ankle up here, in the mist and maybe twenty miles from the nearest person, he was in trouble. Up on the plateau under these conditions, it was nothing like summer.

He walked on, rather more carefully.

The slope steepened to his right and there was a burn. He stopped and checked the map. It might be one of two streams. If he was in Place A, he needed to bear off to the left for four hundred yards. On the other hand, if he was in Place B, he'd overshot and needed to turn back and follow the stream back to the lochan. He really wasn't sure.

He started off to the left then hesitated. It felt wrong. He looked back and at that moment the breeze opened up a long tunnel into the mist and he saw back the length of the stream. It didn't look like it was draining from a lochan. In that case it was heading for it, yes? He checked the compass and carried on into the grey.

He felt very alone. It seemed like days since he'd seen another person. The sense of connectedness he'd had with Stella and even at times with the lads, that was still there, still true. But he was learning the truth of the opposite: that in another way, and at other times, one really was alone. It was down to him, just as it was in the sky. Just as it was for Stella, in front of her screen.

It came to him with a shock, like when the plane had suddenly flipped over on its back when he'd been bombed on take-off, that she really was someone else. She existed for herself, not for him. However loving she might be, she was the centre of her world.

He slowed, faltered. But that's what makes her so worth it, he thought. That's exactly why it's worth while. Because she's not me. Because I'm not her. Because we're not each other.

Then out of the mist came a low sound of water. A few steps more and he was standing at the edge with the tiny wave breaking at his toes. '*Thank you*,' he said again. He'd found the lochan.

22

Mid-September

Foxy Farringdon had asked me out of the blue the week before, just as I was leaving work. Her parents were having a bit of a do. Wedding anniversary. Would I like to come for the weekend to the Hampstead place?

I stared at her, touched and taken aback. I was about to say yes, when I remembered.

'I'm afraid I've made a date with my friend Maddy,' I said.

'No matter,' Foxy said gaily. 'Bring her along as well. We've plenty room and she sounds a fun gal.'

'She is that,' I agreed.

So I put it to Maddy and to my surprise she was all for it. A trip to the Smoke, do some shopping, drink loads of someone else's booze. And *men*! Cartloads of men, smooth, loaded ones who wouldn't stand on your feet when you dance. There'd be music, wouldn't there?

'From what Foxy says, they've got a ballroom and they mean to use it,' I admitted.

'It'll be a scream. A scream,' she repeated.

'Oh come on, let's go!'

Unlike me, she didn't seem in the slightest intimidated by the prospect of staying with a family of posh strangers. Why, they might even have a butler. A hoot.

We'd been warned about the bombing that had been going on for days now, but the way we looked at it, London was a big city and the buildings much stronger than flimsy huts. We were probably safer there than at work. Mrs Mackenzie came over all emotional and even hugged me goodbye in a stiff kind of way, though the hint of water in her eyes might just have been at the thought of the loss of income if I never came back.

It was another warm morning yet high summer was starting to leak away, you could feel it in the air. As we walked to the station, Maddy looped her arm through mine and we swaggered down the road laughing and giggling like any shop girls. I wore a green dress that set off my hair and Maddy was in yellow and her bangles click-clacked all the way. With her golden hair permed up and the dress, more than ever she reminded me of the dandelions that were everywhere that summer, so brazen and irrepressible.

The train was slow and packed and smoky, as they always were during the War. Once we came to a halt for ages in the middle of nowhere. The conductor came by, Maddy grabbed his arm and asked what was holding us up because we had urgent appointments in London. I could have sworn he said 'Swans on the line, miss.' I shook my head to clear my ears then he said it again, pulled his arm free and hurried on down the train. Swans on the line! I could picture them draped over the rails, their long necks drooping mournfully, wings spread wide, like aristocratic suffragettes lying down in front of a race meeting, holding up this entire train of human fears and hopes, yearnings and frustrations.

'I thought he said *Songs on the Tyne*,' Maddy said. 'Or maybe *Some other time*. Trust you to hear something weird.'

Then we giggled and squabbled over it till the train started again, but at intervals throughout the day the image came back to me. Haunting, stately, ridiculous, those swans would always remind me of being young and scared and high-spirited, in the early days of the War.

He took his time then. Walked right round the lochan to get the shape of it so he'd know exactly where he was. Then he sat down behind a boulder out of the wind and had his first sandwich and more tea.

He'd been lucky. The glimpse through the mist at the crucial moment had made all the difference. Gut instinct had told him he was heading the wrong way. So much for gut instinct.

He thought of Stella, wondering exactly where she was at that moment. What she was thinking and feeling. *I love you*, he mouthed silently into his Thermos top. For the first time he felt the true weight of those words, understood that the 'you' wasn't just some projection like the plane silhouettes on the screen when they were doing aircraft identification. *You* was its own centre. And yet we're connected. That's the thrill.

He lifted the Thermos top and silently toasted her.

He considered bailing out off the plateau. All he had to do was follow the stream that ran from the lochan right over the edge, down the slopes and into the valley. Then again, he'd come this far, was sure now where he was. Just one more summit along a single bearing. So long as he didn't miss the cairn. If he missed it, there was nothing but miles more of the same.

He got to his feet. Checked the bearing on the map and reset the compass. He wanted the clean sweep, to do all he'd planned, to do all the summits on this part of the Cairngorm plateau, as he and Leslie had failed to do all those years back. They'd run out of time and daylight — bad planning, not really realizing the scale of things here — and had to leave without the last peak, Monadh Mor. That had bothered him then and bothered him now. This time he'd do the lot.

His ankle was stiff at first and his body cold from stopping. The ground rose, fell, rose again as he held on the bearing. The edge of the plateau came in from the east at this point. Yes, here it was.

He sat down a moment on a rare boulder, right at the edge of the plateau. Then even as he checked the map and readjusted the bearing, the mist started to break up. He saw the slope ahead, then he could look back and see the lochan. Then he looked off to his left and the whole glen was there as the cloud tore open. He could see right across to the far side where the slopes rose again, see the summits of Braeriach and Ben Macdui, the shoulder of Cairngorm itself. Then the sun came through and in a minute he was sitting high up on the world with warm sunshine pouring over his face and hands.

He said *Thank you* for the third time that day and got to his feet with a big feeling pushing up in his throat. Bloody wonderful, so it was. Pity Stella wasn't here to share it. He'd have to appreciate it for two.

He stood and appreciated it. The hours of sensory deprivation had made for this intense delight, just as the proximity of death made him feel life crawling across his skin. At least at those times when he wasn't ill with dread. There had been so much dread, and so much elation. Some of it sick like when he killed. Some of it good and healthy, like when he lay on the bed looking up at Stella as she smiled down. Or standing on the track above the cottage where they'd lived together for one long weekend, suddenly aware of himself, his breathing at the centre of his world.

It felt like he'd lived several months in a week, several years in a month. The cottage seemed an age ago, and he'd come a long way from himself. *A long way from myself*, he repeated quietly.

Across the big valley he saw a herd of deer,

their grey shapes drifting into a corrie. He put his hands to his mouth and hollered though there was no chance of them hearing him. His voice sounded strange to himself after hours of only his footsteps, the faint hissing of mist into grass and heather, the odd torn creak of a passing crow. Maybe he wanted to be sure he existed.

He shrugged the pack higher up his back and set off again, confidently up the slope towards where the summit must be. He pushed on up, whistling vaguely, happy and empty, feeling the sun and breeze drying out his damp clothes. Yes, and there was the summit. He strolled over and rested his hand on one of its big grey stones as though greeting a favourite dog. Done it, he thought. Stuck to it and did the lot. Only me. Feels good.

He found a place out of the breeze where he sat and had his sandwiches. Then he lay down in the sun, smoking and listening to the drag of the wind and the high fizzling of an invisible lark. With the sun filling in the hollow round his eyes, his thoughts slowed and finally stopped, and he was just existing.

Down near the river in the East End it looked as though some giant had walked at random up to a house or shop in the middle of the street, swung a vast boot at it then for good measure ripped off the roof and front wall. Wisps of smoke still rose from some charred timbers and such bomb sites were steaming with water. Usually a policeman was posted to keep children out and make inquisitive passers-by move on.

Maddy and I moved on. The next street was untouched, and the next. The one after that had a small crater in the pavement and all the shop windows blown in. We stopped in front of a greengrocer where a woman was still piling cauliflowers before non-existent glass. The handwritten sign above her head read *MORE OPEN THAN USUAL*.

'Look at this one,' Maddy said. Next to it was a tobacconist and hung in the missing window was another sign that simply said *BLAST!*

I smiled at that all the way down the street, and wondered if jokes could be a sign we would win in the end. Or perhaps there were similar signs hung up in shops in Berlin. What was obvious was that though the city had been bombed steadily for much of the day and the night for the past week, the damage was surprisingly limited. The rumours had been the whole place was rubble but it just wasn't true. Shops and offices were open, buses and trams were running, trains were held up by swans on the line — life as usual, more or less.

We set off towards Oxford Street, wanting to get there and do some shopping before the lunch-time raids started. And it was on our way there that something odd happened.

Maddy was beside me, salivating through a shop window at a pair of shoes I thought frankly tarty but she pronounced smart. A shop assistant came into the window from the side then glanced up at us. She was near our age, nothing special about her, but Maddy jumped back as if she'd been punched. Her face was white. The assistant had her mouth open and looked as shocked as Maddy. In fact, she looked remarkably like her, maybe slightly older and slimmer.

'Come on!' Maddy grabbed my arm and yanked me off down the street. I looked back, saw the assistant still standing staring after us with one green shoe in her hand.

'First time I've seen you run away from a

shoe shop,' I said. 'So who was that — a long lost cousin?'

Maddy didn't smile.

'Sister,' she said out of the side of her mouth. 'Oh, Gawd!' And she pulled me into the nearest shop doorway and turned her head away. She looked in a terrible flap. I glanced back, saw a middle-aged woman walking past. Something about the set of her head, the determined way she was not looking to the side as she passed the doorway, made me wonder if she'd seen us. I looked after her and saw her turn into the shoe shop we'd run away from.

'Is she gone?' Maddy asked in a shaky voice.

'Yes,' I said. 'But — '

'Don't ask,' Maddy said. 'Stella, please don't.'

Then we went on our way, arm in arm, not saying anything. As we turned into Oxford Street the sun came out again and Maddy stopped and finally looked at me.

'My ma,' she said. 'We don't see eye to eye.'

'Seems to me you don't see each other at all,' I said. A feeble joke, and I hated myself the moment I'd made it. 'So what's this all about?'

There was a long pause. Maddy looked at the sky, along the street of shops, at the pavement. She'd never spoken of her family, had always turned away with a joke any of my questions.

'I haven't seen ma or sis for nearly two years,' she said at last. 'We had . . . a bit of a do.'

'And your father?' I said. 'What about him?'

'You must be joking,' she said, and her voice wasn't charitable.

For a moment we looked at each other. Then she shook her head.

'You're a brick, Stell,' she said, 'but it's not something I can say. Maybe someday . . . '

Then she looked at her watch and gave me a big unconvincing smile.

'We're missing valuable shopping time,' she said. 'Let's go to it!'

She crossed the road and I had nothing to do but follow, thinking how you think you've got someone taped then realize you don't know the first thing, and wondering when I'd finally find out.

The answer, of course, was never.

It was late afternoon by the time he struggled over rough ground back up the floor of the valley towards the bothy. His bad ankle was jabbing and his boots were heavy. The river kept getting in the way and finally he had to ford it, running across at the shallowest place he could find, with the notion that if he went fast enough his feet wouldn't get wet.

He got to the other side, damp and laughing, then sat down and took his boots off, emptied out the water, squeezed his socks and left them out to dry for ten minutes while he sprawled in the heather.

Time to get back to base. He put his wet boots on and plodded on up the glen.

★   ★   ★

He saw them some distance off, two figures moving about in front of the bothy. He hesitated, then walked on.

The man in the grey sweater waved as Len came slowly up the slope from the burn to the bothy. He introduced himself as Alec Watson, held out his hand. Len noticed he

310

had a limp and stood slightly off-centre. The other man was coughing inside the bothy, a harsh, tearing sound. Sweet blue-grey smoke rose from a neat stone-circled fire made of dry heather roots and a few bits of wood.

'The kettle's nearly boiled,' Alec Watson said. 'You'll have some tea?'

'Thanks,' Len said. 'I must be a few pints short.'

The cougher came out of the bothy in bare feet, hand over his mouth, introduced himself as James MacIver. Like Alec, he looked in his fifties but he was much paler and more drawn.

The kettle boiled, tea was made, Len offered biscuits from his pack. They sat at ease in front of the cottage in warm sunshine while the breeze and smoke kept midges away. They compared their days — the two men had come down the Lairig Ghru, the longest, roughest pass in the Highlands, were on their way to Braemar. Len found himself both sorry and relieved they were moving on the next morning.

The smoke swirled sideways and Jimmy coughed again, a deep, flat, tearing cough that made Len wince. He coughed himself red in the face but pale about the temples. He gulped tea, put two lozenges in his mouth and eventually the coughing stopped.

'Sorry about that,' he said. 'The mist this morning is bad for my chest. I shouldna have come out, really.'

He got up and went inside the bothy, closed the door. Len could hear the coughing start again. He looked at Alec. Alec stretched out his bad leg, picked up a twig and poked the fire around.

'Gas,' he said quietly. 'In the Great War. Jimmy's embarrassed about it — best thing you can do is ignore it. Can I ask what you do yourself?'

'RAF,' Len said. 'Pilot.'

'Oh aye. Fighters or bombers?'

'Fighters.'

'Hurricanes or Spitfires?'

'Hurris,' Len said, staring into the flames, near-invisible in the brightness of the day, only their heat making the ground behind quiver. 'We've been posted up here from the South for some R & R. Going back in a few days.'

'I see.' A long pause as they both studied the fire. Alec Watson wrapped his handkerchief round his hand and picked up the kettle to pour them out more tea. The coughing inside the bothy had subsided again.

'A nephew of mine — well, my only one — flew Hurricanes,' Alec said. 'My sister's boy. More dried milk?'

'Thanks,' Len said. He blew on his mug and watched the ground quivering as he contemplated that past tense. So many people now past tense, he thought. The worst is that you almost get accustomed to it, as if it were natural.

'And?' he asked. 'I mean, what happened?'

'Oh, he's no deid,' Alec said. He hesitated, glanced sideways at Len. 'But he's awfy badly burned. The surgeon's done wonders on his face and hands, but still. It's a terrible thing to say, but maybe he'd be better off if, you know . . . '

Len nodded. Then they both sat a while, drinking scalding tea and looking into the fire.

23

Mid-September

The raids started early afternoon and went on from there. At first I was very frightened. Then edgy. Then just alert.

It is, I discovered, impossible to be petrified for hours on end. Even if the bad stuff is happening just a mile or two away, that's far enough. As though our fear and our sympathy, like our RDF, has a limited range. Anything outside it is just mush.

I winced for those who were getting it, but mostly I was watchful to check it wasn't going to be me. And those raids were all directed at the river, the docks, the East End.

So the sirens started, people hesitated, moved away from the taped-up windows and got on with their shopping. The longer nothing terrible happened, the more normal it became. There were distant thuds, rumbles, faint sirens from ambulances and fire engines, all from the direction of the docks. As long as the bombing was accurate, in Oxford Street we were safe enough. It was nothing like the attacks on the receiver huts when we'd been the targets.

'Imagine being trapped inside Debenham and Freebody's,' Maddy said. 'Even if there's not that much for sale.'

'I know,' I replied. I think we were helping each other be brave, and somehow we knew being jokey was the form. 'Terrible, isn't it?'

Eventually I selected a pale green outfit on the grounds it made my hair look like it was meant to be that colour, plus a pair of what my mother would call Not Sensible shoes. It took all my coupons. We walked down the flights of stairs — the lifts all being closed — and pushed out through the revolving door and stood in the entrance.

The streets were nearly empty. The odd person went by at a quick walk, head down as if it was safer not acknowledging what was happening in the sky. A police car passed, then an ambulance. Three air-raid wardens hurried along, one suddenly clutched his helmet and looked up at the sky. That moment, that gesture, stuck with me for the rest of the War — his long bony nose, the gleam of his eyes as he swivelled to look up, the way he held his helmet on, his set lips. When someone, like my son, asks me about the bombing in the War, that's one of the two images that come. The other I try to put off as long as possible.

Once the ARPs had gone, we went into the street and looked up. The sky seemed filled with a swarm of midges, mostly very high up, it seemed like hundreds of them. There were some contrails, and the occasional line of smoke heading down, meeting the smoke rising from the direction of the docks. The air smelt of rubber and something sweet and burnt, like caramel.

The droning was faint but continuous. At certain points the long regular lines of bombers were stirred about as if someone had taken a big stick to the blue pool of the sky, and I knew that's where the fighters must be. For the first time I saw directly the odds they were up against and I heard my heart beating in my ears. It was impossible. There were just too many of them. I could never tell Len this.

But right now he should still be in Scotland, safe for a few more days, so I could relax and enjoy myself.

'Come on, Stella! Let's get off the street!'

Maddy was tugging at my arm.

'It's dangerous! They're too near!'

'I know,' I replied quietly, and allowed myself to be led in the direction of the tube station. If the trains were running we'd catch one out to the Farringdons' house in Hampstead. We might be late, but that was understood. All arrangements were rather provisional now. The War was our excuse, and it excused a great deal — just how much, we had yet to determine.

In a way, I admitted, as Maddy and I hurried along, still looking up at the sky, it was all rather exciting, being bombed.

That night the three men lay talking side by side in sleeping bags on the hard dirt floor of the bothy. Jimmy was in the Observer Corps, Alec the Home Guard, in addition to their day jobs in factories in Clydebank. It was good for Len to be reminded that he wasn't on his own. In fact every adult in the country seemed in some way involved in this war, and all had opinions about the way it was run. It wasn't like the Great War. People were somehow more possessive of this one, as if it was their war and their country. It seemed unlikely people would go back to the way things had been, any more than he could.

Lying beside them, listening to their quiet voices doing routines about the trenches, he felt the distance he'd come from himself since the War began, and the unknown distance yet to go. As if there were a long row of earlier selves lying in sleeping bags to his left in what was presumably the big bothy of his life, and another more shadowy series of future selves parked off to his right, stretching into the dimness beyond the reach of his torch.

He smiled to himself in the half-dark. He

appreciated Alec and Jimmy not asking him about the flying and combat. Their stories of their war seemed a kind of sympathy, a way of letting him know they understood both the terror and the dailyness, the exultation and the bewilderment and the weight of the knowledge that one had killed.

Jimmy was talking about the importance of keeping your feet washed and dry. One sunny afternoon his platoon hung their socks out to dry on a radio-telephone line and German snipers had used them as target practice, and he'd lain in the sun darning a bullet hole in the heel and it had been the happiest moment of the war, happier even than the end of it when they'd been too tired to feel much at all.

'Of course, you had to believe you personally wouldn't get it,' Alec said thoughtfully. 'Even though you knew you probably would. Otherwise how could you carry on?'

How indeed, Len thought.

He lay unmoving in his bag as Alec went on to talk about the day he lost that particular illusion. A grey, misty morning, after hours and days of barrage from the guns behind them. Then the silence. Then the men being ordered over the top, slowly breaking out of the trenches like a wave breaking the length of a beach. And when it came to their company and the officer, a Captain Grey, ordered them to attack, leave the trench and advance towards the enemy. As he stood below the lip of the trench, Alec understood for the first time he would die if he went up there. A bullet would hit him, perhaps several, and he'd be dead. He was no different from anyone else. His body was soft, he would be hit — he could hear the machine guns had started up, heard the shouts and the sudden, cut-off cries — and he would die.

He stood in the trench, unable to move as his mates levered themselves from the trench and started off. He stood there, shaking his head. Captain Grey stood on the lip of the trench, pointing his revolver at him. Ordered him to leave the trench. Alec stood looking down at his feet, his precious muddy feet, and shook his head, more in bewilderment than refusal.

'For the last time, Corporal!'

He looked up at Grey, at the gun pointed at his heart, and slowly shook his head. Captain Grey frowned as though puzzled, then suddenly reeled sideways and spilled into the trench. Alec looked at the open emptying eyes, the blood spreading from the throat and more staining the uniform round the chest. Then he shrieked, jumped out of the trench and started running, shouting, after his companions. Then a bullet hit his thigh and he went down and stayed down, cheek resting on the mud. He cursed the deep pain and muttered *Thank God, thank God*, for he was still alive. After a while he began to crawl the short distance back to the trench. He made it, and his war was over.

'I don't know what changed,' Alec concluded. 'Or why. I just woke up that morning and realized I wasn't an exception. You think because you're smart or lucky or just because you're you, you'll get off with it. But I realized I was like anyone else. I would be hit and I would die. Well, I was wrong about that last bit!'

'You were aye a right haiver,' Jimmy said, and then they both turned the conversation to jokes and anecdotes and finally got off the war altogether. But long after they ceased and the torches had gone out, Len lay awake in the blackness inside the bothy, looking up where the ceiling must be and, beyond that, the distant, indifferent night sky, where he too was not an exception.

We got to the Farringdons' pile round five o'clock and were met by Foxy, her parents and brothers, her boyfriend John Goldsmith, and various alarmingly smart (though not too intelligent) aunts. No butler, to Maddy's disappointment, but a couple of maids took our coats. At first sight I disliked John G. for having a high forehead, wavy hair and a long aristocratic nose, but he seemed so high-spirited, so pleased with life and himself (and, it has to be said, me), that I came round to him. I'm shallow and easily led, but it *is* nice to laugh and flirt again.

Meanwhile Maddy was having a wonderful time, being outrageously forward with Foxy's brother Gerald, who looked rather smart in his army uniform, back for a weekend's leave before being sent out to Malaya.

'I expect it'll be gin slings and polo parties and the chance to improve my golf,' Gerald said. 'Should be pretty quiet, not like here.' And indeed as he spoke, we heard the low distant thuds and some sirens nearer by.

The house was enormous. We were shown up to our room, quickly had baths then changed into our new frocks and went downstairs. We rather nervously went into a marvellous public room with a genuine Adam ceiling and there met loads of confident, high-spirited people and had cocktails and chat.

I was trying to be an ironic observer, told myself I was cleverer and better educated than most of these people. But still I felt gauche as I drank and laughed and listened to John G.'s dubious but funny stories.

My body tingled, my mind seemed full of bubbles. I felt the heat and warmth of John's big shoulders brush mine as we sat down together for dinner. (Foxy was further up, wedged in between two stiff aunts, and I had to wonder what the parents' attitude was towards this supposed couple.)

The meal lingers in my mind's mouth still. There was a handwritten menu in front of each of us.

Oysters or smoked salmon or grapefruit
Thick or clear soup
Steamed sole
Glazed chicken with vegetables
Iced puddings
Savouries
Coffee

To accompany this, we had sherry, hock and champagne, and John and I applied ourselves with zeal to all of them. He explained to me how drink numbs the higher centres that control your repressions, thus giving free play to all your lower centres. I pointed out I had no repressions so the drink would make little difference to me.

'We'll see,' he said, and filled my glass again. 'We'll see about that.'

I caught Maddy's eye over my glass; she winked at me. Lacking all decorum, I winked back. Then someone put on gramophone records in the ballroom and John went to have the first dance with Foxy while the aunts scrutinized. Then he came back and danced with me.

He was a marvellous dancer but ooh! sensual to his fingertips. He had a habit of getting your right hand on his hips, where he would play with it in a thoughtful way. Also of placing his lips on top of my head (at least, that's what it felt like). His conversation was excellent too — the best part was his voice, which was deep and very slow and considered, nothing like Len's urgency. He lamented that we hadn't met earlier, not just before he had to leave. He rebuked me for trying to chassé at the end of a three-quarter turn. I pretended to kick his shins and told him I would *chassé* just when I wanted, and his job was to keep up with me.

I kept noticing Foxy looking on, and her aunts, but what could I do? Besides, I was enjoying myself extremely. On a turn by the blacked-out windows, I briefly thought of Len somewhere in the mountains, but he seemed faint and a long way off. And besides, he'd said often enough it's important to enjoy the here and now, so I decided I'd be a sophisticate and do just that.

It was, I should say, a very speedy and passionate foxtrot. At the end of it, he insisted on taking my pulse, said with pride he'd once got a girl's to 130. Mine was 100, his 90, but as his is usually 60, I thought I'd done pretty well.

Then I was made to sit down but he kept me up for two more dances and then finally an eightsome reel, which seemed complicated at first but like anything else you watch other people and catch on and begin to see the point in it. The point is fun, nothing else.

I glimpsed Foxy flanked by guardian aunts and felt sorry for her. But really, if she allows her life to be guided by aged relatives, no surprise she's unhappy.

John G. took my pulse again — 110. He said he'd never met a woman with such marvellous stamina. He lingered longer than strictly necessary over my palm then asked my height. I told him.

'Good,' he said. 'Just the right height for a waltz.'

And certainly we fitted nicely as we spun round the room (which was, I admit, beginning to spin round me). And he liked the right books too — *Cold Comfort Farm*, *Pooh* and *Pygmalion* and *Gone with the Wind*.

Most of the time seemed spent with him, but I also danced with a Derek, another John and a moon-faced calf called Anthony who asked me what pack I hunted with.

Then I sat down a while and talked to Maddy and Gerald (she was sitting on his knee, fairly drunk, I think, her lower centres working just fine). She pointed across the room at Anthony.

'That fat bloke,' she said. 'He asked me what pack I hunted with. And I told him — my girlfriends on a Saturday night. Then he went all pink in his ears. Ooh, I said, you've gone the colour of one of those riding coats.'

Then John G. was sitting beside me and we talked about Life — a thing, he agreed, one was tempted to do after midnight. And we said lots of things about how short and strange and uncertain it was, and how you had to stay up late and enjoy all experience as much as possible. Then we went out into the garden to cool off.

The garden was huge, walled, with big trees at the bottom end. We sat on a bench in what I suppose you'd call a bower, drinking champagne direct from the bottle (which made it go up my nose) and admiring the moon. A fine full moon, low in the sky and still yellow. A harvest moon. A bomber's moon — or is that a clouded one? I wondered. Off in the distance was a red glow and every so often sparks lit up in the sky. It was, in its way, very beautiful.

'Your pulse rate is still raised,' he said. 'I wonder why?'

He had his hand lightly on my wrist. He looked at me, smiling in the moonlight. I saw his teeth shine in the dim light from the moon and the docks on fire, and his eyes were dark in shadow. I knew he was going to kiss me and at that moment I wanted him to. I wanted to feel someone else's lips, the taste of someone else's mouth and their arms round me. He bent towards me. I'd never see him again. I bent towards him.

Maddy pushed into the bower, trailing Gerald behind her.

'Hello, you two! Got anything left in that bottle?'

Then somehow she got between us on the bench, and we chatted for a while till the bottle was finished. She said that we'd go inside and fetch another, but once we were in she steered me up the stairs to our room.

I stood at the window while I tried to unhook my dress. From this height I could see much better the glow around the docks, and even the tips of flames, and searchlights hitting barrage balloons, and ack-ack bursting in the sky.

'Maddy, why is it all right for you to do some things and not me?'

She lay on the other bed in her maroon pyjamas. She raised her head and looked at me.

'You don't half ask some stupid questions, Stella,' she said.

Then I lay down and listened to the distant thuds and sirens, and tried to play back the day, then fell asleep, still hungering for something just out of reach.

24

Mid-September

Next morning he went out for a pee and the mist had come down again. So he lay in his sleeping bag while Alec and Jimmy made their breakfast and packed to move on. Jimmy went outside to cough and Alec handed over a mug of tea.

'Sorry if we went on a bittie last night,' he said. 'It was just yarning and blethering.'

Len nodded as he took the mug, scalding hot, by the rim between two fingers.

'Don't worry about it,' he said. 'It made me glad I'm not in the trenches!'

'Aye,' Alec said. 'Right enough. Still, you do what you must, eh?'

Jimmy came back, pale and drawn.

'Bloody mist,' he said. 'Bloody country. When this is over I'm thinking I'll emigrate to Australia with my wife and the bairn James.'

They shouldered their packs and stood looking down at Len.

'Well, good luck, son.'

'Aye, look after yoursel,' Jimmy said.

'Thanks,' Len said. 'You two go careful.'

'Aw, us!' Alec said. 'Nothing ever happens in Clydebank!'

And they were gone. He'd not see them again, nor forget them.

He lay in a long time, shifting about trying to find a comfortable position, too lazy to get going. Eventually he got up, made breakfast, ate it standing outside. The upper slopes were well wrapped in mist and tatters blew down the empty glen. He checked the map and decided to stay off the tops, take the long track through the Lairig Ghru to Aviemore, get the train back from there.

He slowly packed up his sack and buried his rubbish and left that place.

It's still possible to go there. Corrour Bothy. It's on the map, easy enough to find at the southern end of the Lairig Ghru pass. Anyone can take the train to Braemar and walk in as he did. Cross the same burns, follow the same tracks with the certainty his feet passed here.

Very little has changed in the bothy since he slept there. The dirt floor is now overlaid in concrete, even colder and harder. The fire grate looks ancient and probably is the one he used. If visibility is poor, it's still best to follow the stream up the slope onto the plateau as he did, take a compass bearing and believe in it until The Angel's Peak appears. It's simple to add another stone to the cairn, touch it as he did.

The plateau, like anywhere else, is just as full of ghosts as it's allowed to be.

On good days the cloud level is above 4,000 feet, and unlike for him it's possible to see perfectly clearly, all the way across the undulating plateau, Loch nan Stvirteag. His lochan is easy enough to find; it's the only one thereabouts. What can't be seen — and yet imagined with such certainty it seems it really should be visible — is him. Sergeant Leonard Westbourne, groping cautiously across the plateau, compass held in front of his chest, peering into blindness as he searches for his destination.

'Rise and shine, little star!'

I woke slowly and reluctantly. The room was dim from the blackout blind. The inside of my mouth was an ash-pit. Maddy was standing by my bed in her pyjamas, holding out a mug of tea.

'Oh, God,' I said. 'Oh, God. Maddy, I'll never be superior again.'

'Glad to hear it,' she said. 'I blame your mum.'

I slowly sat up and took the mug and began sipping. I couldn't say I'd forgotten last night. It was all too clear but now looked completely different. I didn't appear a witty, attractive and sophisticated woman. I seemed like a stupid, nearly-drunk, over-impressionable silly girl. And John G.? I went over the things he said, and his charm turned to a kind of patronizing bullying. That remark about me being the right height. And I'd laughed and felt pleased instead of kicking his shins.

No, that wasn't fair. I'd played along with it. And he'd been upset the way the family had kept him away from Foxy. And then out in the garden, I must have known what was happening and really wanted it to happen. I loved Len but a week away from him and this . . .

'Oh, God,' I moaned again. I put down my mug, then began to cry. She put her arms round me.

'I miss him so much,' I sobbed. 'Honest I do. But I'm so scared he's going to die. I don't want to be left alone. I used to, but now I don't and it's his fault.'

She soothed me, held me, stroked my shoulders and kindly said nothing. Then once I'd stopped snivelling and drunk my tea I started to thank her for saving me from making even more of a fool of myself the night before. She cut me off.

'The main thing is to know when you're flirting and when you're serious,' she said. 'And be sure of the difference. Champagne is bloody nice but it muddies the waters.'

'What about Tad?' I asked. 'Is that serious?'

'Go and have a bath,' she said, 'and don't ask stupid questions before breakfast.'

For Len Westbourne it was a long day stumbling about among the boulders that litter the bottom of the Lairig Ghru like tank traps. Aches and twinges came growling up his shins — flying had brought no fitness whatsoever. He stuck burning soles in an icy stream and was surprised they didn't sizzle. He was hobbling by the time the glen started to open out, his shoulders raw from the weight of the pack.

This is how he spent 15 September, which would come to be held as Battle of Britain Day — alone, sore-footed, laboriously covering rough ground like the infantry man his father had been in the previous war.

With the deadline for destroying the RAF in order to launch Operation Sea Lion only two days away, late that morning the *Luftwaffe* sent massive bomber fleets, heavily escorted by fighters, to attack London. Raids were also made on Thames shipping, Portland, and the aircraft factory at Southampton. Part of the strategy was to force the RAF to finally fully engage and send up all its fighters. And fighter aircraft, both sides had now grasped, were the key to the struggle.

The August raids had been bigger. Neither side was now at its full strength. This phase of the fighting is best seen as two depleted, exhausted fighters swinging blows at each other with weakening arms, one desperately seeking a knock-out, the other only to hang on.

The RAF were running low on fighter reserves, and more than a quarter of their pilots had been killed or put out of action. Though the losses overall were in their favour, they could not go on much longer. On the other side, the *Luftwaffe* had suffered significant losses, especially among the bombers. And unlike the RAF, its pilots were not rotated; many had been fighting now for two months without a break. Still, they were assured, the RAF was very nearly finished and would put up little resistance.

As it was, the 12 Group, normally kept back well north of the Thames, for once got a 'Big Wing' of five squadrons assembled in time above Duxford. They flew south, too late to stop the attack but in time to fall on a bomber fleet already shaken and scattered by the 11 Group fighters. Douglas Bader's 242 Hurricane squadron, together with those of the Polish 302 and the Czech 310 — fresh and frustrated at missing the action for so long — cut the bombers to ribbons while the two fresh Spitfire squadrons took on the Me109 fighters.

The result was not quite the massacre proclaimed in the papers next morning, but it made a nonsense of the *Luftwaffe* pilots' leaders' claim the RAF was nearly defeated. Even as Len was hobbling in a happy daze through the deep valley of the Lairig Ghru, the last German planes were limping home.

He came to another bothy late ·in the afternoon, sat down by it to have a precious cigarette, his second-last, and check the map. He'd seen no one all day — a few grey-headed crows and a couple of kestrels were the only living things he'd met.

He went inside and lay down and snoozed a while. While he slept the *Luftwaffe* launched the second wave of attacks on London and the factories. The sequence was the morning all over again: RAF fighters, many of them fresh, falling in numbers on vast formations of tried airmen who had been told to expect no significant resistance. The loss was not just that of aircraft and pilots, it was in airmen's morale, in the *Luftwaffe*'s belief that they were winning this struggle.

The luxury of sleep at any time of day, Len couldn't have enough of it. He stretched, yawned, then went back to sleep again. When he woke again, a bit shivery and cold, he went outside and saw that the evening sun was breaking through, and he decided to stay there the night and go on to Aviemore tomorrow. Still get back to base in time.

When the sun fell behind the hills, it got cool and he gathered materials and built a fire, outside in a blackened ring of stones. It may have been Alec and Jimmy's. He wondered if they were in Braemar now, with Jimmy coughing up what remained of his lungs.

He was shocked to realize he hadn't thought of Stella for hours. In fact he hadn't thought of anything for hours, just putting one foot in front of another as he pushed his way up the great valley to its midpoint then down the far side. His head was still full of it — the wind over the rocks, the occasional harsh cry of a bird, the scuff of his feet and the rattle of pebbles, the great slopes rising high and bare on either side as he picked a way through the valley of stone towards Aviemore.

He had been blank for hours on end though he'd come here to think. Maybe blankness was a kind of thinking. Maybe just feeling here and present was more than enough, was everything. At the end of his life that's all there would be, one last moment.

At least live it, you fool. Don't hang back.

He fed the fire, ate, then looked into the flames again as night came on with a clearing sky. He leaned back on his elbows, feeling cool on one side and scorched on the other. Orion was clear and the Pleiades were rising over the shoulder of Cairngorm. Or setting?

It seemed important to know. He went into the bothy and came out with his sleeping bag, unrolled it on the ground, made a pillow of his spare sweater and trousers then got inside. He lay a long time looking up at the stars. He felt himself expand into the hugeness where there was no terror and no killing and life was much much bigger than a cramped cockpit in a jolting sky.

Oh, and the Pleiades were rising. He noted it in his diary, then curled deeper into his sleeping bag. By the time they were overhead, he was asleep. And the lights had finally gone out in Goering's chateau headquarters near Saint Malo, where the *Luftwaffe* command had been collating the day's climactic events. They were ready to admit not defeat but the absence of victory, which would be enough to have Sea Lion postponed. Still, the nightly bombing raid on London would go ahead.

That evening, after a quiet day — I mean, no drinking and only a few distant explosions — Maddy and I went on the bash with Foxy and the cousins, John G. (who looked rather sheepish, I thought, and distinctly less handsome) and Gerald, out to one of the big pubs that had a dance floor. There were a lot of uniforms there, mostly in small groups talking to each other, gesturing and laughing. I recognized it by now, recognized it from myself, the too-much-brightness, the eager hilarity.

I seemed to have mislaid my sense of connection. There was Len, but he was too far away. Mostly I sat out the dancing and sipped port by the bar, watching John G. and Foxy — now free from the guardian aunts — sashaying past in a passionate foxtrot. I noticed he had the same trick with her, putting her hand on his waist, murmuring in her ear till she threw her head back and laughed. Last night my Len had seemed rather ingenuous in comparison with these people — shy and young, full of silences and sudden blurts. Unsophisticated.

The violinist sawed away, the clarinet bleated, the piano shivered out its tune while the bass thumped and drums swished. They were playing 'These Foolish Things', I remember that clearly. Gerald and Maddy twirled by, his hands were all over her and she winked at me. She was in a sleeveless satin frock with very little back. She must have got it before the War, it wasn't the kind of thing that came with coupons. I smiled back, she waved her glittery bangles at me and whirled away.

Oh we're a fast set. All this laughter and carry-on while we can. The quick, I thought, the quick and the dead. And Len, who I was ready to betray with a kiss last night, seems sincere and open, my only true one.

I ached for him. I longed to tell him what he was to me. That I'd only now ceased playing at love. That though I'd no intention of ceasing to laugh, I was serious.

There were a couple of deep loud thumps that didn't come from the drummer. I looked towards him. He seemed puzzled, head cocked to one side, then there was a roar and the floor reared up and the roof came down and they met in midair where the flash was brightest.

Someone was sobbing. I sat up and saw my hand was bleeding. I grabbed my wrist to cut off circulation and for some reason stuck my bad hand in my mouth. Blood? Only port wine. Steam hissed from a severed pipe, somehow the lights were still on, a few of them. People were slowly getting to their feet, doing foolish things like setting tables upright or running hands through their hair. A man came uncertainly towards me, his head and face and shoulders white with plaster dust, making him look like his own ghost. It was so comical I sat on the floor and laughed as he came closer.

He held out his hand to help me up.

'Stella,' he said. 'Are you all right?'

It was Roger. Good old heartbreaker Roger.

★　★　★

I think I must have fainted for a few seconds, though that's excusable what with the bomb blast and all. I was lying flat on the floor with Roger kneeling by my head. I was gratified to see he seemed quite concerned.

'Are you hurt, Stella?'

I shook my head. I was looking past him to

342

the heap of ceiling and beams piled up in the middle of the floor. I focused on a long bare arm sticking out from under the pile. I saw bluegreen and rose glittery bangles hanging loose around the dropped wrist.

'For God's sake,' I said. 'Help my friend.'

'Had a good time?' Dusty Miller asked as the car swung down the road next morning. 'Head better, I trust. London's been taking a pounding but they've finally left the sector stations alone. And the RDF stations, you'll be glad to hear. The lads in 12 Group are all talking about getting big wings up 'cause we've got more time — I mean, there's bloody miles of bombers coming through, day and night, plenty for everyone. And it seems like the 109s have been ordered to stay close to them, which is good news for us. Bloody wizard, eh? We're heading off tomorrow and we'll be flying the next day so that's what's happening. Oh, and we'll be eating grouse for the next week or so, what with the CO and the chaps having a couple of good days . . . '

I sat back and nodded and grunted at intervals while the stubble fields flashed past. I was gladder than ever that I'd politely refused Dusty's offer to come along for the walk. A nice enough chap but, as Alec Watson would say, a terrible blether. I didn't want blether, or this speed. I wanted more and more silence and stillness.

I pulled out my last cigarette, lit it and inhaled deeply, feeling the sweet rasp off the back of my throat. Silence and stillness were going to be in short supply. It wasn't exactly what a fighter pilot lived for. Now I had to be noisy, assertive, quick, if I wanted to survive and be any use.

The roadside bushes swung away as we shot by. Here we go, I thought. Here we bleeding go.

Perhaps we could have saved her. If we'd been quicker. If we'd been trained. Once we'd torn away the rubble, we might have found a way to make her chest rise again.

If wishes were fishes, my dad used to intone into his beer, *most would swim free*.

But many don't swim free, and so I sat dry-eyed into the small hours back at the Farringdons, remembering Maddy. Roger — who was not on the convoys at all, but back home on leave — came back with us, washed off his ghost-dust and was kind. He brought tea and listened as I talked of the drinks we'd drunk, dances danced, confessions shared. Above all, the laughter. For she, like Tad, knew how to laugh.

At the thought of Tad, my heart squeezed. Either I or Len would have to tell him.

Leave that till tomorrow. For tonight there was the remembering. Roger knew me — well, he was the first man to have known me — and it was oddly easy to glance into his pale eyes and talk about my snobbery with regards to Maddy. How I'd looked down on her bright breeziness as somehow coarse, not to be taken seriously even as I admired and envied it. As if she was somehow less of a person because she had been educated less and laughed more loudly in public places. As if because she was free and easy with men she was not a good woman.

I think it was in the course of that long night that I finally put my insecure snobbery behind me. Just as I discovered that my long-held ache about Roger was that of bruised pride, not undying love. I told him as much. I told him he'd been quite right, he owed me nothing and I'd needed him to leave me to grow up myself. He had been my first lover and he was right not to feel guilty or responsible about that. I now gave that love to another man.

He nodded but couldn't look at me. I think he was embarrassed. I'd never talked like this before. I'd wept, shouted, been silent or sarcastic, but I'd never been open.

Finally I slept, in the bed looking down onto the garden where I'd so nearly made an idiot of myself before Maddy had got in the way. Across the room the other bed was silent and flat. Though there would surely some day be laughter again, and even light-heartedness, I'd left my long drawn-out adolescence behind on a ruined dance floor, under a pile of rubble and broken beams and moonlight pouring in where the roof should be.

25

Mid-September

It was the engines that woke me. Rolls-Royce Merlins passing low overhead, a dozen or more. I was back at base in the same old bunk bed and the early-morning shift was going into action. The new sergeant pilots, Day and Dixon, were soundly asleep, presumably dreaming of death or glory.

I lay in the half-light, remembering leaving the airfield near Aberdeen. That lift as I came unstuck from the earth again. The sense of dreamy freedom, for all the noise, as I watched dabs of clouds passing by beneath, and below them the green fields, roads and farmhouses, as we set our course for the War. I still loved flying, that was something. As Tad liked to say, it was just the shooting I wasn't so keen on.

The brisk double tap on the door. 'Morning, Stevie.' 'Morning, sir.' Mug of tea — a brief memory of being handed tea in the bothy by Alec, that peace already so far behind — sign the chit. How it comes back, the routine.

Day and Dixon were already talking eagerly of getting up there and tangling with the Hun. I couldn't get excited. The rage that had followed Stella's dad and Stella herself getting bombed, even that had gone. All that was left was the routine. I guess that made me an old hand. A near-ace in this desperate pack. Ho hum.

Routine. Yet lying there waiting for the tea to cool enough to drink, listening to the others' eager conversation, it seemed such a bizarre thing to do. To get dressed, have breakfast, then wait to fly and kill or be killed.

But it's the one thing I'm trained and fitted for. So I got some tea down my throat and tried to get myself in the mood. The main thing was to do it, to get up there and break up the bombers and get through to tonight to see Stella again. If I stayed passive and dreamy like this, I was a dead man.

I put my tea aside and swung my legs out of bed. Breakfast, then a game of table tennis with Tad or Dusty or Paddy McNally to get the aggression going and the reflexes on the mark. Trigger-happy, that's what I must be again.

I'm on the train out of the city as the day's raids begin. A neat, white-haired man opposite chats me up in a fatherly way, and the two soldiers by the door keep glancing and grinning, but it's all right. Small things can't bother me today. I'm impervious.

Maddy's weekend case is in the rack above my head, next to mine. I'll take it round to her billet while they try to trace the family she refused to see or talk to me about. But I want to hang on to the gaudy bracelets she wore.

Lord, when this war is over we'll want non-events. We'll not talk about it to our children and we'll try to give them the luxury of boredom, to make life so safe and reliable they'll probably rebel and make something of their own. But not war, please God, not war.

And Len and I, we'll not talk about it in front of the children. At most we'll give them trifles, little silly stories. The real thing, what it really felt like, we'll keep between ourselves. We'll keep it inside ourselves, for it has made us what we are.

The train stops. After a long time we're told we have to leave it and get on another.

No reason is given. That's the War for you. The old man disappears. I stand with the soldiers on the platform and they offer me cigarettes. I take them, smile at their chat-up lines. One of them is even rather good-looking, but that's all right.

Then I think how we'd all be more animated if Maddy were here, how easily she could have been here, cackling with laughter, returning their blue jokes with bluer. And then I have to go and sit inside the Ladies and let the water come down my face for a while.

The new train comes and I go out to meet it. The soldiers share my compartment but see I'm not in the mood now. The authorities are all notified. I gave them her billet's address and phone number and it's up to them to find her family. There's only Tad to tell and I dread that.

I sit back and close my eyes, let the changing sunlight flicker inside my eyelids. As I turn away from the window, her bracelets rattle and clack restlessly in the pocket of my coat.

Hundreds of them, fucking hundreds, spread back for miles towards the south coast. You could practically walk on them all the way to London. The bombers were stacked squadrons, Heinkels and Dorniers by the look of them. I stuck the oxygen mask to my face and pushed the throttle through the gate as we rose to meet them through thin cloud. Then I saw above them the fighter-bomber escort, the Me110s. And above that, tiny midgelike specks I knew to be Me109s. So now the escorts had to be escorted. Surely that was a good sign. We had made a difference.

I was trying to remember how to do this. For the first time I was leading a wing. Checked Coco to my right, Paddy McNally sound to my left, Dixon struggling behind. We were climbing but not quickly enough. Way up ahead the Polish and Czech squadrons in Spits were piling into the escorts, the Big Wing theory working at last. Through the last of the cloud now, 17,000 feet, the city hidden below. They know nothing about us. Maybe Stella is still there.

We're closing on them. Oh, God. What do I do? Time to get up-sun, or take them from below? I'm meant to lead. And here it comes at last, that thick ball rising in my throat, my hands shaking on the shaking controls. Heart-beat thumping in my ears. Here we go.

'*Engaging enemy. Follow me in. Watch your backs, chaps!*'

Oh, my God. My God. Get us through this.

★ ★ ★

So I led my wing down into the bombers and was so busy flying and trying not to collide with anything that I forgot to fire. Simply forgot that's what I was there for. Already I sensed how the week off had made me slower.

Then I pulled out of the dive, came up on one from below, a perfect line of attack safe from his rear guns. I closed on him, flicked off the safety then realized I hadn't set my gun sights. Cursed, sheered off. I glimpsed Coco rushing past. Paddy McNally was still glued to my left. Dixon seemed to have disappeared.

Set the sights with one hand, checked my tail. The 109s were coming down, arrive in maybe thirty seconds. Just enough. I swerved back in at the formation, let off a few seconds of unlikely deflection shooting, saw tracer coming my way and instinctively ducked, as though that could make any difference. A big thump, my kite juddered then fell away, whirling like a sycamore seed. Dropped down right out of battle from 15,000 feet, tailplane looked mostly shot away.

I reached for the hood as we went down through cloud, then remembered London was below. Didn't want my plane to drop onto some poor air-raid chap on the street, some Alec or Jimmy, so thought I'd have another go at controlling it. A long time fighting with the controls then suddenly it came out of the spin. I straightened her up and staggered off towards base, the kite sliding all over the sky.

Below cloud now, creeping away from London. Over open country, high enough to bale out. But no, I was set on bringing this back. Stubbornness, and some vanity. I thought to impress the few people who mattered to me — the CO, Tad, Dusty, Coco and Paddy McNally, the shade of cheery Fred Tate and maybe above all the silent, unsmiling airframe mechanic Evans, who reminded me of my dad.

I was sweating so much the canopy was steaming up. Muttering curses and prayers as I nursed and cajoled that Hurri home. There was the airfield. I got on the R/T and told them to have the crash truck ready in case. Then I took a deep breath and slowly took her down, uttered another prayer — *Please God, let me off with this* — as I took the plane down below baling-out height.

I was committed now. And the damn thing kept trying to flip on its side and the controls were so sluggish it was like flying through treacle as we came in with a lot of right rudder, yawing over the trees where I'd carved my name a lifetime back, hit the new concrete runway, bounced into the air, hit again, slewed sideways but stayed on the undercarriage and bumped to a halt by the control tower.

Thank fuck for that. As Dusty would say. I switched off and sat there a few moments. A morning of misjudgements I'd been lucky to get off with. Must be sharper next time. I could feel a headache coming on.

I unbuckled my harness, opened the hood and got out. As always, the whiff of grass, fresh air, high-octane and glycol, was like smelling salts to me.

I scrambled down from the wing as grim Evans came running up. I looked at the tailplane, there wasn't much left of it, or the rudder. In fact it was like lace, mostly holes. Evans looked at the tailplane, then at me, shook his head and spat at the ground.

'And now I suppose you expect me to repair that,' he said.

It was the longest sentence he'd ever addressed to me. I felt immensely pleased.

I walked down the street in that safe old town with a suitcase in either hand. Hers was heavy in my right hand, I'd repacked it myself with her clothes she'd brought for the weekend and the new ones she'd bought. At least I'd managed to do that dry-eyed, distant and efficient. Now some kind person offered to help me but I said, 'No. Thank you,' and hurried on with my face turned away. Anyone being kind made me tearful. Especially kind for no good reason, for someone you don't know.

I came to Maddy's street and passed the stop where I'd got off the bus so often. I remembered the bus I'd met her on. How she had no money for her fare and I paid it to get up the nose of that bossy conductress, and then we started laughing and joking. Then we'd got off the bus and went for coffee and cake at Lyons and talked for ages while the rain came and went. I was taken with her irreverence, her laughter. They crossed the distance that shyness and my solitary, dreamy childhood had put round me.

By the shops, a child went running to greet

an old lady, probably her grandmother. She tripped and fell, bang, just like that, quite hard on the pavement, and lay there howling, clutching her skinned knee. What struck me was how everyone around, including myself, at the moment it happened leaned towards her. We winced. We felt the hurt. A woman bent to pick her up, another two stood by clucking sympathetically till her granny caught up and embraced and soothed her.

That goes some way to making up for the War.

I went on my way, thinking, What are we? We drop bombs on people we don't know, can't even see. And we're sometimes kind to people we don't know, we wince when we see pain, especially in children. And I know it's the same on the other side. These same people that dropped the bomb on Maddy would in the street of their own town comfort a child with a bleeding knee, soothe and joke until she began to laugh. My opposite number, my ghostly Fräulein, she certainly would.

So what is this happening for? I dunno, as Len would say. I dunno. But it's clear that the only way to end it now is to fight back. It was pure survival at first, but the invasion panic seems to have receded a little. They say it's not going to happen this year. Maybe we're going to make it through.

Often when I'm unhappy I yearn for that cave behind the waterfall, the solitary place where no one can get me, except perhaps the dream gypsy-boy, Fando's spirit. But now I walked slowly up Maddy's street, yearning only for yesterday when she was still alive.

26

Mid-September

I lay on the warm grass, watching Tad play patience. His dark hair had been uncut for weeks and was now flopping over his eyes like one of the university boys in the old days back in late June when we were young and regardless. His hands moved calmly and efficiently, without a hint of the shake I'd noticed in others, including myself. He got stuck, he cheated, he carried on.

He looked up and noticed my expression.

'Hey, I'm only cheating with myself, you know,' he said.

'I'm not disapproving,' I protested. 'I'm just baffled what makes it worth playing if you don't stick to the rules.'

'Who said it was worth it?' he said. He grinned up at me. 'At least I don't spend my evenings tearing beer mats into smallest pieces, or writing in a diary things I already know.'

'That's not fair,' I protested. 'That's completely different.'

'Yes?' he said. 'How is that?'

I was stuck for an answer. Then a new Hurri came dropping down over the perimeter fence and I knew it was the replacement for the one I'd got shot up. So that was me back on readiness once it had been armed. One, maybe two sorties before the end of the day.

I got up to go and check it over. I looked down at Tad grinning to himself.

'Maybe once in a while I tell myself something I didn't already know,' I said. 'Can your cards do that?'

I hurried off before he could reply. The plane was shiny-new, still didn't have its numbers painted on. I was hoping the young woman pilot was delivering it, but instead a short, bow-legged bloke jumped down.

'This for you, pal?' he asked.

'Certainly is,' I said. 'Is she A1'?

'On the bloody button,' he replied. 'You need an oxygen bottle and the guns synchronized then she's ready for the off.'

I stroked the wing then clambered up and checked the cockpit hood runners. Still a bit stiff. I'd put some graphite on it. I'd a good feeling about this plane.

There was a thump on the fuselage. I looked round and there was Evans kicking the rear wheel. He looked up at me.

'Do us a favour and don't mess this one up, son,' he said.

★ ★ ★

We went up again round six o'clock. My flight, Tad on the second wing, plus the new Czech squadron. They didn't speak English that well but they were very good at killing. Like Tad, that's all they wanted to do. I'd talked to one the night before. 'My country is finished,' he said, and made a cancelling gesture with his hands. 'Now I fight here.'

They were very dangerous. They seemed truly regardless. They were true fighter pilots. I admired them and wanted to keep well away.

Luckily they were flying Spits and were always sent to take on the 109s higher up. We were the workhorses, there to disrupt bombers. That suited me fine. I wanted to survive. I was beginning to think it was possible.

I'd thought a lot about that in the hills, and now I was back it seemed we'd entered a different phase of the fight. The numbers were still stacked against us but somehow we'd turned a corner. We were putting up bigger numbers of our own. We'd dropped the fancy formations. We were fighting further inland, which gave us more time to get up in numbers, removed the prospect of baling out into the drink, and cut down the combat time of the 109s to a few minutes. The big question was how the cities would take the bombing.

I was thinking this over in the back of my mind as we climbed. The front of my mind was frightened as always and busy dealing with a suspect oil-pressure gauge. Bloody new aircraft. As we rose up towards the enemy — and there was no problem finding them, there were miles of them spread all the way back to Dover and beyond — I felt just right, on form. An intangible thing, but I was rested, ready, and fairly convinced I could survive this.

We wheeled and came down at them more or less out of the sun. They scattered like startled silvery fish. I got off a couple of squirts to little effect then found myself alongside a very surprised Heinkel. As the rear-gunner wheeled for me, I turned in and let him have it the length of the fuselage, then sheered off.

Lord it was slow. I felt like a cheetah attacking some big lumbering animal. As he wheeled I came in again, got really close, closer than I'd meant to and pressed the button in sheer fright. My kite juddered from the recoil of eight machine guns. Bits fell off the Heinkel, then the port engine blew and it slid out of the sky. I followed it down, against orders but my oil gauge had gone again and anyway I wanted this one for a definite. It spiralled, I dived in a leisurely corkscrew. I saw one man jump out then the other, and I was glad to see it for they were out of the fight. The plane went on to hit the ground and blow up. Both parachutes opened, I came out of the dive and passed close to them. I could see their heads swivelling back towards me, worried I was going to shoot. It was known both sides had done that. So much for chivalry. But I wanted none of it and flew on by with a wave they probably never saw as they floated on down towards the Home Counties.

It was probably the best and most spot-on combat I'd had, and I was humming 'Red Sails in the Sunset' to myself as I flew on, keeping an eye on that erratic gauge. Then a fighter began to fill my mirror. It had come from nowhere and was right on me. I was about to throw the stick into the corner when it stood on one wing and went past showing my squadron's insignia and Tad waving.

I gave him the fingers and flew on like nothing had bothered me.

We landed, Tad doing his slow victory roll

far too close to the ground and me behaving myself. I jumped out. Evans was there, ran his eye over my plane and grunted.

'See you stayed out of trouble,' he said. 'Don't suppose you hit anything.'

'A Heinkel,' I said. 'A definite. Saw the pilot bail out.'

I joined up with Tad and we walked together towards the dispersal hut. He'd picked up one, and a probable. Then he'd been jumped by five 109s.

'So I just high-tail out of there,' he concluded.

I knew he was such a good pilot he could extricate himself from almost anything. Only sheer bad luck would do for him. I told him about mine and he whistled.

'Reckon that makes you ace, my friend. The DFM is good as in the post.'

'You mean I'll get it next year?' I retorted. 'And how come you haven't got a gong yet from the Polish Air Force?'

His hand automatically went up to the *Poland* insignia sewn high on the arm of his uniform.

'But you see,' he said, 'we have much higher standards, you know.'

I put out a foot to trip him but he skipped away, and we were coming over the grass towards Bill Raymond, standing there with his clipboard, and we were briefly happy and high-hearted like in the early days. There was Uncle George, waiting to give Tad a bollocking for his victory roll. Only he looked awkward, embarrassed, chewing away on his pipe.

Then I saw Stella standing outside the Control Tower, in uniform and not smiling, standing straight and alone. She was looking at Tad, not me. There's only one reason for looking at someone with that dread. That compassion.

He saw her. He slowed. I think he knew before she stepped towards us, her hands coming up, her face stiff with not crying.

'Tad,' I said, 'I'm so sorry.'

He stared back at me. I couldn't say any more, my voice wouldn't work.

'Was she having a good time?' he asked abruptly.

'She was . . . ' I cleared my throat, Len took me by the arm. 'Dancing,' I said. 'She was dancing and having a good time. Then the bomb . . . '

He looked straight past me and water began to run from his eyes. I've no practice for what to do when men cry, and it was the oddest crying.

'That's good,' he said. 'When you must go, that is the way. Santa Maria . . . '

He turned his head away and quickly thumbed each eye.

'I'd better report back, and get lecture from Uncle George,' he said. 'Thanks for telling me personal, Stella.'

Then he turned and walked towards the man with the clipboard and the CO. Len and I looked at each other.

'You're all right?' he said.

'I'm fine,' I said. 'Not a scratch.'

'That's good.'

'But it was horrible.'

'It must have been.'

It was having other people around, and the uniforms. We couldn't even begin.

'I'd better be off,' I said. 'I only got permission to deliver my message. Can't make tonight — I'm sitting in for someone who's sick. Tomorrow night?'

'Sure,' he said. 'Stella . . . '

'I know,' I said. 'It's rotten. You be careful.'

He nodded, for a moment looked direct into my eyes. For a moment we met.

'See you later,' he said, then turned away and walked over to the clipboard man. I retrieved my bike, cycled out the gates and went on up the lane in the cool evening.

That's how it was in those days. All arrangements were provisional. Maddy's death underlined that, and it left a hole in my side that never quite went away. Our partings often had a slight delay, a hesitation, then a sudden cutting-off, for there was no knowing which one could be final, and we can't bear that for long.

I turned left at the top of the lane, my calves aching, anticipating the long downhill that was coming next. How can we dare love anyone, I thought, when they're just going to die? And I thought of my father, the wall falling on him, his closed-off face in the hospital bed, and I thought at times our losses are like splits in the heart through which it may grow yet bigger, and there's nothing else to do but love, nothing to be regretted but not loving.

Then I coasted to work with the cool rush of air over my face, the evening filled with dozy bugs, and the bracelets clicking as my hands shook on the handlebars.

★　★　★

We didn't make love when we met up the next night. Not at first. We didn't go out for a drink. Nor did we take a walk, though the evening light was pretty enough.

With remarkable speed we got into each other's arms. Not that there was any of *that*. He held me or I held him. We were held. There were some tears. Mostly there was a silent ache and we lay on the bed sharing it.

The evening breeze grew colder. It blew in the window and furled back the curtains then let them drop then blew them out again. I lay for a long time watching them. Gradually I felt able to tell him about it — the weekend, the party, the dance and the bomb. I thought about telling him about John G. and my absurd flirtation, the kiss in the garden that never happened. I wanted to tell him so as to explain how I'd come to see things differently, how along with Maddy's death that had been part of why I felt different now. Then I realized that even *I* didn't have to be that stupid, and instead grazed lightly on his neck for a while.

Then he told me about his time in the Cairngorms, about how he struggled against the mist and feeling lost even though it turned out he wasn't. About two men he'd shared a night in a bothy with, who had somehow made him feel better, part of something. Above all — and this was the bit that stayed with me — how big and bright the night sky was in the mountains, what it was like to sleep in a warm bag on the heather looking up at the stars. Then we talked for a while about doing that together after the War, and though I like my creature comforts I said I would.

Then we lay for a while, stroking, and I noticed he was beginning to look as if he was being tortured, the way he used to before he kissed me (am I so scary?). I lay there and waited for it. He cleared his throat a couple of times. The curtains blew out and drifted back. I could feel his heart beating hard under my shoulder.

'I should have mentioned this earlier,

Stella,' he said. 'Because it's been true for a while.'

His face endured a few more toenails being pulled out. My heart started hammering as well. There was no way back from this.

'It's just that I love you,' he said. 'Though there's no 'just' about it.'

I'd been told this before, by Evelyn, even by Roger, but it had never made me snivelly before.

'I know,' I said eventually. 'I know that and I'm so glad.'

'You do believe me? I know what I'm saying. I'm in my right mind, never been righter.'

'I believe you,' I said.

No one told me it would be so painful letting go. Letting go of my solitariness. Letting him find me in my secret place.

'I love you like crazy,' I said. 'And seriously. If you know what I mean.'

'I get the idea,' he said, and stroked my face. He touched my lips. His eyes were huge as he looked at me. He put his hand to his chest where his heart was, stared at me then slowly moved his hand onto my heart and left it there. I could feel mine beating under his fingers. He said nothing and it was the most eloquent thing he ever said.

* ★ *

We'd always been quite good at it, and we quickly became much better that night, and a very satisfactory time was had. Especially once I'd tactfully shown him some things, and then there was no stopping us. My heart was in it and my body at last became like one of those burning laurel branches when a leaf twists free and rises out of the bonfire, flaming and crackling as it spirals up into the dark and ceases for ever to be what it was.

'I'm flying,' she'd cried in my ear. 'I'm falling. Catch me!'

I could hear her voice long after I'd finally dressed and left. It echoed inside as I cycled back to base on the adjutant's bike, my body all soft and loose. The moon was up and the road wasn't too hard to see without lights except where it went under trees.

I'd reached saturation point. Maddy, Tad, the big thing we'd finally said to each other — I couldn't think about them any more tonight. Instead I just felt myself alive and sweating slightly in my uniform and my calves aching on the long uphill stretch.

Then I was picturing when I'd closed on that Heinkel in the rush of combat. I watched again the tracers that marked the last of my ammunition, watched them sparkle and seed bright rosy buds along the fuselage. How they suddenly bloomed into one monstrous rose . . .

I bounced into the verge and wobbled back into the centre of the empty road. Death's gardener, I thought, that's me. Getting good at it, too.

My hands were pale and tight on the grips. It seemed unlikely that those hands could touch my lover so, and also press the button and kill men.

I swore out loud and pedalled on. This is not the way for a fighter pilot to think. Surely the other blokes didn't think like this. Or maybe we all do and just keep it to ourselves. If I survive, I want to do something better with these hands, something to soothe and make well . . .

I pictured myself kneeling as I pushed peas into soft earth with my forefinger. Pushing them down somewhere, oh, in Hampshire maybe, a soft rain falling on my gardening trousers, April and the hour before a weekend lunch . . .

I have to marry this woman because whenever I see her now I have this urge to plant, deep and patiently. I can see her face, teasing and laughing and making me blush at my naïvety. But if we live through this, and are to live well later, surely something must grow — children, sweet peas, routines and hollyhocks and marigolds. We must grow them to screen off the war years. Only once in a while will we mention it, out on a walk on our own or late when the children are in bed. And I begin to think I see why our parents kept their war to themselves. It was too horrible yet precious, it had gone too deep.

And so I biked on, too late again, knowing lack of sleep would make me slow tomorrow. I turned the corner and came in through the gates. The guard stepped out with his rifle lowered and a joke ready, he knew me well enough by now.

Outside the Mess I could hear music though it was late. I went in. There was no one in the bar except Bill Raymond the Intelligence Officer, the barman and a figure hunched low over the keyboard playing the same phrase clumsily over and over: Tad. One of the keys wasn't in tune, even I could tell.

Raymond waved to me. I could see he was quite drunk. Watching pilots come and go seemed to affect him as deeply as it did us. The lights were harsh and his face was pale.

'Better get your friend to go to bed,' he said. 'He won't listen to me.'

I went over to the piano and let my shadow fall over the keys. Tad looked up then. After the news he'd sat in the Mess and wept openly for ages, everyone giving him a wide berth and me just sitting by helplessly. He was dry-eyed now and it worried me more.

'Oh it's you,' he said. 'Did you have nice evening?'

He didn't say it nicely. I just nodded.

'Time for bed, Tad,' I said. 'Got to be sharp in the morning.'

'I'm not a child,' he said. 'Go fuck yourself.'

Then his mouth twisted like he'd just chomped on a lemon.

'Leave me be, friend,' he added. 'I'll to bed when I'm good. Now I want more drink and night music. A Polish love song — all very sad; you know.'

Then he bent forward and played the same phrase again, stumbling over the sour note.

'The bar's closed,' I said.

'Uh-huh,' he said indifferently. 'Well I'll just stay here till it opens again. Good night.'

He carried the phrase on, singing in a whisper under his breath. Tad was a man of many talents but music wasn't one of them. It was almost unbearable to listen to though I didn't understand a word. I stood there, waiting.

'She's gone,' he said conversationally. 'She's a gone girl.'

'Yes,' I said. 'It's rotten and nothing can change it.'

He glanced up at me then but kept on playing.

'She was . . . swell,' he said. 'A whole lot of fun. A *bundle* of fun. And a lot more no one knew.'

'Yes,' I said. 'I thought so too. But this is not the way to mourn her.'

He stopped playing abruptly and glared at me.

'Best thing you can do,' I said, 'is get a night's sleep and go back to work tomorrow in decent shape. You know that's what she would want.'

He stared down at the black and white keys like it was their fault. Then he slammed down and played violent nonsense. He broke off, slowly lowered the piano lid and got to his feet.

'Let's go beds, I'm finished,' he said. He draped his arm round my shoulders then looked down at the piano. 'Lennie, one of these days I burn this damn heap so they have to get another,' he said. 'So help me God.'

27

Late September

The trees outside the boundary fence are shedding leaves like old delusions. Already they look rather tired and the last two nights' winds have stripped most leaves away. I have to remind myself that trees are not emotional and stand for nothing but themselves — which these do rather nicely. Their roots must be huge. I've read that there's as much tree underground as over, and even when the wind really blows, they scarcely sway at all. They at least are mature, fully grown, adult.

We've flown three sorties today, four yesterday, and now my wing has been stood down. It seems there's no end to the supply of bombers, though they've been perhaps fewer the last couple of days. Equally, there's no end to us rising to meet them now they've given up bombing the sector stations and the RDF masts, and concentrating on London and the factories. We've more pilots and more planes. (That Sergeant Dixon, no one saw him go or found the plane, he just vanished into the sky.)

I've found the initials I carved. Already the raw cut is filmed over. That's good, because I didn't want to damage the tree. I'm sitting propped against it, telling myself things I already know, as Tad would say.

Not that he's saying much these days. He's given up the cards. Mostly he just sits with the latest Polish 'News of the World' unread on his knee. In the evenings he drinks and plays the piano in the Mess, same lugubrious Polish songs over and over. It's starting to get on people's nerves and the other evening there was nearly a fight when Paddy McNally was called on to replace him at the keys.

Last night I came up to him with the news he'd been moved and made my wingman. I thought it worthy of a bit of a roasting, maybe an evening down in the pub in the village where we could have a proper talk, about Maddy and the rest of it.

'Fine,' he said. 'No problem. I'll cover you.'

Then he went back to his paper and wouldn't look up.

A magazine I was reading spoke of the camaraderie in the Forces, especially among 'our brave airmen'. Within limits, I think to myself. There's still Officers and Men, always will be. Could we even have a war without such distinctions? (The CO dropped a heavy hint today I'd be offered a commission when my DFM came through. Don't think I'm interested. Then again, could do with the extra pay.)

For instance. The other day me and Paddy McNally popped over to Hornchurch to pick up some spares they had and we hadn't. Their main Mess had been flattened and they couldn't have me eat in the Officers', oh no, so the man in charge suggested Paddy ate inside while I had my swill at a table outside the door.

Well there was nothing left to do but spit on their food and leave. So we did. Good bloke, Paddy, for a university type, laughed like a drain all the way home. We got a rocket of course, 'lack of respect for a superior officer', but they're not going to ground us at this stage in the game. We're much too valuable. So sod 'em.

As I walked into the woods earlier, along the broad path to the church in the next village, there were many rustlings and scuttlings. I saw two red squirrels that quickly turned their heads away as if I embarrassed them. Suddenly I'd had it with flying and the War. I couldn't do it another day.

At the stile I met a gamekeeper with a shotgun, and as we chatted it hung from the crook of his arm, pointing at my foot. And I wondered what he'd do if I asked him to shoot. I heard they did that in the Great War. Now I know why.

It's not like when Stella's dad was killed and she was bombed. No purposeful anger, no rage pushing me on. Just weariness at it all. Weariness and habit.

I'm just sitting here till I'm ready to move. It'll come, whatever it is.

This is how it happened. It's in the official report, and there were several witnesses to the final moments.

The report says Sergeant Pilot Leonard Westbourne broke away from combat with his ammunition exhausted, claiming a possible Me110. He dived away and became aware of a Me109 following him down. He took an amount of enemy fire, sustaining damage to the port wing. He went steeper into the dive then at the last moment pulled out. He blacked out and came to moments later to discover he was on an even keel and alone.

Sergeant Westbourne took a compass course for his base. He then became aware of another fighter aircraft ahead. On approaching closer, he identified it as a Hurricane, then saw it was the aircraft of his wingman in Yellow section, Sergeant Pilot Tadeusz Polarczyk (seconded 18/6/40; see file RAF/OS(P)/JHP31b). He passed close by him. Polarczyk was flying on a level course, apparently uninjured and in control of his aircraft, which seemed in sound mechanical order. He made a friendly gesture as Westbourne passed close by him, and informed him over the R/T he had shot down a Dornier 17 (confirmed). He then overtook Westbourne and approached the airfield ahead of him.

Westbourne reports that Sergeant Polarczyk approached the airfield low, estimated at less than a hundred feet. He then turned the aircraft on its back and flew inverted over the runway at roughly sixty feet, causing personnel to scatter. (It has to be said that Polarczyk was an expert pilot, one of the most skilled in the squadron.)

Westbourne then landed and waited in his cockpit for his fellow pilot. Sergeant Polarczyk was ordered by his CO to land in good order. No intelligible reply is recorded. He approached the runway very low as before, then went into the manoeuvre known as a 'victory roll'. He lost height while doing so, and on coming out of the inverted position his starboard wing tip brushed the ground. The aircraft immediately spun out of control, hit the wall of one of the aircraft pens, and burst into flames.

Sergeant Pilot Westbourne had to be restrained from approaching the burning aircraft too closely. There was no possibility of survival. The remaining ammunition began to explode and the fire tender kept its distance till the flames began to die down, whereupon the fire was extinguished.

The remains of Sergeant T. Polarczyk were removed for burial. He has been recommended for a DFC (posthumous). The incident is best seen as a tragic accident that occurred to a very fine but overtired pilot. It has been stressed to the remaining pilots that such unauthorised manoeuvres will be severely disciplined.

In light of the above — the pilot in question had flown twenty-four sorties in the previous five days — it has been decided to withdraw the squadron for a week before returning them to battle.

★ ★ ★

So the report ends. It's dated 30 September, the last of the massed daylight raids, when the German losses were proving unsustainable and the RAF stronger than they'd been in the weeks before. From then on all major raids would be conducted by night.

The Blitz was to go on for many months, but the Battle, though it officially ended on 31 October, was almost won. That is, it wasn't lost. The sustained bombing of London hadn't panicked the population into demanding peace as all pre-war strategists had assumed. Without German air superiority the invasion of Britain was impossible. Hitler cancelled Operation Sea Lion and ordered his Chiefs of Staff to start drawing up plans for the invasion of Russia.

The man who had directed the Battle and whose strategy of limited engagement had defined it, Sir Hugh 'Stuffy' Dowding, was summarily retired from his post, and in the first official history of the Battle of Britain his name isn't even mentioned. His abrupt and uncommunicative manner had made him many political enemies; worst of all, he'd committed the crime of being right.

The Allied pilots (the Poles alone made up more than 10 per of Fighter Command in south-east England, followed by the Czechs then Commonwealth and American pilots, many of whom were outstanding) who'd survived the Battle of Britain now had a much better chance of getting through the rest of the War, though this wasn't clear to anyone at the time.

In a different way that time remains unclear to us. Though we have better access to the records, something in the air, in the flavour of the times and people's minds, is lost to us. It's so close yet out of reach, like the dead of that vanishing generation, like the dirt floor below the concrete in Corrour Bothy.

28

Beginning of October

I stand in the empty Mess, the bar is closed but I've a half-bottle of whisky in my hand. A big party tonight to celebrate our being rotated off-duty. Someone new on the piano for the inevitable singsong, the CO's new adjutant, bloke called Bates. Knew all the songs, played fine.

A wingman. Everyone should have at least one. A guardian angel, a right-hand man.

I look down at the piano and open the lid. Brush my hand over the light and dark keys. Hear the old music stir dust in an empty Mess, Sniff Burton playing the rags and popular songs. And Tad's efforts, more humorous before Maddy died.

'It's easy, Lenny! You play the left hand, yes? Don't they teach you peasants anything? Loosen up, eh! Loosen up, my friend.'

He was a light partner to my dark, he told me that once. *Regardless* is the word. Regardless and ruthless, the ideal fighter pilot.

The ideal fighter pilot does *not* try a

victory roll fifty feet above the deck.

Who would hear me fingering the black notes at two in the morning? I've this notion that Captain Nemo in, what was it, *Twenty Thousand Leagues Under the Sea*, he used to play the organ, black notes only. I try it. Sounds like a dirge.

I wish I could break into something light-hearted and silly, a ripping 'Jeepers Creepers'. A quick 'Boomps-a-Daisy'. But I don't have the ability. I was never taught. Besides I've hugged my life too close. Been full of death, Tad, full of it.

'*One of these days I burn this damn heap . . .* '

I pour the spirit over the keys. I take out my lighter. Now I must be both of us. I must be leader, and the wingman. I must be victor and the victim going down. A pyre for the dead.

The flame is tall in my unsteady hand.

Roger phoned me — would I see him before he went off on convoy again? I hesitated, thought about my new seriousness with regards to Len. Then I thought, It's quite possible he'll get torpedoed. So let's exhume the past and give it a decent burial.

'Fine,' I said. 'Drive on up.'

He picked me up in his brother's car. He looked supple and intelligent, assured. He looked at me and raised his dark eyebrows. I admit I looked rather swish. I'd put on the party frock I'd danced with John G. in, just to remind myself how foolish I can be (also because it suited me). We went out for a meal in a restaurant that wasn't serving much. We had a bottle of wine to make up for that, then ordered another.

And we talked. About the convoys, which sounded frankly terrifying. Cold and wet and long drawn-out fear, fear of things you couldn't even see. Fear that at any time of day or night, the deck might heave up under your feet and the boat be ripped apart, sink and leave you swimming in a sea of burning oil. Horrible. The air war is clean in comparison.

But he also talked of nights on watch on the voyage to Newfoundland, and how the stars were brilliant at sea, how they moved across the sky while the planets went their own way. Of phosphorescence, when the ship's propellers dug white fire into the water. And the northern lights like pale searchlights meeting at the top of the sky.

He grew quite passionate about it, and watching his face I began to see what I'd once seen in him. The sense of superiority that hung around him like a mist had disappeared, burned away by the War.

I talked about Maddy, our friendship, what she was like and how we'd met. Already it was starting to sound like a story about someone else I'd once known, though she was still sharp and real in my heart. I hoped she would be for a long time. What with the wine, I got a bit emotional, and he put his hand on my arm while I gulped and tried to get some breath.

Then I told him about me and Len. About how it wasn't that serious at first, how the things we'd been through separately and together had forced a deeper connection between us. How sometimes when I looked at him there was a glow around him, especially in his eyes or his mouth, and at other times there wasn't but he still seemed emotional, funny and vulnerable. And brave, in his way. I meant, in the way of someone who gets scared but does it anyway.

'But do you love him?' Roger asked, and looked straight across the table at me.

I bowed my head and considered. Do I love Len? More than as a piece of rhetoric, or a thank-you for some great sex? I listened to myself for an answer then raised my head and looked my first lover in the eyes.

'It's like this,' I said. 'I breathe all the time, though I'm often not aware of it. But anytime I ask myself, I can tell I'm breathing. That's how I love him. All the time, even when I don't feel it.

'And these days', I added, 'he's not *out there* any more. I've let him in — '

I broke off. He looked at me, and I thought I saw envy in his eyes.

'So do I take it you're, ah . . . ?'

'Yes,' I said firmly. 'And very well too.'

I thought he seemed slightly put out. Which was gratifying, but I'd said it because it was true. Indeed, as I'd spoken, I began to see for the first time the flight path of me-and-Len, and where it had landed us now.

'Good,' Roger said. He raised his glass to me. 'Just be careful you don't get pregnant.'

'Well,' I said defiantly, 'I don't mind too much if I do.'

And there I'd shocked him. His mouth stayed open then he looked down and lowered his glass and we were both silent for a while, he thinking whatever, and me a bit shocked, at what I'd just said. It had been the wine talking, but it had come out.

★　★　★

We finished the second bottle then he drove me home. He talked on the way, about his fear, the necessity of what he was doing, and the moments of beauty and strange new experience.

He'd always been an aesthete, that was his creed. The pursuit of beauty, in art and in life. In practice that seemed to mean the pursuit of whatever woman had crossed his path and seemed lovely. I had been one of them, and it hadn't been so bad. He had made me feel lovely and fascinating and the source of all light. So I'd fallen in love with him, because of that feeling he gave me and the sincerity of his own feeling. Because it was sincere. It was just temporary, that's all, and he felt bad about it when the source of all light moved elsewhere, to another face.

It was love, just not a very mature one.

He drove the last bit in silence, then stopped outside the house. He switched off the engine then turned and looked at me in the half-dark.

'You know what moves me most these days — apart from your lovely face, of course?'

'Of course,' I said. 'No, tell me.'

'Beauty and sacrifice,' he said. 'We must take what beauty there is, and sacrifice is all around us. That's what's going on here. Involuntary maybe, but no matter, that's what it is. And I think it'll destroy and justify our generation.'

Beauty and sacrifice. It was like being back at one of our seminars. Discuss. Roger at least made me think.

'Well, good night,' I said.

'Goodbye,' he said. 'I'll think of you. Good luck.'

Then he kissed me, a little too close to the mouth, smiled sort of apologetically. I got out of the car, he started up and was gone into the night.

'Goodbye,' I murmured to myself. 'Good luck.'

I went to fit the key to the lock but the door swung open. Mrs Mackenzie glared at me, and I knew she must have been watching through the window.

'Your young man telephoned,' she said. 'I

called but you'd gone out.'

'An old friend,' I said and squeezed past her. 'We went out for a meal.'

'Oh yes,' she said, making it sound like I'd gone to Gomorrah for the weekend. 'And drink taken, no doubt.'

'Loads,' I said. 'A bucketful. A whole ocean.'

Then I went up the stairs and lay giggling on my bed, thinking of Len and wishing he'd been there, stretched beside me, his arms around.

29

Early October

Our squadron was rotated off-duty for a week. We were moved north of London and stood down, so Stella and I were able to meet and go together to Tad's funeral. Maddy's was still delayed while the authorities tried to trace her family, so effectively had she cut off from them.

Something was over, like simple happiness, like laughter. It was too early to say what was left for us.

After the funeral, after the near-empty crematorium and the brief roar of flames and the few words said, we walked down to the river in silence with a picnic. Some sandwiches, tomatoes and eggs, biscuits and two bottles of beer. I ducked under the barbed fence and held it up for her, then we walked slowly down through the long grass of the big field. The middle of the day was hot and still and flies hummed continuously in the shadow under the dusty elms.

I stepped over the stile into the next field. I held out my hand and she took it as she stepped down. She went past me along the yellowed path and I attended almost without thought to her passing by, the faint rustle and sway of her summer dress, her hair piled up but spilling down her freckled neck.

The path turned, dropped down a bank and came out by the river where a faint breeze brought coolness over our arms and faces. The river slowed here into a deep brown pool that cut into a far bank screened with trees. A rope swing hung down from one of them. The grass looked like it hadn't been beaten down for weeks. On the pebble spit on the near side were the remains of two fires.

'This'll do,' I said.

I stood on the stones, hands on hips. I flexed my fingers, feeling yet the brass handle pressing deep. It was the flames that were the worst, the finality of it. And even then it had been hard not to snigger, thinking of the pointlessness of burning again what had already been burnt.

I shook my head at my own drunken vandalism of the Mess piano. How the black varnish had split and bubbled, flared briefly then went out. Pointless.

I knelt and placed the beer bottles in the edge of the pool, rolled up my damp sleeve and went to join Stella where she sat on the bank flanked by tall grass and cow parsley, hugging her yellow dress about her knees as she stared down-river.

A faint sound of the sea in the elm trees overhead. A wood pigeon calling in the leaves somewhere. A pop and burble from the downstream shallows. I lay back with my eyes closed and let it all drift.

★   ★   ★

Lord, I feel old. I'm a veteran at twenty-two, antique and scarred by careless handling, one arm awry, the right elbow joint for ever slightly forced. I feel like a chair I want to rest for ever in. I want only to be left out in the sun all day, brought in again at night . . .

I wash my face carefully each morning with the hottest water I can run. I shave then peer earnestly in the mirror. Even after this few days' rest, you could pack everything you need for a month in the country in the bags beneath my eyes . . .

Never thought to live this long. Before Stella, when the War and I were young, that didn't seem to matter so much. That's the trouble with women, they make us want a future. Dusty Miller has finally been promoted to a desk, too old at twenty-seven. Now he'll survive. And yet, at the bash we had to celebrate, he seemed down and out of sorts, for he was no longer one of us.

The wind stirs her dress, the wood pigeon calls in the wood. We lie sprawled on the bank while the beer cools, fingers touching lightly.

Sometimes it seems that touch is our only excuse. In the distance there are engines, whining faint as river gnats . . .

$$\star \quad \star \quad \star$$

' — Hey you!'

'Who, me?'

Her hand inside my shirt, easing buttons open. Sun hot on my skin.

'Yes, you. Do you fancy — ?'

'What, here?' I said.

'Where else?'

I opened my eyes, looked at her grinning down at me, full of mischief and life. Looked across the river at the screen of trees, then behind us at the long undergrowth. No one had been here for ages.

'Now?' I asked.

'When else?' she replied.

'I haven't got . . . I mean, is it safe?'

'What's safe?' She opened the last button and stared down at me. 'Safe enough,' she said. 'Come on.'

I crouched at the river's edge and washed. The water was fresh but surprisingly mild. I looked back at him but his eyes were closed, dozing again. He sleeps so much.

I walked further into the pool. It looked deep and fine, the water clear near me and dark green by the far bank, reflecting the trees. I wanted to drink it all up. I wanted it all over me.

I loosened the dress from my shoulders, chucked it back onto the stones, took off my underwear then launched myself in.

God, it was cold. The shock burned along my entire skin. I ducked my head, came up and then it was fine. I felt the water everywhere, all around me.

He was propped up watching me. I waved then turned on my back and watched myself bob. The trees arched overhead, so tall and deep tired green. I did a fast crawl across the pool, turned at the bank then followed it up to the top, then back down to the bottom end of the pool. I suppose I was showing off a bit, knowing he couldn't swim well and I could. Thanks to my dad. Then I felt regret like a bayonet plunge and twist in my chest.

But I was alive. I pulled myself up onto the far bank and let the sun begin to dry me. I felt self-conscious being naked yet it was kind of wonderful. I studied the water drops drying on my arm, began to count the emerging freckles.

You might wonder, I thought, how anyone can take the plunge and love somebody who might be killed in the next few weeks. But how is that different from giving your heart to someone who might die in the next few years? As sooner or later, die they must. And that will hurt so much. The longer you've been together and the more you care, the worse it will be.

I stroked my upper arm for comfort. It was dry already, the skin smooth and firm. I'm young, I thought with some surprise. The dying bit will come anyway, sooner or later. The main thing is to live first.

I looked to my left and saw a rope hanging from a branch over the river and knew what to do. I stood up and made my way along the bank, very aware he was watching me as I pushed through the long grass like some soft-soled Eve. I hoped he liked what he saw because it was me.

I scrambled up the rock that hung over the pool, leaned out for the rope and pulled it back to me. It was warm and rough in my hands, looked strong. I looked at the pool — a long way down but it seemed deep enough. As I stared down I saw myself looking back up at me, my ghostly reflection, my other side, and I wondered how my Fräulein was doing and how we could ever cross the distance that lay between us.

I hesitated and looked across the river at him. He was sitting up now, watching and waiting. I knew if I'd been alone I wouldn't do this, but with him watching I had to for my own sake, and I was glad it was like that.

I took a few steps back, gripping the rope. It was a big drop and the prospect of letting go clenches the stomach. Live a little first, I told myself. Think of it as flying.

I ran forward and flew.

⋆　⋆　⋆

In mid-air, the river shining below. Poised for a moment in his gaze. Everything clear, stopped. My reflection, my Fräulein looking back up at me. Then the drop, blur and *Smash!* into the water. The shock of it. Under the surface, water into my ears and eyes so cold, then surfacing back into the world. Sunlight, trees. United with it all again, with myself. My laughter, his applause as I swam back across the pool.

He took my arm as I staggered awkwardly from the water.

'Reckon that calls for a beer,' he said. 'I'm impressed.'

'Jolly good,' I said. 'Wizard. Can you pass me my dress?'

He picked it up, held it out towards me, open like a boxer's dressing-gown. I backed into it.

'I'm starving,' I said.

'I love you,' he said conversationally.

I turned my head. His face was inches from mine. I felt like I'd been born for only a few seconds. I licked salty sweat from his top lip.

'Yes,' I said. 'Ain't it terrif?'

'Is that terrific or terrifying?'

'Both,' I said. 'Definitely both.'

It's all in the letting go. I knew that then.

30

Mid-October

My other wingman was Paddy McNally, who'd arrived as a sergeant but quickly became an officer, for which he received much ribbing from us lowly types. He was a steady pilot, and I trusted him. We flew together when I was very jumpy, couldn't stop thinking about death, about Tad. I slept badly and dreamed too much. Paddy and I began to play table tennis together, trying to sharpen our reactions and get in the right split-second mood.

It was the third sortie of our fourth day back in the front line. We engaged a cluster of bombers at about 15,000 feet, with their escort around them and their escort's escort above being taken on by the Spits. I checked on the position of Blue section, told them to get higher. They were being led by a new chap who had no combat experience whatsoever. I ask you. I was feeling pretty calm till just before I gave the order to attack and then that fur ball of fear and raw adrenalin choked in my throat and down we went.

I came in at the wrong angle, missed everything, was vaguely aware of the Me109s turning my way. There was a patch of cloud up ahead and I made for that with Paddy sticking close.

'Oh Christ! No!'

His shout in my headphones. Even as I put on hard right rudder and saw the fighter shoot past, I saw Paddy's plane slew across the sky with half the wing gone. I thought I saw his arm come up, reaching for the cockpit hood, his other hand clawing at his face. Then I was into the cloud and he was gone.

★ ★ ★

Two days later he lay, quite calm, in the hospital bed and told me the story. Said he had something to tell me. Something important. But first I had to hear the story.

His face was tilted up towards the ceiling as I sat on the edge of the bed. The ward was painted blue, pale blue like the sky on a morning patrol way back in the early days.

'They're telling me a shell splinter nicked my optic nerve,' he said, and put a hand up to his bandages. 'I was instantly blind. It hurt like hellfire. But I found the canopy catch, opened it up and fell out.

'I could hear engines, a lot of them, and I didn't especially want to get tangled up with them or shot at, so I thought I'd count down twenty seconds. One elephant, two elephants, you know the routine. Then I pulled the cord.

'It opened. Sweet merciful mother, it opened. My next problem was landing. So I listened. Listened till I heard a dog barking, then a lark, then voices. Time to brace for impact —

'A ploughed stubble field,' he said. 'I got lucky. It could have been anything but it wasn't. I spat the dirt out of my mouth, lay on my back and bawled 'Stardust' till they found me. God, Len, that earth under my back felt good! A gift, somehow more than I deserved. You know?'

His head turned in my direction. I was picturing Stella, swung naked out across the river, mid-shout as she fell. Her shriek as she entered. Her laughter as she surfaced.

'Yes, reckon I do,' I said

He turned on his side and lay facing the window. It was a fine early evening outside. I'd come straight from the airfield once I'd been stood down.

'Blind,' he said. He spoke carefully, slowly. 'Blind isn't a blackout, Len. Not like you'd think. It's milky blue. Funny thing is it brings the world closer. More solid, you know?'

His hand moved over the coverlet, stroking, and for a moment I could imagine what he meant. Having everything in touching distance. Was this what he had to tell me?

He grinned. 'It's the last months that were a blur,' he said. 'Really we didn't look properly at anything. We couldn't see.'

I sat there, suddenly sweating. Couldn't speak. He sat up, reached for a tin under his mattress and began to roll a cigarette. He wasn't very good at it yet, but I let him get on with it. He'd have to learn.

'And Len,' he said, 'half of them are mad, you know. Quite mad. And most of the rest — oh, brave enough, but either numb or dumb. Then they die not knowing . . . And that's a waste. Wouldn't you say?'

He lit up, smiled in my direction.

'And now I've shocked you,' he said. 'But we both know it's the truth. I'm sorry I never said this earlier, instead of just playing table tennis and drinking pints. But it wouldn't have been playing the game, eh? Now I see no reason not to say what I want to.'

I sat there. My mouth may have been open. No one spoke like this. Even with Tad I'd kept my thoughts mostly to myself. Maybe we all thought the same but kept it to ourselves.

I watched the shadow-branches close and open on the far wall, caught in the low sun and projected past my shoulder. I watched and felt them as though they parted in my chest.

'Easy to speak from the sidelines!' he laughed. 'But I'm here to tell you this, my boy. *Just being alive is being in love.* It's a gift, and you don't hang on to gifts too tight. You pass them on, right?'

He winced, broke off, his hand went up to his bandaged eye then came down slowly.

'Anyhow,' he said. 'How's Stella? And are you taking that commission?'

'Well,' I said. 'Thriving. I reckon not.'

A horn sounded outside. I went to the window and looked and for the first time thought it wonderful to be able to look.

'Got to go,' I said. Put my hand on his arm. 'That's the adjutant. Thanks for the tip, I'll try and take it.'

'Sure,' he said. 'It's nothing at all. Thanks for coming.' His hand tightened on my arm. 'Heard you got your DFM,' he said. 'Congrats.'

I mumbled something modest, though I was quite chuffed about it. He patted my hand, like he was an old man or I was a child.

'Ta-ra, Paddy,' I said. 'I got to go.'

He nodded in my direction, grinned.

'Be seeing you!'

I left him then, walked down a long pale green corridor through a series of doors.

No anger, no pity, my God, no fear. Blind isn't as imagined. And dead is not lying awake in the dark for ever. Whatever it is, it's not that.

I thought of how, when I had flu as a child, the dressing-gown on the back of my door became a monster, and how it was so frightening I didn't dare move all night, nor scarcely breathe in case it spotted me. But when morning came and my fever dropped, I saw it for what it was. Just a dressing-gown. I made myself put it on to go to the bathroom.

I put it on. That was it.

I walked out the final set of doors, clear-headed, resolved, into the difficult light.

There is darkness everywhere outside the circle of our lamp. It's nearly ten and he seems to have dozed off. But I'm awake to what we've done. I sense it already, even if he doesn't. I know it in my core.

My eyes are open and I see. I see further than he does, I think, from my place of greater safety, the place he flies to protect me in. That's the deal we make.

The dead are more present than the fears, as they should be. I hope they'll walk with me for years. I hope in peacetime they come back to me and make me stumble or smile as I walk our child to school. My dad, Maddy, Tad — may I feel them near me again as I dust their frames, then carry on with whatever my life may be.

One day there may be a generation without a great war. What will they do then to know themselves?

Len's deep asleep, I think. I must wake him soon and send him back to his station. He dreams of flying and surviving, of being careful, I hope. We have been careful in every way but one, and that is my fault.

But it's right. It is, I know.

I know.

Say it straight, if only to yourself as she lies silent by your side.

Say the myths we live by.

Planes will burn, but not this plane.

Men will be killed, but not this man.

Loves will sour, but not this love.

These are the rumours that keep us going to the end. Pass 'em on, pass 'em on.

Think clearly now, for there's no other time. Why should we prove exceptions when the rule's made up of those who thought themselves exceptions?

But there's no fear, only this acceptance, vast and calm as the night beyond her blackout blind.

I used to think to love, and to fight this war, were at odds. And now I think I must fight on, not from habit or exhilaration at the adventure or simple obedience to the voices that guide us. Not even in anger any more. But I'll go up again tomorrow because I believe that what we fight is against life, against love.

So in this case to fight is to love. That's the only way we can do it and remain human.

Everything we have we lose, that's for sure. But everything we lose we've had. And I must come to take it lightly.

My hand rises and falls on her breathing ribs. The fragility.

18 October 1940
You walk across the grass to the pens,
parachute bumping the back of your thighs
— yourself, Coco Cadbury and a new
wingman whose name you're struggling to
remember, Andy someone. It's getting harder
to remember new info and faces these days,
as though your memory is a waiting room
that's full up with earlier arrivals so new ones
are left outside.

How well you can picture them, still hear
their voices as they eat and read, play cards,
wait and drink and sing. Handsome Geoff
Prior next to young Johnny Staples, his hair
all tousled and sticking up, gentle St John
murmuring aristocratic advice, Bo Bateson all
hail-fellow and terrible jokes. Sniff playing
boogie-woogie, Shortarse Madden with his
cheeky grin, cheery Fred Tate. And Tad.
Above all, Tadeusz, from his gleaming brown
brogue on the fossilized tree stump to the last
drunken songs on the piano. And all the
laughter and killing in between.

You feel dense with the dead. You carry
them all packed inside you. No wonder at

413

times you find it hard to breathe.

But not this morning. It's a fine morning, dew heavy on the grass and the air cool, almost chill. It's proper autumn now, you can hear the pheasants cackling in the woods. How good it would be to sit on your sister's swing, surprise your mother as she went outdoors, meet up with your father, go to the pub and finally have that talk you've never had. Next leave, definitely.

These days you try to attend to everything as it happens, so while you talk with Coco about the football match coming up this weekend and keep an eye on Andy and try to include him, you notice the cloud cover building up from the west and wonder whether you'll find yourself above or below it. At least it's somewhere to hide in the sky.

As the aircraft are wheeled out of the pens and you nod to sombre Evans, you think of the letter to Stella you left unfinished between the pages of a detective thriller. You were saying how sorry you are you can't go with her to Maddy's funeral this morning. You wanted to attend for Maddy, for her above all. You know what it is to lose your closest wartime pal. Then you found yourself writing about after the War. About marriage and children, in a way you haven't done to her face. You wonder if you should send it.

Your tie is too tight, you loosen it as you step onto the wing and into the cockpit. Respectably dressed for another day's work at the office. Cramped little office, the bright yellow Mae West a bulky nuisance as always.

Fact is, you reflect as you run through the checks and Evans attaches the accumulator, you and the others may have won a victory of sorts. A breathing space at the very least. For the flow of bombers that flooded across the sky day after day, endless as ripples of the sea, has dried to a trickle, abruptly as if someone had turned off a tap.

At night the cities are still getting a pounding, and there's very little can be done about that until they sort out RDF carried in night fighters, but the mass daylight raids have stopped and nothing has replaced them but small-scale nuisance raids. Stella tells you she sits in front of her screen for hours on end and next to nothing shows up.

Maybe you've made it through.

You fire up the engine and Evans drags away the accumulator batteries then pulls away the chocks. You look across to Coco and Andy, wait for their thumbs up. It's all very orderly, just another recce patrol. Gone are the frantic scrambles, the bombs raining down on the airfield, the enemy fighters coming in low, the worry about Stella's safety in the unprotected huts. The invasion barges have been bombed or dispersed, there'll be no invasion this year.

You think of a game of chess that was really Ludo and you smile, shake your head as you taxi over the grass and turn on to the new concrete runway. At the far end are the trees where you have walked and carved your name. As you gun the engine and begin to roll, for some reason you picture a table tennis bat propped at a slight angle on the little white ball, exactly as you left it. Then the ground is a blur and your speedo needle rises so you ease back on the stick and you come free of the earth one more time and it feels good.

(Leaving Mrs Mackenzie's on the way to Maddy's funeral, she stumbles then steadies herself, one hand on the garden wall. A brief wave of nausea has plummeted through her, and a feeling like she's missed a step in the level pavement. She stands in the sunlight with sweat along her hairline, not sure what has just passed, smiling uncertainly at the morning as Len enters the fire he became.)

31

She would keep the photograph beside her bed wherever she slept for the rest of her life. He is in uniform but his tie loosened, his cap pushed back, leaning against a tree with his arms folded, his eyes narrowed by the light he grins into.

The leaves above him are thick and dark. High summer, then. Taken by a path crossed by shadows and light. Behind him, a fence then a field of some tall crop, probably wheat.

With such details, it could be anywhere in southern England. There's no one alive now who can say. Evelyn, steady, patient Evelyn who raised the child as his own, had his heart attack ten years ago. And she has now finally gone into the silence to join the rest of her vanishing generation, whose code was sacrifice and whose quest was a decent normality, though it was one that had never quite existed. Who were so baffled by our turning away from what they made.

All that's left are the letters, his diaries, the stories she told near the end. The long-delayed stories that told what you came from, that seemed more vivid and real to her than the room she lay in. Also this silver-framed photo, gathering dust and glances through the years. And three dusty yet gaudy bangles. They gleam on the table, blue-green shot through with rose, and at last you know what they mean.

And at the very bottom of the hat box in the wardrobe, there's another photo. Black and white of course, though their world wasn't, any more than ours.

It's of her, taken down by a river. Behind her is a deep still pool, then the far bank dark with trees, and if you look closely a rope swing hangs down from one of the branches. She is wearing a loose print dress, buttoned down the front, and her damp hair is plastered about her head as she moves between light and shade, holding an open bottle of beer in her left hand. Judging by the trees, it is late summer, and she is smiling, by God she is beaming, life streaming from her face towards the viewer and fortunate man who raised the camera to his eye in that moment, that summer.

Acknowledgements

This novel has its origins in the narrative poems 'A Flame in Your Heart' by Andrew Greig and Kathleen Jamie, Bloodaxe Books, 1986.

There are many books about the Battle of Britain period, but this story particularly benefited from: *Fighter* by Len Deighton; *The People's War* by Angus Calder; *The Last Enemy* by Richard Hillary; *The Forgotten Few* by Adam Zamoyski, a history of Polish pilots in the Second World War.

And the book itself benefited a lot from dedicated editing by Jon Riley at Faber, and the close reading and support of Lesley Glaister.

We do hope that you have enjoyed reading this large print book.

Did you know that all of our titles are available for purchase?

We publish a wide range of high quality large print books including:
Romances, Mysteries, Classics
General Fiction
Non Fiction and Westerns

Special interest titles available in large print are:
The Little Oxford Dictionary
Music Book
Song Book
Hymn Book
Service Book

Also available from us courtesy of Oxford University Press:
Young Readers' Dictionary
(large print edition)
Young Readers' Thesaurus
(large print edition)

For further information or a free brochure, please contact us at:
Ulverscroft Large Print Books Ltd.,
The Green, Bradgate Road, Anstey,
Leicester, LE7 7FU, England.
Tel: **(00 44) 0116 236 4325**
Fax: **(00 44) 0116 234 0205**

Other titles in the
Ulverscroft Large Print Series:

THE UNSETTLED ACCOUNT

Eugenia Huntingdon

As the wife of a Polish officer, Eugenia Huntingdon's life was filled with the luxuries of silks, perfumes and jewels. It was also filled with love and happiness. Nothing could have prepared her for the hardships of transportation across Soviet Russia — crammed into a cattle wagon with fifty or so other people in bitterly cold conditions — to the barren isolation of Kazakhstan. Many did not survive the journey; many did not live to see their homeland again. In this moving documentary, Eugenia Huntingdon recalls the harrowing years of her wartime exile.

FIREBALL

Bob Langley

Twenty-seven years ago: the rogue shoot-down of a Soviet spacecraft on a supersecret mission. Now: the SUCHKO 17 suddenly comes back to life three thousand feet beneath the Antarctic ice cap — with terrifying implications for the entire world. The discovery triggers a dark conspiracy that reaches from the depths of the sea to the edge of space — on a satellite with nuclear capabilities. One man and one woman must find the elusive mastermind of a plot with sinister roots in the American military elite, and bring the world back from the edge . . .

STANDING IN THE SHADOWS

Michelle Spring

Laura Principal is repelled but fascinated as she investigates the case of an eleven-year-old boy who has murdered his foster mother. It is not the sort of crime one would expect in Cambridge. The child, Daryll, has confessed to the brutal killing; now his elder brother wants to find out what has turned him into a ruthless killer. Laura confronts an investigation which is increasingly tainted with violence. And that's not all. Someone with an interest in the foster mother's murder is standing in the shadows, watching her every move . . .

NORMANDY SUMMER/ LOVE'S CHARADE

Joy St.Clair

NORMANDY SUMMER — Three cousins, Helen, Tally and Rosie, joined the First Aid Nursing Yeomanry. Helen had driven ambulances through The Blitz, but it was the Summer of 1944 that would change their lives irrevocably.

LOVE'S CHARADE — A broken down car, a mix-up of addresses and soon Kimberley found she was stand-in fianceé for a man she hardly knew. What chance had the pair of them of surviving this masquerade?

THE WESTON WOMEN

Grace Thompson

Wales, 1950s: At the head of the wealthy Weston family are Arfon and Gladys, owners of a once-successful wallpaper and paint store. It had always been Gladys's dream to form a dynasty. Her twin daughters, however, had no interest, and her grandson Jack had little ambition. And so, it is on her twin granddaughters, Joan and Megan, that Gladys pins her hopes. But unbeknown to her, they are considered rather outrageous — and one of them is secretly dating Viv Lewis, who works for the Westons but is not allowed to mix with the family socially. However, it is on him they will depend to help save the business.

TIME AFTER TIME
AND OTHER STORIES

Mary Williams

In this collection of mysterious short stories the recurring theme of 'time after time' is reflected upon with varying intensity, and in several as a haunting reminder of life's immortality. Time itself has little meaning in the wheel of eternity, and it is more than possible that the vital spark or soul of any human being could by chance contact that of another known to him or her in a previous existence on earth. Some stories concentrate on the effect of wandering apparitions about the ether and in all of them can be found love, tragedy, emotional yearnings and sheer terror.